M000222891

HIDDEN FROM SIGHT

SALLY RIGBY

TOP
DRAWER
PRESS

CRIME FICTION BOOKS

and ignoring her. Rude. 'Will you take my case or not?' the statuesque woman said.

'It's not a decision I'm prepared to make without knowing further details.' Seb stepped to the side, his face set hard, and ushered Annabelle into the large hall.

Tension hung in the air. Did Seb still have feelings for Annabelle? Is that why he was acting weird? All he'd ever told Birdie about their break-up was that they'd wanted different things in life. She'd always imagined that it was mutual. Maybe it wasn't.

'Let's go to the kitchen,' Birdie suggested. 'The kettle's only just boiled for our coffee. I'll make one for you too, Annabelle. It's instant. I hope that's okay.' She moved ahead of the others and headed to the rear of the house and into the large farmhouse-style kitchen.

Following the outcome of the case concerning her husband, Seb's cousin Sarah had decided to up sticks and fulfil a lifelong dream of travelling the world, and so she'd offered Seb Rendall Hall to live in while he got back on his feet after a rather inauspicious exit from the Metropolitan police, thanks to a member of the team he was on being on the take, and it had now become the base of operations for his private investigation services. Birdie had been here so often in the last year that she felt practically at home in the place. And most importantly, knew exactly where the coffee was kept.

Annabelle and Seb sat in silence at the table as Birdie busied herself making the drinks. When they were ready, she joined them, placing a steaming cup in front of their guest, hopefully hiding the chip she'd just noticed on the edge.

'Right,' Birdie said, taking charge. 'What's the problem?'

'Jasper's gone missing. I haven't heard from him since Tuesday.'

'Jasper?' Birdie queried.

'Jasper Pemberton. Annabelle's fiancé,' Seb said, his voice flat.

Yikes. Not even a year since she'd split with him. She hadn't taken long to move on.

'Have you been to the police? Surely they would be the first place you'd go?' Birdie frowned. Was she missing something?

'No. It's best this is kept quiet. Will you find him for me?'

'Five days isn't a long time, Annabelle. Are you sure he hasn't gone somewhere and neglected to tell you?' Seb picked up his mug and drank.

'Why would he do that?' Annabelle drummed her fingers on the wooden table.

'There could be many reasons. Perhaps he was somewhere with no signal for his mobile, for example. Or, he's been tied up in meetings. Has something happened to make you believe that he's in danger?' Seb leant in slightly.

'What sort of danger?' Annabelle looked concerned.

'That's what I'm asking you.'

'Nothing that I'm aware of. I… It's just a feeling I have. He simply wouldn't disappear without letting me know.' She looked over at Birdie. Was she wanting her support?

'Have you contacted his friends or colleagues?' Birdie asked.

'No. I've come to see you first.'

'I'm sorry, Annabelle, but this isn't a case for us. You haven't given me cause to believe there's an issue.' Seb waved his hand dismissively. 'I'm sure he'll turn up soon.'

Birdie stared at Seb, open-mouthed. She wasn't privy to the business plan yet, but why would he turn down good

money? It wasn't like they were rolling in cases. Okay, so Seb was right, Pemberton would probably turn up. Most missing people did. But … saying no to working for Annabelle made no sense.

'And is that your final decision?' Annabelle pushed.

'It is.' He sat back in his chair with his arms folded across his chest.

Could he make his feelings any more obvious?

The lines tightened around Annabelle's eyes. 'I see.' She drew herself up to her full height, leaving her coffee mug untouched. 'I'll let myself out. Thank you for your time.'

She walked out of the kitchen, leaving Birdie and Seb staring after her.

'Don't you want to say goodbye?' Birdie asked to the sound of Annabelle's retreating footsteps on the old stone floors. This rudeness was a side to Seb that Birdie had never seen before. It was most disconcerting.

'No.'

'I don't see why we couldn't have taken the case. It's not like—'

'There is no case,' Seb interrupted. 'Pemberton has probably gone away and not mentioned it to her. It's simply Annabelle wanting to be in control.'

'But—'

'No buts. This discussion is over.'

Chapter 2

Birdie had planned on arriving at work a good hour before the morning briefing to hand in her notice, but it hadn't happened, and with only fifteen minutes to go, she decided to wait until after.

'Are you listening to me?'

The sound of her partner DC "Twiggy" Branch's voice cut into her thoughts.

'What? Yeah. Of course. What did you say?'

'I asked if you had a good weekend.'

'Yes. And yes. Something major has happened, but I can't tell you until after I've seen Sarge,' she said, referring to their boss, Sergeant Jack Weston. She bit down on her bottom lip. 'Then again... Promise you won't say anything.' She glanced at the other members of the team, who were seated at their desks in the large office, to make sure they couldn't hear. Not that she didn't trust them – they were a great team – but it was only right to speak to Sarge first... Apart from Twiggy, because of their close relationship.

'Promise.' Twiggy rolled his chair over to her desk until they were seated side by side.

'I'm handing in my notice.'

'You're what?' Twiggy shouted.

'Shhh. Everyone will hear you.' She turned back to Twiggy, who was still aghast. 'I'm leaving. I'm going to join Seb's company. You know I've been thinking about it. Well, this weekend, I finally made up my mind.'

'But you can't leave. I need you. You're my partner. Not his.'

Guilt coursed through her. But she couldn't throw away the opportunity of working with Seb.

'Are you worried because of your illness? Because if you are, I told you I'll always be here for you, and that hasn't changed. I just won't be sitting next to you. You know you can call me anytime. Day or night.'

Twiggy had been diagnosed with frontotemporal dementia, and it had left him devastated but determined to carry on while he could. He could carry on working for years, and he did have his wife Evie and their kids to help take care of him when he'd eventually have to step down.

'No. It's nothing to do with that.' He paused for a moment. 'Okay, maybe it is a little. But I don't want to stand in your way. If only it wasn't Clifford.'

Twiggy had resented Seb the moment he'd begun working with Birdie on several cases, accusing him of stealing his partner, but it hadn't been like that. Birdie had been the one who had wanted to work with Seb when he was investigating the suicide verdict of his cousin Sarah's husband. At the time, Birdie had been stuck in the office on desk duty following an accident she'd caused. He'd phoned wanting the police and coroner's reports, and she'd only allowed him access if she could help with the case. The rest, proverbially, was history.

'Thanks, Twig. I—'

'Morning, all.' Sarge arrived in the office, cutting short the conversation.

Birdie sat through the briefing, forcing herself to look interested and to answer any questions Sarge had. Finally, it was over, and she hurried to catch him before he had a chance to leave.

'Sarge, have you got a minute?'

'What is it?'

'I'd like a word in private.'

'What have you done now?' Sarge rolled his eyes.

'Nothing. I promise.'

'Okay, but I have a meeting in thirty minutes, so it had better not take too long.'

She followed him into his office that was so untidy it was a wonder he could find anything. She sighed. She'd miss all this.

She sat on the only empty chair opposite him and sucked in a breath. 'I'm leaving. I'm going to join Seb... I mean Sebastian Clifford, at his new company as a partner.'

Sarge sat back in his chair and stared at her, his eyes unblinking.

'It's a big step to take. Are you sure that's what you want to do?' His tone was calm and neutral. It was almost as if he was expecting it.

'As I'll ever be, Sarge. Look, I do love the force and working here, but you've got to admit that I might be better off not having the constraint of so many rules.'

'Just because you're a PI, it doesn't give you free rein to break the law.'

'I didn't say that. You know Seb. He's not like that.'

'Well, we'll be sorry to lose you – although there will be decidedly fewer headaches for me without your antics, and I won't miss that – but I'm not going to try to persuade you to stay if you've made up your mind. So, with your notice period, you will—'

'Actually, Sarge. I was working it out. With all the annual leave I'm owed, I could leave today. I know it's short notice, but we haven't got any big cases on, and it's not like you're going to miss me.'

Was she pushing her luck? Well, why break the habits of a lifetime, as her mum was so fond of saying. And if she didn't ask, she wouldn't get.

'I'll have to contact HR and confirm, but... I suppose, if that's what you want, then I won't stand in your way.'

'You mean, I can? Wow. Thanks, Sarge. I'll have some leaving drinks tomorrow at the pub. You will come, won't you?'

'Wouldn't miss it for the world. Now, buzz off. I'm busy.'

Seb glanced at his watch. Birdie had ordered him to be at the pub for her leaving drinks by six. But he'd waited until seven because he didn't want to muscle in on proceedings. He wasn't at all sure of the reaction he'd receive, especially from some of Birdie's colleagues, who would perceive him as stealing one of their team.

He pushed open the door to the Old Bell, the red-brick pub in the centre of Market Harborough town centre, and the noise hit him instantly, coming mainly from the back of the small bar, where he could see Birdie standing, surrounded by her team.

'You're late.' Birdie glared at him as he wandered over.

'Sorry, I had a phone call. Can I get anyone a drink?'

'As you're asking, I think we're all ready for one.' The

group around her cheered, and Birdie reeled off a list of drinks. 'Do you need a hand at the bar?'

'I'll be fine. You stay here.'

'Okay. But don't be too long – all this chatting is thirsty work!'

Birdie returned to her conversation, and Seb walked over to the bar and gave the order.

Leaning against the old oak bar top, he turned to survey the party and caught sight of Twiggy heading in his direction. That hadn't taken long. Was the man going to start already? Seb braced himself as Birdie's former partner approached.

'Clifford,' Twiggy nodded.

'Twiggy,' he nodded back.

'I'm telling you now, you'd better look out for Birdie, or you'll have me to deal with. Got it?' The man folded his arms and stared up at Seb, who towered over him.

'You have my word. Although, you do realise that she's perfectly capable of taking care of herself. And anyone else she's working with, should the occasion arise.'

'That doesn't mean you should let her get carried away with things. I've known her a lot longer than you, and she can get herself into trouble.'

He wasn't being told anything he didn't already know.

'It will be fine.'

And it would cut both ways. Birdie wouldn't stand for him acting rashly. Not that he usually did. With perhaps the exception of his response to Annabelle.

Had he been rash, and a little childish, by refusing to even consider looking into Pemberton's disappearance? Birdie had thought so, but he'd dug his heels in. He wasn't ready to revisit his previous life.

'Just make sure that you're there for her,' Twiggy emphasised with a sharp nod, cutting into Seb's thoughts.

'I will. That's a promise. Now you're here, will you help me with the drinks?'

'Okay,' Twiggy said in a gruff tone.

Was that it? Seb had got off lightly, considering.

They headed back to the tall table the team were standing around, and before Seb even had a chance to take a sip of his beer, there was a tap on his shoulder. He turned. It was Sergeant Weston.

'Yes?' he said.

'Over here, son,' the man said.

Seb sighed and followed him to a quieter area of the pub.

Was this what it was going to be like all evening. Everyone wanting to take him to one side to give their opinion?

'How may I help you?'

Sergeant Weston locked eyes with him. 'I know our Birdie's a handful, but she's one of us. You keep her on the straight and narrow and treat her right. I don't want to hear of her being involved in anything illegal. If you become involved in anything dodgy, you'll have me to answer to.'

'I can assure you that won't happen. You have my word.'

'Good. That's all I wanted to know. And good luck. With Birdie on board, you're going to need it.'

Chapter 3

'Are you sure that Sarah won't mind us moving the furniture around?' Birdie asked the next day as they shifted the antique desk from the smaller study into the larger one of Rendall Hall.

'Well, it's either that or you work in the smaller study, which is in the other wing and means it won't be easy for us to discuss matters.' He grinned. Birdie wouldn't want to be away from the hub of the operation in case she missed anything.

'Okay, that makes sense. How long are we going to make this place our base?'

'Before we make any rash decisions, we need to have some cases to work on and then we'll reassess our situation. At the moment, it's ideal unless Sarah returns early from her travels overseas.'

'As much as I love the place, driving back and forth here every day is no good for my old Mini, which, as you know, is on its last legs.'

Seb had the money to buy her a new car, but Birdie wouldn't accept it. When they'd discussed the possibility of her joining him, and he'd suggested that her input be paid over a period of years because she was saving up for a house deposit, Birdie had refused, insisting that if she said yes she'd invest all her savings. She said that if it had been otherwise, she wouldn't have felt like a "proper partner."

He admired her for that.

But although her enthusiasm inspired him, he couldn't quieten the niggle at the base of his stomach… Now it wasn't just his livelihood on the line; what if the business failed and she was left penniless?

No, he couldn't think like that. It wouldn't. He'd make sure of it.

'Once we have established a client base, we'll lease you a company car,' Seb suggested as an alternative.

'How exciting! Something fancy like yours?' she asked, referring to his BMW. 'Then again, probably not, because I'd be too scared to drive it, in case I bashed it. Perhaps something smaller would be better. And more economical, as we are meant to be making a profit in this business of ours. Which reminds me. I still don't understand why you turned down the case that Annabelle offered us.'

Not that again. Birdie hadn't stopped mentioning it since he'd said no.

Okay, so he'd dug his heels in. But, there was more to it than just taking on a missing persons case. Annabelle came from his previous life, the life from which he'd successfully managed to distance himself.

Annabelle had been his girlfriend for several years, until he'd left the Met. They'd known each other most of their lives because their families mixed in similar social circles. Seb's father was a viscount, and hers was a duke. A match made in heaven … so everyone believed. Except with hindsight, it wasn't. When Seb had decided to go into the police force after university, it hadn't been well received, especially by Annabelle.

They'd stayed together, although not seeing much of each other because of his shifts and his refusal to attend any society functions unless absolutely necessary, until he'd left the force and she'd tried to persuade him to work on his father's estate in Winchester, alongside his older brother Hubert, who would inherit the title of viscount on their father's death.

Not long after their split, Annabelle had started dating Jasper Pemberton and, more recently, became engaged to him. It wasn't that he followed her movements, but his mother had told him after it had been announced in *The Times* newspaper. Seb suspected that Annabelle had been seeing Pemberton prior to their split, considering the short time it took before their engagement. Seb had known Pemberton by name but had no idea what sort of man he was.

He stopped moving and lowered the end of the desk he was holding to the ground. Birdie followed suit.

'For the last time, Birdie, and then this discussion is permanently closed. First, Annabelle has no real evidence that Pemberton has disappeared. He might have decided to go somewhere and not told her. The trouble with Annabelle is, she's very controlling, and if she doesn't know everything, then her nose gets put out of joint. Second, and more important, is that I have no desire whatsoever to become involved in that social circle again. And that's final.'

'Even if it means losing out on business?' Birdie pushed.

'Yes. We still have the work with Rob, which is ongoing until such time as I end the arrangement,' he said, referring to the consultancy work he'd been doing for his friend and ex-colleague at the Met. He took hold of the desk. 'Now, lift.'

'And when's that going to be?' Birdie asked, doing as instructed.

'I don't intend for us to be working with Rob for too much longer.'

'Unless you keep turning down cases. You know we'll have to take some of the stuff we'd rather not. Like following cheating spouses and being bored to death.'

He glanced across at Birdie, who had a glint in her eye.

'I can assure you I will not be turning down work unnecessarily, and—' His phone began ringing. They rested the desk on the floor, and Birdie hopped on top, swinging her legs, while he pulled out his mobile and stared at the screen. Damn, just what he didn't need.

'Good morning, Annabelle,' he answered, walking away from the desk. If she was going to ask him again to help, then he'd have to be more insistent.

'Sebastian, I need your help.'

'We've already had this discussion, Annabelle, and I—'

'No, Sebastian. Listen to me. I have proof that Jasper's missing. A letter's arrived demanding that I contact Jasper and tell him to return what isn't his or there'll be consequences. I have a week to find him. Now do you believe me? He's taken something which doesn't belong to him and gone somewhere. You have to help me. If we don't find him…'

'Did the letter come through the post?'

'There wasn't a stamp on the envelope, but it was mixed up in today's postal delivery that had been pushed through my letterbox. I picked it up from the floor of my apartment.'

'Was it handwritten?'

'No, it was typed on a plain A4 sheet of paper in large

font. The envelope was an ordinary white one, with my name written on it in capital letters.'

'Have you contacted the police?'

'No. I want you to deal with it for me. Please. Daddy's got an important business deal coming up, and any adverse publicity could be detrimental to it. I can't risk the press getting wind of it. We have to do it ourselves. That's why I asked you.'

If he refused and it turned out to be life-threatening for Annabelle and Pemberton, then he wouldn't be able to live with himself. But agreeing meant having to spend time with the society set he'd turned his back on, which was something he didn't relish. But what choice did he have.

'It might not be possible to keep the police out in the long term, but for now, we will investigate. Return the letter to the envelope and don't touch it. I suspect there will only be your fingerprints on there because the person who sent it would have worn gloves, but if there is anything on the envelope, we want to prevent any further contamination. Are you alone at the moment?'

'Yes. I'm at my flat. I have a busy day. I've arranged to go out with a girlfriend for lunch, and this afternoon I'm having a dress fitting for a charity gala dinner I'm helping to host next month.'

He glanced at Birdie and forced back a chuckle. What would she have to say about Annabelle's "busy day"?

'Okay. Leave it with me, and I'll get back to you shortly.'

'When? This is urgent.'

He stiffened. This was exactly why he didn't want to have anything to do with the woman.

'Soon. There are certain logistical issues to consider and meetings to be rearranged.' On principle, he didn't want her to know that they were free to begin work immediately.

'Well, make it quick. I am a paying customer, after all.' Annabelle ended the call.

You're welcome. He replaced his phone into his pocket with a sigh.

'What is it?' Birdie asked.

'That was Annabelle.'

'Yes, I gathered,' she said, placing her hands on her hips and rolling her eyes. 'What did she want?'

'She's received an anonymous letter demanding that she tells Pemberton to return something that doesn't belong to him.'

'Or what?' Birdie frowned. 'Was she threatened?'

'Not overtly. All that it said was there would be consequences. It didn't say for whom. They gave her a week to find him.'

'Was she upset? Worried? Why didn't she go to the police?'

'Perturbed is how I'd put it. She's concerned that it will have a detrimental impact on her father's business.'

'Not another viscount?'

'Oh no, much higher. He's a duke. In order of importance it goes duke, marquess, earl, viscount, and baron.'

'Wow… You mean that to him you're just common like me.' She laughed.

'Not exactly, it's—'

'I'm joking, Seb.'

'I know that,' he said, giving a tiny shrug. 'Anyway, she's asked for our help. So, I guess we'll be taking her case after all.'

Chapter 4

Birdie jumped off the desk, waving her arms around in excitement, the moment Seb had told her he'd agreed to take Annabelle's case. She couldn't believe it. Her first ever case as a PI.

'So, what are all these mysterious appointments that you told Annabelle have to be rearranged?' She tried to keep a straight face but failed miserably.

'I didn't want Annabelle to think we were hanging around here doing nothing, desperate for a case to cross our threshold. It isn't good for business,' Seb said as they manoeuvred the desk they were carrying through the door into the study. She'd been in there plenty of times before, but it still wowed her. The room was south-facing and had large French windows that overlooked the beautiful gardens that were tended by a man from the village who visited once a week. And the walls were lined from top to bottom with books.

Never in a million years had Birdie ever imagined working in such luxurious surroundings. It certainly beat the cramped sixties building where Market Harborough Police were stationed.

They placed the small desk opposite the much larger one that Seb worked from.

'Not good for business, or not making you look like a failure in front of your ex?' Birdie locked eyes with him. 'And what about payment? I hope this isn't going to be another one of your freebies.'

So far out of the three cases they'd worked on, Seb had only been paid for one, and that was because he'd been asked by a DCI from Lenchester Police to investigate a cold case concerning a relative of hers.

'This is different, and in my conversation with Annabelle, she referred to remuneration. When I contact her to make arrangements for us to meet and discuss the way forward, I will inform her of our rates.'

'Do we even have any?'

'Nothing is set down because each case will be individual.'

So that's how he was spinning it. 'Will Annabelle get "mates' rates"?' She did quote marks with her fingers.

They did need to get paid for their work, but perhaps she was being harsh. After all, when they'd investigated into the parentage of the little girl Birdie's aunt was fostering, it wasn't done for money. She'd understand if he didn't want to charge Annabelle much, or at all. But it didn't mean she wasn't going to tease him about it.

'She will be charged what is fair and equitable.'

'What if she asks for a discount?'

'I doubt she will. Money isn't an issue for her.'

'Fair enough.' She shrugged. 'What about a contract? I'm assuming all clients will sign one. Or are we going to be dodgy PIs, not averse to crossing the divide between what's legal and what isn't?'

'For goodness' sake, Birdie. We...' He paused. 'Another joke?'

'Yep. One day you'll get the hang of me. Though, to be honest, I thought you already had. Maybe I've just upped my game and you're slow to catch up.' She placed a hand on her hip and stared up at him. Unfortunately, being about a foot shorter meant trying to look superior wasn't exactly successful.

Seb rolled his eyes and shook his head. 'What the hell have I let myself in for?'

'And you're only asking that now? You seriously must be losing the plot.' She gave him a gentle nudge on the arm.

'In answer to your question about the legalities of our services, my solicitor is currently drawing up a terms and conditions agreement for clients, which we will look over together once it's complete. But in this instance, we can trust Annabelle will pay for our time, whether or not the investigation is successful.'

Did he still have a thing for Annabelle? On the surface it appeared not, but Birdie couldn't be sure. Maybe he was jealous over her relationship with Pemberton and he was pretending it was a nuisance having to work for Annabelle.

'Where does Annabelle work?' She was bound to be an influencer or have her own designer business of some sort.

'She isn't in paid employment, but volunteers for several charities.'

'Nice work if you can get it.' How cool would it be to not have to work for a living? To have enough money to spend all day, every day, chilling and mooching around the shops in whatever foreign country took your fancy.

'You'd hate it.' Seb gave a dismissive wave of his hand.

Would she? He could be right, but she'd certainly love

the opportunity to find out for herself. It was very easy to dismiss the benefits of money when you had loads of it. Not that Seb was super rich, or if he was, he didn't flaunt it.

'Perhaps. But as I'm never going to find out, it's pointless discussing it. So, what are our plans now regarding Annabelle?'

'Before I call her back to arrange a time for us to meet, let's look into her fiancé Jasper Pemberton. I've heard of him but know very little detail. You start while I fetch another chair.'

Seb left the room and his dog, Elsa, a yellow Labrador, moved from where she'd been lying by the window and settled herself at Birdie's feet.

'Are you comfortable, girl?' Birdie leant down to give Elsa a pat, and she wagged her tail furiously. 'Of course you are. Right, let's find out more about *Her Ladyship's* boyfriend.'

She googled the name Jasper Pemberton, and there were several, but she managed to find the correct one after seeing a photograph of him standing next to Annabelle in a society magazine article. Digging a little deeper, she discovered that he worked at the Nelson Art Gallery in Mayfair, London. His social media presence was negligible, to say the least, so she checked out Annabelle's and that was the same. Was it an aristocracy thing? Did they like to keep their lives more private than everyone else?

It wasn't much to go on, so she undertook a search on the art gallery to see what that might bring up. There was plenty to check. She clicked on a recent newspaper article and her jaw dropped.

'Oh. My. God.' The squeak of wheels from the chair being pushed along the wooden floor outside the study

caught her attention, and Seb appeared in the doorway.
'Seb, quick.'

'What is it?'

'You'll never guess what I've discovered. Although why on earth Annabelle didn't tell you, I don't know. It turns out that the art gallery where Jasper works had a painting stolen last week and a forgery put in its place. It was discovered on the Thursday. According to this one article, it was worth a million pounds. Wow! One million. Who on earth would pay that much for something to put on the wall? Don't tell me this is a coincidence. Jasper goes missing at the same time as the painting, and Annabelle gets a letter demanding *something* to be returned? It can't be.'

Seb dragged the chair over to the desk where she was sitting and sat beside her.

'Good work. What do we know about this painting?'

'Nothing because it hasn't been disclosed which one it is. But we still need to know why Annabelle kept it quiet.'

'And the gallery?'

'It's one of three owned by the Nelson Group. They're based out of Germany, but there are galleries in Paris, Vienna and then the one in London where Pemberton worked.'

'I'll give Annabelle a call and see what she has to say.' Seb picked up his phone from his desk and pressed a number.

Interesting that he still had her on speed dial. Whenever Birdie broke up with someone, she eradicated them from her life. No photos. No social media presence. Nothing. It was as if they didn't exist.

'Put her on speaker.'

'Sebastian. Finally. I was beginning to think you'd forgotten me.' Annabelle's clipped tones echoed around the room.

If the woman spoke to Birdie like that, they would be falling out, big time.

'We've done some research and discovered that the gallery where Jasper works had a valuable piece of art stolen last Thursday. It was replaced with a forgery.'

'Oh. And you think that might be relevant.'

'Well, yes. Surely Jasper must have told you,' Birdie said.

'Am I on speaker? I didn't realise,' Annabelle said pointedly. 'In answer to your question, I hadn't seen him for a while.'

'But it was in the media.'

Seb gave a sharp shake of his head. *Don't.* She hadn't meant to sound so accusatory, but how could the woman not know about this?

'Sorry,' she mouthed, and he nodded.

'It might well have been, but I wasn't aware of it.'

'We believe that this is most likely what was being referred to in the letter you received. We—'

'I'm sorry, Sebastian, I have to go. I'm expected at a meeting and can't be late.'

Birdie exchanged a glance with Seb, who rolled his eyes.

'Of course, I understand. We'll be in London tomorrow and wish to meet with you to discuss the case and our involvement.'

'I'm busy in the morning. Meet me at three, at The Savoy.'

'Okay. Put the letter into a sealed plastic bag and bring it with you.'

'Will do. Got to dash.' Annabelle ended the call, and Seb returned his phone to the desk.

Birdie frowned. 'She can't be that worried about him if her meetings are taking priority. But at least now we have our first case, although I did notice you didn't mention our fee.'

'And you would have also noticed that she didn't give me a chance. Now, let's discover what we can about Jasper Pemberton and the gallery where he works. I don't want any surprises.'

Chapter 5

'If this is where we're going to hold our client meetings, then we'll have to quadruple our fees. This place is amazing.' Birdie said as she followed Seb into the Thames Foyer of The Savoy, where afternoon tea was being served. Mesmerised by the grandeur of her surroundings, she stared up at the glass atrium where the natural light shone through, bathing the room in warmth from the sun's rays. 'It's not exactly private, though, is it, with all these people having their tea.'

'There will be enough hustle and bustle that people won't hear what we will be talking about.'

'I suppose so. Especially as we'll be serenaded.' She nodded at the pianist. 'Concerto in F. I approve.'

Seb turned to her, his eyes wide. 'You know Gershwin?'

'Don't look so surprised. I'm not a total pleb.'

'But—'

'But, how can a working-class girl like me know about him?' she interrupted. 'I'll tell you, it's because that's what I grew up listening to. *The Great American Songbook* was a favourite of my parents and grandparents.'

'It was nothing to do with your *class*, whatever you mean by that. My reference was regarding your age. Although, you've never mentioned your taste in music before.'

'It's never come up. I don't recall asking you what music your parents listened to when you were a child. Although, I'm guessing it was opera and classical.'

'Now who's being stereotypical?' Seb arched a brow.

'Touché.'

'Even if it is true,' he added, a wry grin on his face.

Birdie didn't respond, her attention distracted by a trolley being wheeled past them, piled high with mouth-watering sandwiches and pastries. 'I take it we'll be ordering afternoon tea.'

'I wouldn't be so cruel as to say no, knowing how much you enjoy your food.'

'Good.' She glanced around the room, which was full. 'Did Annabelle book us a table?'

'I assume so. But knowing Annabelle, they'd fit us in, even if she hadn't. We'll ask the maître d' if she's arrived yet.'

'Am I dressed okay?' Birdie glanced down at her navy-and-white gingham dress, which she was wearing with a pair of white trainers. She'd never been into such a posh place before. It was where all the celebrities hung out, and she didn't want to look out of place. Which reminded her, she'd have to check out whether there was anyone famous in the restaurant so she could tell Tori. Her friend would be so jealous if Birdie did see someone, especially if they were from *Made in Chelsea* or *Love Island*.

'It's smart casual and that's exactly what you are. Ah, there she is.' Seb detoured away from the maître d's station and headed towards the far end of the room where Annabelle was seated at a table.

'She must've arrived early. That's a surprise. I'd have bet on her being late and making an entrance,' Birdie commented.

'That's where you have analysed Annabelle incorrectly because she's a stickler for being on time. Obsessive, in fact. So, if anything, she would have been early.'

As soon as Seb said the word *obsessive*, Birdie could see it. Annabelle was the epitome of a walking, talking Type A personality.

'I stand corrected. What time do we have to be back at your place?'

'No time in particular, why do you ask?'

'I was just wondering about Elsa because we've left her alone.'

Birdie had fallen in love with Seb's apartment in Chiswick, where they were staying while they were in London. It wasn't huge, but it was cosy and had two bedrooms, both with an en suite, which meant she had her own bathroom – a massive treat, because at home she had to share with her two younger brothers and there was always a fight to see who could get in there first. It was perfect for Elsa, too, because it was on the ground floor and had a small garden.

'Don't worry – I've already arranged for Jill from next door to let Elsa out during the day and, no doubt, she'll take her for a long walk. There's a park close by. Jill loves looking after Elsa and was a godsend when I was doing shift work at the Met. I know she's missed Elsa while we've been living in East Farndon.'

A looming thought hit Birdie's stomach. Did that mean that when Sarah returned, Seb would want to move the business to London? They hadn't discussed it. Would she want to move away from all of her friends and family? It hadn't worked out when she'd moved to Manchester to attend university. But the circumstances that caused her to drop out weren't likely to reoccur; she'd found herself in a toxic relationship, and the only way she'd been able to maintain her sanity was to escape.

Still, there wasn't any point in thinking about relocating now because Sarah could end up being away for years.

'That's okay then because Elsa's our top priority.' Birdie's tone was flippant, but she meant it. She couldn't bear it if the dog was left alone and became upset.

They continued to the table and when they arrived, Annabelle glanced up at them, face blank, staring directly at Seb. 'I was only expecting you.'

Was she meant to leave?

'I believe I said *we* when we spoke yesterday. Birdie and I will be working on the case together. Have you already ordered?' Seb gestured for Birdie to sit before Annabelle had a chance to reply.

Birdie relaxed, pulled out one of the chairs around the circular table, and sat opposite Annabelle.

'Yes. I have ordered tea for two. I'll have to change it.' Annabelle tutted and then signalled to one of the waiters who was hovering close by. 'Please change my order to *three* teas.' She glanced at Birdie. 'You're not vegan or vegetarian, are you?'

Birdie really wanted to say yes just to wind her up because she was sure that Annabelle would think she was being a nuisance but didn't want to miss out on the cream-and-jam-filled scones.

'A normal tea would be fine, thank you.'

'I don't want you writing notes or recording our conversation on your phone – people might think that you're from the press and wonder why I'm giving you an interview,' Annabelle said once the waiter had left.

Then why arrange to meet here and not where she lived, or a place where they'd be less on show? The woman was a walking contradiction, for sure, and Birdie couldn't envisage them becoming friends any time soon.

'There'll be no need for that because I recall everything,' Seb said, relaxing back in his chair.

'Surely you know that Seb has HSAM? That's highly superior autobiographical memory in case you wondered.' Birdie said, chuffed that, for the first time, she'd got it right.

'I do know what it stands for and am fully aware of the fact that Sebastian has it. But *you* might have wanted a record. I assume you don't possess the same talent…?'

Birdie didn't get the woman. She wanted their help, yet she was doing her hardest to be confrontational.

'I don't need a separate recording – Seb has it covered.' Birdie glanced at Seb, who was frowning.

Was she being rude? She didn't intend to be, but it wasn't easy when Annabelle was making it so hard for Birdie to like her. Just because Birdie's dad wasn't a duke or some other aristocrat didn't mean her views weren't important.

Although Birdie's family could be traced back to Henry VIII. That was according to Birdie's uncle, who'd been doing their family tree. The link was via one of the king's illegitimate children, but it still counted. She had royal blood. Would that impress Annabelle? Except … she'd been adopted, so that might not count. But Annabelle didn't need to know that.

Anyway, Birdie was hunting for her birth mother, and it could turn out that they, too, were related to royalty.

'Since we spoke yesterday, have you checked the news regarding the missing painting from the gallery?' Seb asked, getting down to business.

'Yes, and I was astounded. It was the first I'd heard

about it. Jasper hadn't even mentioned having the painting at the gallery.'

'Did you often discuss his work?' Seb asked.

'I have an interest in art, yes, and would attend exhibitions there. That was why it surprised me that he hadn't mentioned that the gallery was acting as caretaker for such a valuable piece.'

'How does the process of caretaking work?' Birdie asked.

'It would have been brought to the gallery specially wrapped and handled carefully by whoever transported it and then placed in the vault. According to the report I read, it was at the gallery for cleaning by one of their specialists.'

'When was the last time you saw Jasper in person?'

'We went to the theatre on the Thursday before, the seventeenth, to see *Hamilton*. He came back with me to my place, stayed overnight, and left in the morning to go to work. Nothing out of the ordinary.'

'And when were you due to see him next?' Seb asked.

'Not until the following weekend, which is the Friday just gone. But I did telephone him on the Tuesday beforehand and got no reply. Ditto with several text messages that I sent him. That's why I came to see you. Jasper has never ignored me like this before.'

'Could he have had an emergency crop up that involved him going somewhere, and he didn't have time to tell you?' Birdie suggested.

'How hard is it to pick up the phone or send a message?' Annabelle said, a tremor in her voice. 'He's missing, and the note I received confirmed it. I was right in my assumption.'

'As yet, we don't know anything about this painting other than it's been stolen and that an anonymous person believes Jasper has taken it. But what's puzzling me is that, according to you, he disappeared *before* the painting was declared missing on the twenty-fourth. So where was he? And how did he get his hands on it if, in fact, he is guilty of stealing it?' Birdie asked.

Annabelle gave a frustrated sigh. 'I don't know. None of this makes sense.'

'For all we know, he might have nothing to do with the painting. Whoever sent you the note might have got it wrong. But we won't know until we investigate further. Do you know the names of any people he's involved with? Friends. Acquaintances. Is there anyone who might have a grievance against him? Can you think of anything that might help us?' Birdie pushed.

'You're making him sound like some sort of gangster. It's ridiculous.'

'Where does Jasper live?' Seb asked.

'He has an apartment in West Brompton.'

'Did you check to see if he was there?' Birdie asked.

Annabelle exhaled loudly. 'Obviously. I have his spare key and visited before driving to East Farndon. He wasn't there.'

'Did you have a good look around to see if there was anything unusual there?' Seb asked.

'I didn't rummage through his possessions, if that's what you mean, but at a glance, nothing looked out of place. His neighbour saw me go in, and I didn't want him to think I was snooping.'

What a weird thing to say. Why would anyone think that? She was his fiancée.

'Have you been seeing Jasper for long?' Birdie asked.

'We've been dating for a while and are engaged to be married. My family approve of the match. His father was a colonel in the British Army, and his mother is one of the

Brigstocks from Hampshire. You know him, don't you, Sebastian?'

'I met him several years ago at a ball. That was the only time.'

'I thought you lot knew everyone really well,' Birdie said.

Annabelle glared at her from under her eyelashes. 'What an absurd statement to make. And what do you mean by "you lot"?'

'Nothing. Sorry, no offence.' Birdie said, conscious of Seb tensing beside her.

Had she pushed it too far?

'After we've had tea, I suggest you take us to Jasper's apartment,' Seb said. 'We'll see if we can find anything that may help us discover where he is.'

Chapter 6

'Hello, Ted.' Annabelle nodded to the concierge on duty when they walked through the entrance to the building where Pemberton had his apartment.

'Don't we have to sign in?' Seb asked as they walked along the dark green and cream carpeted corridor, with mirrored walls and a single chandelier hanging from the ceiling.

'No, because he knows me.'

'These are fancy.' Birdie gave a wistful sigh, her head turning from side to side. 'What floor is he on?'

'The fifth. We'll take the lift.'

'Okay. If we have to.' Birdie had a thing about lifts and only took them when absolutely necessary.

'You can walk and meet us up there if you like,' Seb said.

'I'll be fine.'

Annabelle stared down at her. 'Are you claustrophobic?'

'If I have a choice, I'll take the stairs, but I can manage a lift if necessary. It certainly doesn't get in the way of me doing my job.' Birdie didn't want to give the woman the chance to find fault.

'Do you have the same issue with the Underground when you're going through the tunnels?'

'No. I'm perfectly fine with it.' She hadn't travelled much on the Underground, to be totally honest, but she wasn't going to admit that.

The lift opened up onto a long hallway. 'There are only three apartments up here. This one's Jasper's.' Annabelle slid the key into the lock of the door immediately in front of them and turned it, opening onto another grand entranceway. 'I don't want you making a mess.'

'We're not here to loot the place.' Birdie rolled her eyes. Did the woman think they were total amateurs?

'I realise that, but Jasper has some valuable objets d'art which you need to be mindful of while you're searching. I'm sure you'd rather be warned to take care than accidentally cause damage, for which Jasper would need compensation.'

'Okay, okay. I understand.' Birdie pulled on some disposable gloves and handed a pair to Seb.

'Should I be wearing some of those, too?' Annabelle asked.

'Your fingerprints will already be in here, so it's not necessary,' Seb said. 'We don't wish to contaminate the scene any more than we have to, in case there's some valuable evidence. It's best if we can start in his study, if he has one – I'd like to examine what he's been working on recently.'

'Yes, he does. It's this way.'

She led them down a corridor, stopping at the second door on the left, which opened onto a large square room with an antique desk in the centre, a light oak filing cabinet against one wall and next to it a large bookcase.

Seb headed over to the filing cabinet and Birdie to the desk.

'I see that Jasper's a gambler.' Birdie looked up from searching through the top drawer and stared at Annabelle, wanting to gauge her reaction.

Annabelle frowned. 'What makes you say that?'

Birdie held up a wad of papers in her hands. 'These are all betting slips, and most of them are from the last few weeks. I'd say that's more than the occasional flutter, wouldn't you?'

Annabelle headed over and stared at the slips in Birdie's hand. 'I've seen him bet on horses when we go to the races, but nothing excessive. Are you sure all of those are his?'

'Why else would he have them? He bets on horse racing and most sporting events, by the looks of things. I just want to see if I have found them all.' Birdie slid her hand back into the desk towards the back and pulled out more paper.

'Betting slips?' Annabelle asked, her voice flat.

'Yes, I'm sorry.'

So, if Pemberton hid his gambling habit from his fiancé, was it deliberate or an oversight? And would Annabelle want to continue her relationship with him now she'd discovered something she'd known nothing about?

'Who owns this property?' Seb called out.

'Jasper does. His father bought it for him ten years ago. Why do you ask?'

'To give me a better understanding of his financial situation. I've been going through his bank statements and they make for worrying reading. He has several bank accounts that are overdrawn, and the current account in which his salary is paid contains just over one hundred and fifty pounds. His next pay isn't due for two weeks, and he has several direct debits set up for utilities and other purchases he's made. How does he support his lifestyle? Does his father help him out?'

Annabelle sighed. 'I don't know about his finances, but he certainly doesn't act as if he has no money and is in financial difficulty. This day is going from bad to worse.'

'I've found his laptop. You don't happen to know the password do you?' Birdie called out.

'Yes. It's *Rembrandt* with an exclamation mark at the end. Use a capital R. It's spelt—'

'I know how to spell it,' Birdie interrupted.

Birdie keyed in the password and began going through the documents. But there were too many. 'Seb, nothing is jumping out at me, but there's a lot on here, including his diary and emails. Shall we take it with us to go through more thoroughly later?' Birdie said.

'Would that be okay?' Seb asked Annabelle.

'Of course. Take whatever you think will help.'

'There maybe something on there that will help us discover who sent you the note. Do you have it on you?'

'Yes. You asked me to bring it.' Annabelle opened her handbag and pulled out the letter, which was in a clear plastic bag. She handed it to him, and he placed it into his pocket without even taking a look.

'Thank you. We'll inspect it later.'

'Do you suspect Jasper of stealing this missing painting?'

'It's too early to say. He's clearly been living beyond his means. And he's been gambling. That doesn't mean he stole it, of course. But searching his laptop and other financial documents will enable a fuller assessment to be made.'

'However much in debt you believe him to be, stealing a painting worth a million pounds isn't something Jasper would do.' Despite the confidence of her words, the reticence in Annabelle's voice hung in the air.

Did she believe he was guilty?

'That's what we'll be investigating. Do you have the names of his friends, so we can interview them?' Seb asked gently.

'There's Charles Bosworth. I'll text you his contact details. They've been friends since school, and he's the person I would class as his closest friend.' She paused a moment. 'Probably his only real friend.'

'Thank you. Where does Jasper keep his passport?' Birdie asked.

'I have no idea. Is it in any of the drawers?'

'It's not in the desk,' Birdie said.

'It's not in the filing cabinet either,' Seb added. 'Perhaps he has it in his bedroom. We'll check there next.'

'Or he might have it with him. If he has stolen the painting – and I'm not saying he has – then he may have gone overseas,' Birdie said.

'Transportation could be a problem, depending on the painting's size. Which we don't know because so far nothing about it has been publicised,' Seb said.

'Did Jasper ever talk about having money issues?' Birdie asked.

'Not directly.'

What was she hiding?

'Indirectly?' Birdie pushed.

'Recently he made several comments regarding pooling our resources. But I didn't take that as meaning he needed money.'

What else could it have meant? Either Annabelle was seriously deluded regarding Pemberton, or she wasn't prepared to admit that he wasn't all she'd thought he was. Birdie doubted she'd admit much to her anyway. Maybe if

Seb spoke to her alone – aristocrat to aristocrat – he might extract more information.

'Did you think his comments strange?' Birdie asked anyway.

'No. They were made during conversations regarding our future. I'll show you to the bedrooms, and then you can continue searching there and the rest of the apartment. I don't want to get in your way.'

Once they were in the bedroom, Annabelle left them to it.

Birdie checked under the mattress and the bed, while Seb checked the drawers and went into the wardrobe.

'I think Annabelle's hiding something,' Birdie said from her position on the floor.

'She's just on edge.' Sebastian replied. 'The threatening note has disturbed her more than she's admitting.'

'If you say so. I don't know her like you do.' She pulled open the drawer to the bedside cabinet but slammed it shut again. 'I don't think there's anything useful in here.'

'Agreed, let's go back to Annabelle.'

They headed back to the kitchen, and the woman was sitting at the table staring into space.

'We've finished our search, Annabelle,' Seb said, drawing his ex out of a trance. 'I think our next port of call should be to visit Charles Bosworth.'

'Actually, hold that thought, Seb,' Birdie said. 'Annabelle, are there any CCTV cameras in the entrance to this apartment block? If there are, we can see when Jasper was last seen entering and exiting the building.'

'Yes, I believe there are. We can ask Ted.'

They returned to the front desk and waited until Ted had finished on the telephone.

'Is there something I can help you with, Miss Annabelle?' the man said once he'd replaced the handset.

'Yes, Ted. I'm a little anxious about Mr Pemberton. He hasn't been seen for a while, and I've asked Mr Clifford and his associate to investigate. Do you have the CCTV footage from last week for us to look at?'

Ted frowned. 'I'll have to ask permission from my manager to show you, I'm afraid.'

If Birdie was still in the police, she could have flashed her warrant card and they would have the footage in a flash. The whole point of leaving the force was to avoid the red tape, not face more. 'What about if you look and then tell us?' Birdie suggested. 'That will save you the bother of having to contact management and ask permission.'

'Um… I suppose that would be okay,' Ted said.

'Thank you, Ted.' Annabelle gave him a beaming smile. 'We wouldn't be asking if it wasn't terribly important.'

They waited in silence while he sat at his computer screen and, using his two index fingers, slowly tapped the keyboard.

'The last time Mr Pemberton left the building was last Tuesday, the twenty-second, at ten o'clock in the morning.' Ted said after five minutes. 'He wasn't dressed in his usual work clothes. He was more casual, like he dresses at the weekend. He hasn't been in or out since.'

'That's over a week ago.' Annabelle turned to Seb. 'This can't be right. Where is he? You must do something.'

'We now have a date to work with. Go home, and we'll be in touch once we have something to report.'

Chapter 7

The walk from Pemberton's apartment in West Brompton to the flat of his friend, Charles Bosworth, in Fulham, only took fifteen minutes, but during that time, Seb was deep in thought and hardly uttered more than two words to Birdie.

She glanced at him, the lines tight around his eyes. Was it having to spend so much time with Annabelle that was putting him on edge?

Birdie totally didn't get how they could've been a couple. They were so different. Okay, she was tall, sophisticated, and elegant. But there was no warmth. And although she wasn't openly rude to Birdie, it didn't take a genius to spot that she thought Seb had gone into business with someone beneath him.

'Another rich one, by the looks of it,' Birdie muttered as they arrived outside the Victorian mansion block.

'Don't jump to conclusions. Mr Bosworth may rent the flat. We don't know of his circumstances,' Seb said, correcting her.

'Rubbish. Even if he rents the place, I bet, per week, it would be more than I pay in board to my mum in a whole year.' She paused for a moment. 'Not that I'm saying I don't give my mum much for my keep, but—'

'I understand what you mean.' Seb smiled, the tension in his body seeming to disappear for the first time since they'd been with Annabelle. 'And you're most likely right.'

The front door was held open by a doorstop, and they walked into the entrance hall.

'No security. That's bad.'

'I expect someone is waiting for a delivery and propped open the door.'

'Yeah, but still – anyone could walk in. And why isn't there a concierge, like at Pemberton's place?' She glanced around the hallway to double-check that she was right. 'Mind you, it's probably good that there isn't, in case Bosworth refuses to see us.'

'You make a valid point. By the way, how am I to introduce you? It's not very professional to refer to you as Birdie when I am giving my full name.'

He was right, but no way could she be known as Lucinda Bird.

'I'm not sure. Definitely not my proper name.'

'I realised that. What about Ms Bird?'

'How's that going to work? Unless you call yourself Mr Clifford?'

'What about Birdie Bird?' Seb suggested.

Would that work? It was weird, but there were plenty of people around with much stranger names.

'I suppose we could try it and see.'

When they reached the flat, Seb knocked, and they waited. Shortly after, the door was opened by a slightly overweight man who stood at about five foot eight with a shock of dark brown, almost black, hair that curled over his eyebrows and covered his ears.

'May I help you?' The man's voice a dead ringer for

Seb's. Did private schools teach their pupils to all speak the same? She totally got the saying that someone spoke with a plum in their mouth. Because that was how it sounded.

'Charles Bosworth?' Seb asked.

The man took a step back, as most people did when faced with Seb's imposing stature.

'Yes.'

'My name is Sebastian Clifford, and this is my colleague Birdie Bird. We'd like to ask you a few questions about your friend Jasper Pemberton.'

Panic crossed his face as he glanced first at Seb and then Birdie, his manner very shifty. She didn't trust him for one minute. He was clearly hiding something, but whether it was to do with Pemberton remained to be seen.

'Are you the police?' he asked.

What had he been up to that he was scared of the law? Maybe she should ask him. Except she wasn't part of the force now, so it was hardly relevant.

'We're working on behalf of Annabelle Frankland, investigating Pemberton's disappearance. Your name was mentioned as being his closest friend, and we thought you might be able to help. May we come inside?'

Seb did his usual trick of taking one step forward, which at his height usually intimidated the other person sufficiently to make them move back, leaving enough space for them to enter the premises.

Birdie stared at him enviously. If only she could do that. Not that she couldn't stand her ground; she might be on the short side compared with Seb, but she could pack a hefty punch when necessary.

'Yes, okay, but I doubt there's anything I can tell you because I haven't spoken to him in a while.' The man held the door open for them to walk inside.

Although it wasn't as amazing a place as Pemberton's,

it was still a lovely flat and Birdie would be very happy to live there. She adored the high ceilings with the ornate covings, and it was furnished to her taste in a very modern and minimalistic way.

They followed Bosworth into the lounge, and he gestured for them to sit on one of the striped sofas.

'When was the last time you saw Pemberton?' Seb asked when they were all seated.

'A crowd of us went to Goodwood several months ago. We were in the Richmond Enclosure, as guests of the duke.' He coughed. 'I have to admit that luck wasn't with me, and it ended up costing me more than I'd have liked. I have no idea whether Pemberton won or lost over the day.'

'Did Annabelle go with you?' Birdie asked.

'Absolutely not. It was boys only. A boozy day out. You know the form,' Bosworth stared at Seb.

Did he? Probably, in his former life.

'And you haven't seen Pemberton since?' Seb asked.

Bosworth glanced up to the side and remained silent for a few seconds. 'Not that I recall.'

Birdie frowned. The man was being way too theatrical with his pondering. How could he not remember whether he had seen his friend?

'We found a large number of betting slips belonging to Pemberton, some of which came from Ascot a couple of weeks ago. Were you with him then?' Birdie asked.

Bosworth shifted awkwardly in his chair. 'I might have been there, but I don't think we spoke.'

'What you mean you "don't think"? He's a close friend. Why can't you remember?' Birdie fixed him with a stare, and he visibly squirmed. Did he know more than he was letting on?

'Okay, yes, I did see him, but we only spoke a couple of words. We were with different parties. That's not unusual.'

'Tell us about your friendship with Pemberton,' Seb said.

'We were at prep school together, and then both went to Winchester College and on to Oxford, although we were in different colleges and studied different subjects. I went into business, and he studied history of art. I'm his oldest friend. But more recently, we haven't seen much of each other because of other commitments on both of our parts.'

'In your opinion, would you say that Pemberton has a gambling problem?' Birdie asked.

'He does like to have a flutter on the horses. We all do. Why do you ask?'

Did he really have no idea of what Pemberton was like, or was he wanting to distance himself from whatever it was that his friend was involved in, for reasons they were yet to discover?

'The betting slips that we found in his study amounted to more than an occasional bet.'

Bosworth shrugged. 'I don't know. I'm not privy to that side of his life. Is that all? Because I'm due out shortly – I have an appointment with my broker.'

'Do you have any idea why he might've disappeared?' Seb asked.

'Are you sure it's not just Annabelle trying to keep tabs on him?' He stared at Seb, his eyes narrowing slightly. 'Of course. I remember now. That's why you seemed familiar. You used to date her, didn't you? You know what she's like, in that case. Wasn't there something…?' He paused a moment. 'The police. That's it. There was a scandal…'

'That's immaterial,' Seb said coldly. 'We're talking about Pemberton's disappearance.'

'Yes. He'd have gone somewhere and not told Annabelle. The way she always wants to know where he is and what he is doing drives him mad.'

'Yet they're engaged to be married, so surely he can't be that unhappy?' Birdie said.

'There are other, more important, things to Pemberton which mean he is willing to put up with Annabelle's obsessive behaviour…'

Had he told them more than he'd intended? His face was impassive and gave nothing away.

'What things? Are you saying that he is after Annabelle's money?' Birdie was unable to come up with anything else that it could be.

'You'll have to ask him. It's not my place to say.' Bosworth folded his arms and tapped his foot on the floor.

'Do you mind if I use your bathroom?' Birdie asked, frustrated by his lack of cooperation.

A look of panic momentarily crossed his face but was gone within a second. 'Yes, it's down the hall, the second door on the left.'

Birdie followed his directions to the bathroom. She didn't need to use the toilet but wanted to have a bit of a look around. He was being shifty and had aroused her suspicions. She pulled open the drawer beneath the sink. It was full of bathroom products, like shower gel, toothpaste, razor blades. Nothing out of the ordinary. She ran her hand along the back of the drawer, and tucked in the corner, she found a small black bag. Inside were two small packets of what she suspected was cocaine. She replaced it and returned to the lounge.

Seb glanced at her and arched an eyebrow.

Birdie nodded. 'Mr Bosworth, while I was in your bathroom, I found evidence of drugs—'

'What?' he spluttered, jumping up from his seat. 'You have no right to search through my belongings.'

'I was looking for soap,' she said. 'Does Pemberton also indulge?'

Bosworth's arms dropped to his side. 'It's only occasionally. I'm not an addict. And no, Pemberton doesn't partake. Not as far as I know. He most definitely hasn't while with me.'

'Who's your supplier? And, by the way, I'm an ex-police officer and do have links with the Met, so I suggest you tell us the truth if you don't want me to call in my discovery and you find yourself spending the rest of the day at the nick.'

Panic shone from his eyes. 'Look, it's recreational use only, that's all. I get stuff from my friend. I'll tell you what you want to know about Pemberton, but please don't report me to the police. I'm already on a warning. If I get caught again, they'll prosecute.'

'Okay. Fire away. You tell us something useful about Pemberton, and our lips are sealed.' Birdie pretended to zip up her mouth.

Bosworth sighed loudly. 'I wouldn't be surprised if he has vanished on purpose. He has money problems mainly resulting from his gambling and extravagant lifestyle. That's why he's with Annabelle. She has money, and he's hoping that she'll be able to bail him out.'

What a bastard. Birdie might not like the woman, but she didn't deserve that sort of treatment.

'Has he asked Annabelle for money?' Seb asked.

'No. That was going to be his last resort. He didn't want to risk it in case she ended their relationship and refused to marry him. His latest plan was to ask one of his special clients, a woman called Felicity, to buy an expensive painting from Nelson Gallery in Mayfair, where he works. He said the commission would go a long way towards covering all of his debts.'

Special. Did that mean what Birdie thought it did?

'What's this woman's surname?' Seb asked.

'I don't know, but he was fairly confident she'd help him.'

'When you say that this woman is "special", in what way? A good client? A sexual partner on the side?' Birdie asked.

Bosworth's cheeks turned pink. 'I've told you more than enough. Pemberton's a friend, but I have no idea where he is. Please leave now so I may attend my meeting.'

Birdie exchanged a glance with Seb. They now had a lot more to go on, and it wasn't worth hanging around.

'Thank you for your assistance. Please contact me if you recall anything that might help or if Pemberton gets in touch.' Seb handed the man one of his cards, and they left the flat.

When they got outside, Birdie turned to him. '*Birdie Bird* seemed to work okay. He did look weirdly at me when you said it.'

'My sentiments exactly. From now on, that's how I'll introduce you.'

'Good. All that matters to me is not having to mention the name Lucinda. I take it our next mission is to track down the rich and *special* Felicity?'

'Yes. We'll do that tomorrow. For now, we will go back to the flat and look through Pemberton's laptop and see what we can ascertain from his diary. We need to discover his last known movements.'

Chapter 8

Seb opened the door to his flat, and Elsa bounded over to see them, her tail wagging furiously.

'Hello, girl, have you had a good day?' He bent down and rubbed the rear portion of her back; her favourite place.

'Shall we take her out before we start work?' Birdie rubbed behind Elsa's ears once she'd left Seb and had nuzzled up to her.

'Jill texted earlier saying she's been out twice already, so I expect within a couple of minutes, we'll find her fast asleep in her bed. We've got work to do.' Seb stretched his arms over his head and yawned.

'Are we keeping you up?' Birdie arched an eyebrow. 'You do know that it's not even seven.' Her stomach grumbled. 'Which reminds me, all I've eaten today is the tea we had at The Savoy, and that's not enough to keep a sparrow alive. What do you have in the cupboards?'

'Not much. We'll order a takeaway. What you fancy?'

'I could seriously murder a pizza.' Her stomach grumbled again. 'Excuse me – but at least you know that I'm telling the truth about being starving.'

'I've got a menu somewhere.' Seb pushed open the kitchen door and headed over to his junk drawer.

'You know we can do it online.' Birdie walked up beside him, pulled out her phone and pressed a few keys. 'What do you fancy? All I need are your card details. I'm assuming that as we're at work, we can claim it as an expense.'

'Whatever you're having is fine.' Seb took out his wallet and handed over his business credit card.

'Are you sure because I'm going to order lots of chillies?'

'Yes.' He hoped that she'd been joking about the number of chillies because he didn't enjoy his food too spicy.

She bit down on her bottom lip while concentrating on her phone and pressing various options. 'Right, it's going to be thirty minutes, which gives us time to do some work.'

They went into Seb's small study, which had a desk under the window overlooking the street, and two chairs. Birdie opened Pemberton's laptop and positioned the chairs so they were both facing the screen.

Seb had often worked from home in the past until he moved to Rendall Hall. If his cousin came back, then the company would have to relocate. He'd assumed that his flat would be ideal, but now there were two of them, it felt a little small. He'd have to investigate renting an office, which would be costly in London. Perhaps they should make their base in Market Harborough. He was sure there would be suitable premises there. Also, he'd enjoyed living away from London's hectic hustle and bustle. Although, he hadn't yet discussed with Birdie where she would like to be based. He couldn't assume she'd fall in line with his plans because she most certainly wouldn't if it didn't suit her. And rightly so.

'Earth to Seb. Can you hear me?'

Seb started at the sound of Birdie's voice. 'Yes? Sorry, I was miles away.'

'You think? Do you want to look through the laptop with me?'

He stared at the two piles of letters on his desk.

'No, you look, and I'll make a start on these.' He nodded towards the mail that was demanding his attention. Considering that most things were done online these days, he still seemed to receive an inordinate amount of post.

'Sure.' Birdie shrugged and turned back to look at the laptop.

Picking his way through the envelopes, it appeared to be a stream of circulars, old magazine subscriptions he hadn't cancelled and the inevitable bills. Except… 'Bloody hell,' he muttered, opening a large cream envelope that sat on the top of the pile and pulling out a gold-embossed invitation.

'What is it?'

'It's my parents' fortieth wedding anniversary, and they're planning a big party at home in Winchester a week on Saturday. I should have replied by now, but I've been too busy.'

'Show me.' Birdie held out her hand, and he passed it to her. 'Wow, your parents sent you an invite to their party. That's crazy. How many people are going?'

'It's not huge, maybe three hundred of their closest friends and relations.'

'Three hundred is small?' Birdie spluttered. 'What happened to a booze-up at the local pub? That's what my parents did for their silver wedding anniversary. Well, it was a bit more than that, but nothing like yours. These invites are amazing.' She ran her fingers over it. 'I see they didn't say Sebastian, plus one. Does that mean I can't go with you?'

'Would you like to go to their celebration?' he asked, calling her bluff.

'No fear. I'd crap myself just visiting the "estate".' She used quote marks with her fingers. 'Why do you need to RSVP? Surely they know that you'll be attending.'

'Yes, they do. But by responding, the staff member who's handling the arrangements will also know, in case my parents forget to tell them. Anyway, back to Pemberton's laptop, which is the reason we're here. I'll leave going through my post for another time.' He pushed the remainder of the two piles of letters to one side of the desk and focused on the screen. He had too much going through his mind to concentrate on anything else other than looking for Pemberton. 'What have you discovered?'

'Well, I don't think he'd planned a trip away in advance because he has appointments booked for all this week. If he was going away, but not telling Annabelle, like Bosworth suggested, then surely he would have cancelled them. It wouldn't be good for his reputation for him to stand everyone up.'

Seb nodded. 'I agree. What appointments are in the diary for this week?'

'He has a meeting with Felicity A, tomorrow at eleven. I'm assuming that she's the woman Bosworth mentioned because there isn't another Felicity in his diary. I think we should keep that appointment for him. Providing we can find her address. I'll see if it's in his contacts.' She stared at the screen while clicking on various contacts. 'I've got it. Felicity Allen and she lives in Grosvenor Crescent, Belgravia. Is it nice around there?'

'It's the second most exclusive area in London.'

'Why doesn't that surprise me. And the first?'

'Kensington Palace Gardens. There you can mix with royalty and billionaires, should you desire to.'

'No, thanks. So do you agree, about seeing her?'

'Definitely. She's the best lead we have so far.'

Seb wanted to get the case over quickly so he could investigate several incidents that had occurred recently. At present, he was unclear whether or not they were connected. He hadn't mentioned anything to Birdie because he didn't have anything concrete to go on, and she might jump to unjustified conclusions. He'd had several calls from a withheld number, and the instant he'd answered, the line had gone dead. Furthermore, twice he'd thought he was being followed by different cars, but when he'd tested it by taking diversions, the cars had disappeared. It could turn out to be nothing. But nonetheless, he was on the alert.

'Agreed.'

'What else does he have planned?'

'A meeting with DM at the Fox and Hounds in Newham tomorrow at six. Is that far from where he lives?'

'It's a forty-minute drive at least, and even longer by train. It's not the sort of area I'd expect Pemberton to frequent.'

'So why is Jasper going to such a dodgy area? Oh, hang on.' She paused for a moment, her fingers clicking on the keyboard. 'This isn't the first time he's met DM. Over the past six months, he's been to the pub three times for a meeting. Always at six in the evening. Look.' Birdie scrolled through the weeks in his diary and showed him the appointments.

'There were also two meetings with a JD within the last month. But no address or phone number.'

'Yes, I noticed those too, but came to a dead end

because there have been no other references to them,'
Birdie said. 'But back to DM, I reckon he could be a loan
shark, and Pemberton met him to borrow some money?
Or pay it back, maybe. What do you think?'

It appeared that even if they found the man, Annabelle
would be far better off without him. Not that Seb would
ever make his feelings known on the matter. It was nothing
to do with him.

'I think that's most likely. We'll keep his next appointment and find out for ourselves.'

'If it's in a dodgy area, we'll need to be careful,' Birdie
said.

'I'll go on my own.'

'You're kidding, right? We're partners and if you're
going, then I'll be with you. It's called safety in numbers.
And it's not like it will be dark. It will be fine.'

Seb sighed. It was pointless trying to dissuade Birdie
because she'd wear him down with her persistence.

'Fine. If that is what you'd like to do, then we'll go
together. Is there anything on the laptop regarding the
painting or the forgery left in its place?'

'Nope. Maybe he was nothing to do with it. Although it
would be a bit of a coincidence, after the note that
Annabelle received… Hey, I've had an idea. Would Rob be
able to identify DM?'

Birdie was referring to Seb's friend and former
colleague at the Met, DI Rob Lawson, who was employing
him as a consultant. 'He may, but it's not exactly the area
in which he works. I'll phone him and ask.' He picked up
his phone and pressed speed dial for Rob.

His old colleague picked up on the second ring. 'Seb,
mate. How are you?'

They'd met years ago and had trained together. He was
one of very few officers who couldn't care less about Seb's

dad being a viscount. He treated him like one of the boys. They were very close, and Seb would miss him when he stopped working for the police.

'Very well, thanks. We're in London investigating a case, and I wondered if you could help. We have the initials DM and suspect it belongs to a local moneylender who operates out of the Fox and Hounds pub in Newham. Can you take a look for me?'

'You'd better be careful hanging around there. That's a definite no-go area for most people, or have you forgotten?'

'No, I haven't, but we're trying to trace a missing person, Jasper Pemberton, and that's one of the leads. He's had several meetings with a DM. Our guy also has financial problems, which is why we suspect the guy is a moneylender.'

'They could have got rid of him for non-payment of debts,' Rob said.

Seb shuddered. How would Annabelle cope if that was the case? For all of her bravado, this whole situation had unnerved her. 'That's a possibility, but the last meeting was three weeks ago, and the next one isn't scheduled until tomorrow.'

'Leave it with me. I'll ask around and get back to you.'

'Thanks.'

'Any chance of meeting up for a drink while you're up here, especially if you've got Birdie with you? I could do with a laugh.'

'If we have time.'

'Cool. Say hello to Birdie for me?'

Rob and Birdie had only met once but had got on famously, despite Birdie only being a detective constable at the time while Rob was an inspector. But the difference in rank hadn't appeared to bother either of them too much.

'Will do.' Seb laughed as he ended the call.

'What's so funny?' Birdie asked.

'Rob sent his best wishes and wants us all to go out for a drink if we've got time.'

'Oh, great, that would be nice. At least now I'm not a DC, I don't have to worry about dropping myself in it! Does he know who DM is?'

'Not offhand, but he's going to ask around and let us know.'

'Good. The more we know, the sooner the case will be over, and we'll be paid.'

Chapter 9

'So, if this is the second best street in London,' Birdie said as they stood outside the house belonging to Felicity Allen – a five-storey terrace with an ornate entrance flanked by fancy white pillars and a big black door with a gold knocker, 'then how much do you reckon this place would be worth?'

It was a nice enough place. Looked big. But it fronted onto a busy road, and there was no garden at the front, and there couldn't be much at the back because space was at a premium in the city.

'I'd hazard a guess at around thirty million pounds,' Seb said.

Birdie's jaw dropped. 'You what?' she spluttered. 'You're telling me that someone would pay thirty million smackers for a terraced house! It's totally beyond me.'

Talk about how the other half lived. This was that, and then some. Felicity Allen must be mega rich.

'It's more than just a terraced house, Birdie, as you will see if we're invited inside. Plus, as they tell you on the TV programmes, it's always location that counts.'

'I know. I watch the shows, but I still think that it's crazy for anyone to pay that much for somewhere to live.'

She'd always known that London prices were much higher than everywhere else, but who on earth could afford to live there? And more to the point, where did Felicity Allen's money come from? That she'd be very interested to know.

Seb pressed the gold bell, and after a short time, it was opened by a man in his fifties wearing what Birdie assumed was a uniform: black jacket, trousers, waistcoat, and tie with a white shirt. Was he the butler?

'Good morning, my name's Sebastian Clifford, and this is my associate, Birdie Bird. We'd like to speak to Felicity Allen.'

'May I tell Mrs Allen what it's about?'

'She had an appointment with Mr Jasper Pemberton, and we're here in his place. He's missing, and we believe Mrs Allen may be able to assist us in locating him.'

Birdie kept her eye on the butler. His eyes narrowed at the mention of Pemberton's name. What did he know that they didn't?

The butler opened the door and stepped to the side while they walked into a square entrance hall with high ceilings.

'Please wait here, and I will ask Mrs Allen if she is prepared to see you.'

He turned and walked down the corridor until out of sight.

'He certainly isn't a fan of Pemberton.'

'Yes, I noted that, too.'

She did a three-sixty, checking out the place. 'This house is totally ridiculous, and I've hardly seen any of it. Is the floor real marble?'

'I imagine it is.'

'And the staircase.' She stared at its sweeping curve. 'It's like something from one of those old movies. Can you see me gliding down them in a long, fancy ballgown?'

'A sight to behold, I'm sure.' Seb grinned. 'I agree. It's a lovely residence.'

'I would expect it to have solid gold toilet seats and taps for it to be worth thirty million, though.'

The sound of the butler's footsteps echoed as he approached.

'If you follow me, Mrs Allen will see you now.'

He led them into a large reception room, which appeared to span the entire width of the house. It had high ceilings and two beautiful fireplaces.

As they had entered the room, an elegant woman was seated on a rolled-arm pale blue sofa. She stood as they approached. 'Good morning, I'm Felicity Allen.'

'Sebastian Clifford, and this is Birdie Bird. We are looking into the disappearance of Jasper Pemberton, with whom you were due to have an appointment today.'

'So, I understand. Do take a seat.' She gestured to the matching sofa opposite her. 'Would you like coffee?'

'That would be lovely, thank you,' Birdie said, having got up too late to even have a drink that morning. It was all Seb's fault because they'd been talking about the case until two in the morning, and she hadn't slept well, despite the bed being comfortable.

Her mind had not only been full of the case, but also on the hunt for her birth mother and when she was going to find time to continue with her search. For a long time, she'd been fixated on finding out who her birth mother was and she'd already made some progress. She knew her mother's name and that she'd moved away to Canada with her family as a teenager but had come back to the UK with her own family.

'Ben, please arrange coffee for everyone,' Felicity said.

'Yes, madam,' he said before leaving.

Madam? This was a whole new world to her, although working with Seb, she should start getting used to it. Maybe he'd give her some lessons on what to expect.

Felicity remained standing until Seb and Birdie had taken their seats. The woman was probably in her late fifties, and overly tanned like so many women of that age. Her perfectly made-up face had hardly any lines, which had to be due to Botox or some other work. Her style was elegant, wearing a pair of silk wide-leg trousers in navy with a pale blue shirt over. She had a string of pearls around her neck and matching pearl earrings. She'd certainly made an effort for her appointment with Pemberton.

'Do you have any idea where Jasper is?' Worry shone from her eyes.

'Not at the moment.'

'Oh, my goodness. I hope he's okay. How can I help?'

'We'd like some background information if you don't mind. How long have you known Jasper Pemberton?' Seb asked.

'For just over two years. After my husband died following thirty-two years of marriage, I was left grief-stricken but with a healthy bank balance. I missed him terribly and, to compensate, went on a spending spree. I met Jasper at the Nelson Gallery in Mayfair, where he works. We hit it off instantly, and he understood my taste. I have bought several pieces of art from him. We developed a friendship, and he would often visit, ostensibly to let me know what they had in the gallery, but it was more than that.' The woman coloured slightly.

They were having an affair? Is that what she meant?

'And how often would he visit?' Seb asked.

'That depended on my social calendar. Usually, once a fortnight, occasionally more often. I haven't seen him for six weeks because I've been on a Caribbean cruise. He was due to see me today, as you know.'

Ah, that explains the tan.

'When were you last in contact with him?'

'We texted one another a couple of weeks ago to arrange today's meeting. He didn't mention there being any issues or that he was going away. But he did tell me that he'd put aside a painting he thought I'd like. I'm very much into the impressionist movement.'

Surely not the one that had gone missing. No. That would make no sense at all.

'Mrs Allen, we believe that Jasper was in considerable financial difficulty. Were you aware of this?' Seb leant forwards in his chair and steepled his fingers.

The woman paused and stared at them. 'He didn't actually tell me… But…' She hesitated.

'But?' Birdie prompted.

'The last time we met, just before my cruise, he was quite insistent about me purchasing a sculpture that he'd brought around to show me. I said no because it was ghastly. I was surprised he'd chosen it, knowing my taste as he does. He made some comment about needing the commission, which I laughed off. He often makes jokes. We have an easy relationship like that. But later in the day, I noticed that a small silver box of mine, which I kept over there' – she pointed to a white-and-gold sideboard beside one of the fireplaces – 'had gone missing.'

'And you believe that Jasper took it?' Birdie said.

'I'm not sure. I was going to ask him today. If he'd needed money, he only had to ask and I would have lent him some.'

'We believe his debts might have amounted to several

thousands. Would you have given him that much?' Seb said.

She adjusted the glasses perched on the end of her nose. 'Probably not without having an agreement drawn up by my solicitor.'

'Why didn't you report the theft to the police?' Birdie asked.

'I didn't want to jeopardise our relationship. I might be much older than Jasper, but we connected. I can afford the loss of a trinket and—' She was interrupted by the door opening and the butler bringing in the tray, which he placed on the table between them. 'Thank you, Ben,' Mrs Allen said.

'How would you characterise your relationship with Jasper?' Birdie said once the butler had retreated. She wanted confirmation of its intimate nature.

'Jasper's good company, and sometimes, when I'm lonely, we spend time together. There's nothing more to it than that. We're friends, and he could have asked me for money. If he's in trouble, then I want to help him. As I've already said, I don't care about the silver trinket.' She picked up her cup and took a sip of coffee.

'Did you have a physical relationship with Jasper?' Seb asked.

Birdie's eyes widened. Nothing like getting straight to the point. She'd been trying to ask in a roundabout way, judging that the woman wouldn't appreciate the direct approach.

Felicity was silent for a few seconds, biting down on her bottom lip. It had been the first time she'd come across as being remotely rattled. 'Yes, I suppose you could say we did. But it wasn't anything permanent. More like a fling.'

Well, next time, Birdie would try the direct approach because it clearly worked. Well done, Seb. Whether or not he'd actually thought it through before asking remained to be seen, though.

'Are you aware that he's engaged to be married?' Birdie asked.

Did the woman have a conscience when it came to sleeping with another woman's fiancé?

'When we're together, we don't discuss our personal lives. We both like it that way. It's not like there's anything going to happen between us. What we have is just a dalliance.'

A dalliance? Very interesting. But Pemberton still had no compunction about stealing from the woman. What sort of man was he? And why would Annabelle, who could hardly be described as stupid, stick with him?

'You might not be aware of this because you were on your cruise at the time, but when Jasper disappeared, so too did a valuable painting that was being looked after by the gallery. It was replaced by a forgery. We're working on the assumption that the two disappearances may be linked,' Seb said.

'No, I had no idea. When on holiday, I make a point of not reading or watching any news. I like a complete rest and can catch up with anything I've missed on my return. For all Jasper's faults – and yes, I'm aware there are many – I can't imagine that he could mastermind the forgery of a painting and then steal the original. He's not the brightest of men. He'd have needed help.'

Exactly what Birdie had been thinking. Despite the man attending Oxford University.

'Is there anything else you can tell us that might assist in finding Jasper?' Seb asked.

'No, I'm sorry, I have nothing further to add.'

'Here's my card.' Seb handed it to her. 'If anything does spring to mind, please let me know.'

Felicity picked up the bell, which was situated on a small table beside where she was sitting, and rang it. 'Ben will show you out.'

'Thank you for your time,' Seb said.

Once they were away from the house, Birdie turned to Seb.

'So, we've discovered that Pemberton was knocking off one of his clients and has also nicked a silver box, presumably to sell and pay off some of his debts. Are we going to tell Annabelle?' Birdie felt sorry for the woman. She'd have never thought that would happen.

'We definitely need to talk to Annabelle, but we'll play it by ear regarding how much we tell her about Felicity Allen.'

Chapter 10

'I suppose we should be honoured that Annabelle has deigned to see us straight away,' Birdie said as they stepped out of the taxi and made their way to the woman's apartment in Chelsea Harbour.

It didn't look as affluent as the areas where Pemberton and Bosworth both lived, but Birdie could be wrong about that. The fact that the block was central with, she suspected, some incredible views would most likely mean that it was also worth megabucks. Having met Annabelle and witnessed the way she lived, then Birdie guessed it was hardly going to be anything else.

'Birdie, you need to temper your dislike for Annabelle in order for us to keep working on this case together. I understand that she's very different from you, and I know she can rub people up the wrong way, especially those who don't know her well, but you must learn to be objective and not let your personal prejudices get in the way.'

Warmth flooded her face, embarrassed at being called out by Seb. But he was totally right; she should make more of an effort and behave appropriately. They were running a business, not a nursery school, which is the age range her behaviour had amounted to. Annabelle was a paying client, with a case for them to investigate.

'You're right, and I'm very sorry. I didn't mean it. It was just me being flippant. I'll act professionally from now on. I promise.' She glanced up at him, and he smiled.

'Thank you. That's all I ask.'

They walked up the two white marble steps, and Seb pressed the button to Annabelle's flat.

'Hello?'

'It's Sebastian and Birdie,' Seb said.

'Come on up,' Annabelle said.

The door buzzed, and Seb pushed it open.

'Hang on a minute,' Birdie said as, out the corner of her eye, she spotted something. 'Look, there are post-boxes for every apartment on the outside wall. Didn't Annabelle say that the post was dropped through her letterbox onto the floor of her apartment and the note was with it? How is that possible if all of the post is left outside?'

'We'll have to find out.'

They walked inside and over to the lift.

'What floor is it? I'd rather walk,' Birdie said. Without Annabelle's presence this time, she didn't feel the need to force herself inside the confined space.

'She's on the top floor. The penthouse.'

'Of course she is… Not that I mean anything in it,' she quickly added. 'Okay, let's go in the lift. I don't think my legs will take me that far.'

The lift whooshed smoothly up to the top of the building, and the door opened out onto sumptuous dark red carpet.

'Nice,' Birdie said, nodding.

'There are two penthouses up here, and Annabelle's is

the one on the left,' Seb led the way, stopping outside an open white door with a gold *P2* on it.

They walked straight in, and Birdie couldn't help her jaw dropping. It was magnificent. An expansive open-plan modern room with the kitchen in one corner, the dining area leading off it and a large sitting room in the lower half. Floor-to-ceiling glass windows ran along the whole of one side with sweeping views over the harbour.

Wow!

'Coffee?' Annabelle said.

'Yes, please,' Birdie said, dragging her gaze from the fantastic view. 'This place is simply incredible. I've never been anywhere like it before.'

'Thank you. I've recently had it renovated. I worked with Brie Falcon on it. You may have seen her work on interiors in the magazines. She was booked up for six months, but it was worth the wait. It's very different from the traditional style it used to be.'

'I'm not surprised you love it. It's fantastic.'

Annabelle poured some coffee from the barista-style machine she had on the side into three china cups and led Seb and Birdie over to the sitting area. The sofas were an oatmeal colour and probably cost more than Birdie earned in a month when she was in the police. Birdie took her coffee with shaking hands. What if she spilt anything on one of them?

'I assume that you have unearthed something, or you wouldn't be so insistent on seeing me straight away, Sebastian.' Annabelle stared directly at Seb.

'Now you do understand that some of this isn't going to be pleasant to hear.' Seb's tone was gentle and kind.

'I can take it. Just tell me what you have found out – I don't care how sensitive it is.' Annabelle picked up her coffee cup and took a sip, but it didn't hide how rigid her body had become.

'We spoke to Charles Bosworth, and he confirmed the extent of Jasper's financial and gambling problems.'

'Yet Jasper never asked me directly for a loan.' Annabelle stared directly at Seb, her empty fist balled in her lap. 'Why not?' Annabelle's face was set hard, the lines tight around her eyes. It was clearly taking all of her reserve to maintain her cool.

'He's been trying to raise the money elsewhere. He had an appointment with a client today, who we went to visit in his stead. He'd been hoping that she would purchase an expensive item from him. Recently he tried to persuade her to buy a sculpture that she didn't want, and we've assumed that today he was going to try to sell her something else. She...' Seb paused for a moment.

'Continue.' Annabelle closed her eyes for a moment and gave a long sigh before focusing on Seb.

'She believes he might have stolen a silver trinket box of hers the last time he visited. But she hasn't seen him since to ask and confirm.'

'No. That I can't accept. I'm sure he wouldn't stoop that low,' Annabelle said, uncertainty in her voice belying the words she uttered.

'You'd be surprised what people will do when faced with difficulties. Although, this woman didn't go to the police, which could indicate she wasn't totally convinced either,' Birdie said.

'Reporting him to the police would be the first thing I'd have done if I'd discovered something had been taken. So, why didn't...?' Annabelle looked first at Seb and then at Birdie. 'Oh. I see. It's written all over your faces. There's more to this relationship, isn't there? Tell me the truth. Was

Jasper having an affair with her, and that was why she gave him the benefit of the doubt and didn't report him?'

'Yes, we believe so,' Seb said.

Birdie could only imagine what was going through her mind. Her fiancé had not only done a bunk, but he had also cheated on her. That would affect anyone, whoever they were.

'We came across the initials DM in Jasper's diary. It was someone he met on a fairly regular basis in a dodgy pub in Newham. Do you have any idea who this person might be?' Birdie asked.

Annabelle sighed. 'No, I don't.'

'We're working on the assumption they might be a moneylender. Why else would Jasper visit somewhere like that so regularly?'

'A moneylender who operates from a pub? Even I know that means he's not above board. Do you think this has something to do with why Jasper has disappeared? Does he owe the person money and is frightened for his life? These things do happen in real life, don't they, and not just in films or on the television?' Annabelle said.

'Yes, they do, but not to the extent we see in the media. Having said that, it's certainly a possibility and something we are investigating. But we don't want to jump to any conclusions. We'll keep you informed of everything we discover,' Seb said calmly.

Annabelle leant forwards and rested her head in her hands. 'This is too awful to deal with.' Her voice cracked, and she coughed. 'Sorry. I'm trying to be strong, to cope with this in my usual way, b-b-but I don't think I can.'

Birdie exchanged a glance with Seb. Judging by the puzzled expression on his face, he was as taken aback as she was. No way had she expected Annabelle to break down.

'Look, Annabelle. We're here to help you get through this. We'll find out what's happened to Jasper and sort it out. All we need is your help. Well, as much as you can give us.' Birdie reached out and rested her hand on top of Annabelle's.

The woman flinched, but she didn't pull away. It reminded Birdie of how Seb was when she was affectionate towards him. It had to be the shared stifled upbringing that made them both so unresponsive to normal niceties.

Annabelle looked across at Birdie. 'Thank you. I appreciate your support.'

'You're welcome.'

'It would be really helpful if you could tell us as much as you can about your relationship with Jasper,' Seb said.

Annabelle sucked in a loud breath and sat upright again, appearing to be back in control. Did that mean the barriers were now back up?

'Things haven't been right between us for a long time. I will admit that. I had my suspicions that there was something wrong, but I wasn't sure what it was and, to be honest, I didn't want to enquire. I had too much on my plate. I wish now that I'd listened to that inner voice of mine.'

'Listened about what?' Birdie asked.

'We got engaged quite quickly after we'd met, which wasn't long after we had finished, Sebastian. Occasionally I have wondered if it is my money and status that he is attracted to. I broached the subject once, but he assured me that was furthest from his mind. Turns out, he's made a complete fool out of me.'

'No, he hasn't. You weren't to know. He must have been convincing because you don't strike me as someone who would normally be taken in. You're way too scary,' Birdie said with a grin.

'Thank you, Birdie.' Annabelle smiled politely. 'I imagine you think I should walk away and forget all about him and whatever it is he's mixed up in, but…'

'Relationships aren't that easy. We've all been in difficult situations. And sometimes it isn't possible to leave. The fact that you've received a warning note puts you right in the centre of what is happening,' Birdie said gently.

'It's not just because of me that I have to be careful. It's the rest of my family and the damage that it could do them. And as much as it seems like he was using me, I do still have feelings for him. There was such a big splash in the media regarding our engagement, and if we were to call it off now, especially with him being missing… Well, you can imagine what would happen.' Annabelle gave a helpless shrug.

'We'll take it one step at a time and see if we can find him first. After that, you can deal with him in whatever way you deem most appropriate. Actually, there is something that has been puzzling me. You said that the note you were sent ended up being pushed through your letterbox here. But downstairs are postboxes for each apartment.'

'Yes, that's correct. All post is put in there, but mine is brought up by the housekeeper who looks after the old man in the penthouse next door. I gave her the code. She's here every day.'

'Is there any CCTV, so we can identify who was dropping post into your box?'

'Not at the moment, although there are plans to install a camera in the future.'

'Crap. I was hoping we might have been able to identify who left the letter.'

Seb's phone rang, and he pulled it out of his pocket. 'It's Rob – I'd better take it.'

He got up from the sofa and walked over to the other side of the room.

'Rob's his contact at the Met. We've asked him to investigate the person with the initials DM,' Birdie said, trying to make small talk.

'Yes, I know Rob Lawson from when Sebastian and I were together.'

'Oh yes, of course.' Birdie sipped her nearly empty coffee sheepishly.

They sat in silence while Seb was on the phone, with Annabelle watching him the entire time. When he'd finished, he came back over.

'DM stands for Declan Murphy. We were right. He's a moneylender and is known to the police. Not a nice guy.'

'What are you going to do?' Annabelle asked.

'We had planned on going at the time Jasper has his appointment. Going instead of him. But I'm not sure that's a good idea. It's better that, initially, he doesn't suspect the real reason that we're there. We'll go to the pub out of which he operates earlier and pretend that we're there to borrow some money.'

'*If* he'll speak to us,' Birdie added, frowning.

'Be careful,' Annabelle said. 'Both of you.'

'We've been in a lot worse situations, Annabelle,' Birdie said. 'Don't worry about us.'

Chapter 11

'You're looking worried,' Birdie said to Seb as they walked up the stairs from East Ham Underground station in Newham and headed along the street towards the Fox and Hounds.

'Not *worried* exactly, but wondering whether or not we've done the right thing by going to the pub together. With hindsight, it might've been advisable for me to go alone.'

Birdie stopped in her tracks and turned to him. 'You're kidding, right? We've been over this, Seb. For a start, there's safety in numbers. We don't know what's going to happen in there and it's better that we're seen together in the pub rather than you just being on your own. It's a lot harder to get rid of two people than one. I'm not saying that you can't protect yourself, because obviously, you can, but in my opinion, two of us is better than one. That's if there is any trouble, of course. Which I hope not, but we don't know.'

Was she right? What would they think about Birdie and him being together? They didn't look like a couple, so would they be suspicious? In this part of town, they might stick out. Or was he making a big deal out of something over which he needn't be concerned? They could easily be friends or relatives. There's no blueprint out there for who should be out drinking together.

'You make a valid point,' he said. 'But my main concern is that they'll think we're with the police. If they do, we'll get very little out of them.'

'You say that, but sometimes if there's an element of doubt, it can serve as protection for us. Anyway, we don't even know if we're going to find this Murphy guy at the pub, and even if we do, we've no idea how it's going to proceed. So, let's just go there rather than trying to work out what might or might not happen.'

It took them a further five minutes before reaching the Victorian pub. Situated on the corner of two streets, its double entrance doors were painted racing green with brass handles, and when Seb pushed them open, the smell of beer hit him. The floorboards were pale in the places where the varnish had worn off, and the wooden furniture looked like it had seen better days. It was even more of a dive than he thought it might be. It was busy, with a predominantly older clientele who Seb suspected might have been regulars because when the pair of them entered, all eyes focused on them, unlike most other pubs when people hardly noticed who was coming and going.

He turned to Birdie. 'Find us a table and I'll go to the bar for the drinks.'

'Sure, there's one over there by the window.' Birdie nodded towards a small wooden round table with two chairs facing one another.

He skirted around some people standing by the bar until he found a space.

The barman, in his fifties with a shaved head and gold earrings in both ears, approached. 'Yes, mate?'

'Half a bitter and a bottle of dry cider, please.'

'Coming right up.' The bartender reached for a half-pint glass and held it under the beer tap. 'I haven't seen you in here before.'

'It's my first time.'

'It's mainly regulars here. We're not exactly a trendy pub.' He grinned. Several of his teeth were missing, and of those remaining, most were blackened.

'I'm looking for a Declan Murphy. Do you know if he's here?'

The man momentarily froze, suspicion shining from his eyes. 'Never heard of him, mate.'

No way did Seb believe that.

'Are you sure?' he pressed.

'Yeah. Totally.' He placed the beer in front of Seb and then reached for a bottle of cider and, after flipping off the top, put it next to the glass. 'That's seven pounds fifty.'

Seb pulled out some cash from his wallet and paid. He then took the drinks over to the table.

'Any luck?' Birdie took the bottle from him, lifted it to her lips and took a sip.

'Most definitely. I asked whether Murphy was in here, and the barman denied all knowledge of knowing the man, but his body language told me otherwise. He clearly knew him but didn't want to admit it. Whether that's because he's been told to say that or he's frightened, we don't yet know.'

'So now what?' Birdie lifted up the bottle and took another drink. 'Mmm. You got my favourite, thanks.'

'You're welcome. My guess is that someone in the pub will be scrutinising us and deciding whether to approach us.'

'That makes sense. If Murphy does work out of here, then he's got to get his business from somewhere. So we just have to sit tight and see what happens. We could do with a photo of Murphy, so we know who we're looking for. Didn't Rob have one?'

'I didn't ask, which was remiss of me.'

'Me too, for only just thinking about it. Text him now.'

Seb sent a message to Rob and within a few seconds, his friend had replied.

'Damn,' Seb said. 'He doesn't have one to hand – he's not in the office today. He'll try tomorrow.'

'Never mind. We might not need it,' Birdie said, shrugging. 'While we're waiting, we can go through what we know so far about Pemberton's disappearance.'

Seb frowned. 'Let's not discuss anything here. We don't know who's listening.'

'Oh no, does that mean we need to make some small talk? I know how you love that.' Birdie smirked. 'Shall I start? Seb, what are your holiday plans for this year?'

'None at present. Now it's my turn. Why don't you tell me what you're planning on doing regarding finding your birth mother. We haven't spoken about it much recently.'

'I've decided that if there's any spare time while we're here, I'll do some more research. I'll start with her school, St Augustine. Marie Davis, her neighbour from back then, told me that was where she went. And when I visited the medium, it was suggested I look there.'

Seb shook his head in disbelief. No matter what he said, Birdie's belief in what she had been told by this so-called medium was cast iron. 'You do realise that there's no scientific proof to back up psychics' claims?'

'You can say what you like, but she knew too much for it not to be true. She was right about me leaving work, and coming to work with you, remember. I'm not saying that I'd fall for everything, but she was different.'

He was fighting a losing battle.

'Yes, but it would be easy to guess that someone was going to change job.'

'That aside, as I keep saying, she knew too much about me for it to be fake. And it wasn't her directly who suggested starting at Kim's school. A spirit from my birth family came forward – who, by the way, had issues with timekeeping just like me – and said that's what I should do. You can think what you like. I've got to carry on and find my real mother.' She paused a moment. 'Even if she doesn't want to see me.'

The fly in the ointment had been that Birdie's mother had told the Adoption Contact Register she didn't want to be contacted. But that hadn't stopped Birdie trying to find her.

'You know that I'll help you in any way I can. You only have to ask.' Although he did draw the line at accepting what the medium had told his partner.

'Thanks, Seb, but I'm going to do this on my own. Whatever I do will be done in my spare time. I've lasted this long without finding her – a little while longer won't make much difference. I promise it won't interfere with any of our work.'

He didn't for a moment believe that it would. Birdie's work ethic was second to none. She'd always go over and above what was required if it got the job done.

'Don't feel it has to be done outside of office hours. There will be times when we're quiet, so you can use that…' His voice fell away as he noticed Birdie had totally lost interest in what he was saying and was instead peering over his shoulder. 'Birdie. Are you listening to me?'

'Don't look now, but there's a man standing by the

door to the gents' toilet staring at you. At least I think he's looking in our direction.'

'Describe him to me.'

'Mid to late forties. Grey hair curling over his ears. Thick eyebrows. Muscly. Dodgy looking.'

'I know the man you're describing. He was seated with a woman at the second table past the bar on the right.'

'How do you know? Oh, forget that. Because you scanned the room when we arrived.'

Seb's HSAM meant that whatever he saw, he remembered. Forever. Sometimes it was a curse. Other times a godsend. Having said that, there were many times when he'd rather not have the ability. It was like having a search engine on in his head. All. The. Time.

'If you're right and he's trying to attract my attention, I'd better ensure that he knows he's made the connection.' Seb turned his head and stared back at the man. They locked eyes, and the man nodded his head towards the toilet door.

'He wants me to go over to the gents. Stay here while I see what he wants.'

'Okay. But if you're not back here in five minutes. I'm coming in to find you. Even if you are in the loo.'

'Give me ten.' Seb pushed back his chair and stood.

'Whatever. Five. Ten. I'll be keeping a close eye on the door. Good luck.'

He left the table and marched over. The man had already gone into the gents, and when Seb pushed open the door, he was standing by the sinks, his arms folded tightly across his chest. He locked eyes with Seb, his top lip curled.

Seb stiffened, bracing himself for whatever was going to happen next. He stood a good seven inches taller than the man, but height wasn't always beneficial if weapons were involved. He glanced at the leather bomber jacket the man was wearing. Was there a gun or a knife in the pocket?

'You asked at the bar about Declan Murphy,' the man growled.

'That's correct.' Seb kept his voice calm.

'Why?'

'I've been told by a friend that he might lend me some money. My friend said to come to the pub and ask for him.'

'What's his name?'

Seb paused and sucked in a breath. 'Okay. He's a friend of a friend. I don't know his name, but I did meet him at the races the other week. Are you him?' Seb didn't believe for one moment that he was, but it might ease the situation.

'No. Murphy will be in the pub from five-thirty tonight. Come back then and sit at the table in the far left corner.'

'And if it's already taken?'

'It won't be. Don't be late, or there won't be a meeting.'

The man brushed past Seb, knocking him out the way, and left.

Seb waited for a few seconds and then returned to the table and Birdie.

'Well?' she said the moment he was in earshot.

'We've got a meeting with Murphy later.'

Chapter 12

'Ready?' Seb asked as they made their way back to the pub for the meeting.

Birdie pulled her denim jacket around her and glanced up at the sky as several drops of rain splattered on her head.

Great. That was just what they needed, especially if they had to make a hasty exit and neither of them had an umbrella.

Seriously? She was making an issue over the weather?

She was becoming her dad, who even used to insure against rain when they went on their annual two-week summer holiday when they were kids. Was she spending too much time with people of a different generation, aka Seb, and was in danger of turning into one of them? When the case was over, she'd drag Tori and others out on one of their nights out. Before irreparable damage was done.

'Yes, Seb. We've planned how we're going to act when we're in there. You're taking the lead, and I'm going to be the eyes. Although, with your superpower, surely it should be the other way around,' she teased.

'I'll ignore that reference. They're expecting me, and it would be suspicious if now the customer turned out to be you.'

'I know. I was just… Oh, never mind.' She glanced at her phone. It was twenty minutes past five. They'd decided to be a little early to give them time to check out the place. 'Come on, let's go inside.'

She pushed open the door to the pub, and they hurried past the bar, not stopping until they'd reached the table in the far corner where Seb had been instructed to wait.

'Cider?' Seb asked once she'd moved one of the chairs slightly and positioned herself so she could see everywhere without it being obvious.

'No, thanks. I'll have a lemonade. Even a half pint might slow my reflexes, and I want to be on my guard because we have no idea what's going to happen. You're not drinking, are you?'

'I'll have a small beer. It might appear odd if both of us have soft drinks.'

Birdie watched him stroll over to the bar. Was he acting too relaxed? Surely someone wanting to borrow money from a dodgy loan shark might be a bit twitchy.

She scanned the room, starting in the far left and sweeping her gaze to the right. After each sweep she paused for a couple of seconds and refocused her eyes. She'd always found this methodical approach to be the most beneficial.

Even though it was only six o'clock, the place was busy. During her scan she wanted to see if Murphy was there, but it was impossible to be sure. Apart from a few loners at the bar who sat on stools staring into their glasses, most of the patrons were seated at tables, some of which had all men, some all women and some mixed. It was a typical pub atmosphere with nothing out of the ordinary that might have put her on alert.

Seb returned from the bar and placed their drinks on the table. She picked up her lemonade, took a sip and grimaced. 'This is diet.'

'Sorry, that's all they had. Would you prefer something else?'

'No, it's fine. I just wasn't expecting it. I wonder how long we'll have to wait for Murphy? I've been checking and can't see anyone staring at us or acting like they expect us to be here. Such a shame we haven't received an image from Rob yet.'

'He did say he wasn't in the office today.'

'I suppose. But surely it can't be that hard. He's a DI, for goodness' sake. He could've got someone to do it for him.'

'Birdie, Rob was doing us a favour, and isn't at our beck and call. He's busy with his other work, as you well know.'

Ouch. Touchy.

It was most unlike Seb. Was he more nervous than he was letting on? Or was the fact they were working for Annabelle finally getting to him? It wouldn't surprise her if it was. She doubted she could be so accommodating to any of her past partners.

Whatever it was. She knew better than to push him on it.

'Yeah, sure. Sorry.' She smiled, and his face relaxed. 'I'm surprised there wasn't a reserved sign on this table.'

'I suspect that if anyone did try to sit here, they'd be ordered to move. When I went to get the drinks, the bartender gave me a knowing nod, implying that I was expected.'

'So he must have been told you were coming and to

look out for you. Interesting that this table is situated well away from anyone else so no one can hear our conversation. Do you think the pub's management is part of this whole moneylending operation?'

'Possibly, or they're paid to allow Murphy to operate from here and to turn a blind eye. We might learn more when we—'

'They're coming,' she whispered, catching sight of two men heading towards them.

In front was a small man who looked to be in his fifties, barely above five foot five, with a shaved head and a thick gold chain around his neck. Could he have been any more clichéd?

Behind him was a man almost as tall as Seb but twice as wide. He stood next to the table, his chest out and his shoulders back, clearly attempting to be intimidating. A deadpan expression was plastered across his face. He'd have been more at home as the villain in a Disney cartoon.

The small man, who she assumed was Murphy, sat on the chair between her and Seb.

'Before we talk money, I want to know how you found me.' He squeaked like a kid whose voice hadn't quite broken.

Birdie forced back the giggle that was threatening to erupt and bit down so hard on her bottom lip that she could taste blood.

Murphy's voice was at total odds with his appearance. She hadn't been expecting that.

She glanced at Seb, but his face was expressionless. How did he do that?

'An acquaintance of someone who's borrowed from you in the past.' Seb steepled his fingers and stared directly at the man.

'Names. I want names.'

After several seconds of silence, Seb spoke. 'Jasper Pemberton. You've lent him money in the past.'

Murphy tensed. 'Who are you, and what do you want? It's not for money – I can tell by how you're acting. Why are you really here?'

What was Seb going to do? Tell the truth? They didn't really have an option if they wanted to know about Pemberton.

'My name's Sebastian Clifford, and this is my associate, Birdie Bird.' He gestured with an open palm to where she was sitting. 'We're investigating the disappearance of Jasper Pemberton, and this has led us to you.'

'Why didn't you say so upfront?'

'Would you have spoken to us if we had?' Birdie asked.

'No.'

'Well then,' she said, about to roll her eyes but thought better of it. She didn't want to wind the man up.

'We understand that Pemberton has been borrowing money from you over a period of time,' Seb said. 'Although we don't yet know for how long or how much he currently owes.'

Murphy glanced over his shoulder. 'Pemberton owes nothing,' he said, his tone altered. Anxious.

Was he scared?

Why?

'If that's the case, then how come he had an appointment to see you at six this evening? Or was it a social visit?' Seb leant forwards slightly, and Murphy slid his chair back a few inches.

What was going on? The man was a known villain, and he was acting like a frightened child.

'His debts have been paid. He owes me nothing, and I don't know where he is.'

Birdie nudged Seb's foot with hers. The man was lying,

but whether Seb could get anything out of him remained to be seen.

'How much did he owe you before the debt was repaid?'

'A few thousand. I don't remember.'

'Liar.' The word had slipped out of Birdie's mouth before she could stop it. Murphy glared at her.

'Who paid off his debts? Because we know Pemberton had no money.' Seb said, taking the focus from her.

'I don't know.'

'Don't be ridiculous. Who gave you the money?' Birdie said.

'The money was at the bar with his name on it. Now piss off.'

'What do you know about Pemberton's disappearance?' Seb said. 'Because it seems to me that you're more involved than you're letting on.'

'Don't push it.' Murphy gave a slight nod of his head, and the man standing beside him stepped forward.

'Boss?' he grunted.

'Escort these two out of here.'

'There's no need for that.' Seb stood, and Birdie followed suit. 'Thank you very much for your assistance. If it becomes a police matter, then I will pass on what evidence I have, and they may wish to question you.'

What the…? There was no talk of police in the plan. What was Seb doing?

'Are you threatening me, mate?' Murphy snarled. 'Because I'd be very careful if I was you. The cops don't bother me.'

'No threats,' Birdie said, holding up both hands. 'All we wanted was information about Pemberton. If he's paid off his debts and you haven't seen him, then that's fine with us.'

'It had better be.'

Seb and Birdie left the pub in silence and headed down the street. Once they were well away, and she could see that they weren't being followed, she turned to him.

'What's with you getting all aggressive and threatening him with the police? I've never seen you act like that before.'

'I was trying a different tactic from normal.'

Birdie frowned. Something wasn't right.

'Ask me before you do it again because it wasn't a wise move. What we don't want is for Murphy to send one of his guys after us. We have enough on our plate without that.'

'He won't. What's more interesting is who paid off Pemberton's debt. And why Declan Murphy, who is not a man to be toyed with, was so reluctant to converse about it. Did you notice his slightly raised eyebrows and his half-open mouth. He was scared.'

'Meaning?'

'That whoever took care of Pemberton's loan was a much bigger fish than Murphy.'

'And, presumably, finding out who that is will be our next task. But how?' She paused a moment. 'Why don't we wait for Murphy to leave the pub and follow him? He might lead us to who we're looking for. Then again…'

'Then again?' Seb prompted.

'Surely he'd just phone them.'

'Unless he was scared that his phone was being tapped.'

'He'd use a burner.'

'True. But as we don't have any other leads at the moment, I agree we should follow him.'

'We've got nothing to lose. Let's stand over there in the doorway of that abandoned shop and wait for him to leave. Hopefully, he won't be too long because it's cold, and I'm getting hungry,' Birdie said, looking up at the grumbling sky. She wasn't up for getting soaked on surveillance.

'We'll give him an hour and then reassess the situation.'

Chapter 13

Seb clenched his jaw at the sound of Birdie tapping her foot against the wall of the shop entrance. It had grated after they'd only been there for a couple minutes, and she'd now been doing it for thirty.

'I think he's in there for the duration,' Birdie said, continuing with the incessant tapping. 'This is so boring. Shall we call it a night?'

'First of all, PI work can be boring. And second, if it means no longer having to listen to your constant tap, tap, tapping against the wall, then I agree we should leave.'

Birdie stared up at him, her eyes wide.

'Seriously, Seb. You need to get over yourself. What's going on? You're acting so out of character it's not funny. Is it because of seeing Annabelle again? Is there unfinished business between the two of you, and it's getting in the way?'

'No, it's not. And no, there isn't. Your mind's running on overdrive. I'm perfectly fine.' His lips pressed together in a slight grimace.

Birdie was right. He wasn't himself. But he didn't want

to burden Birdie with his issues. Particularly as they could amount to nothing, and if he did tell her about the strange phone calls he'd been receiving, it would mean he was blowing everything out of proportion. The trouble was, when he worked for the Met, he was instrumental in putting away some hardcore criminals. Any one of them could be trying to intimidate him. But until he had anything concrete to go on, it was pointless informing Birdie, or anyone else for that matter. If only his mind wasn't constantly whirring, trying to work out who might be after him.

If it did amount to anything, then Birdie would be the first to know, but up until that point, it was best kept quiet. Although, he needed to be more cognisant of his behaviour when with her because she was clearly picking up on changes in his manner.

'If you say so. And I take exception to you implying that I'm unfamiliar with the nature of PI work. Of course I know what it entails. It's exactly the same as police work. Except usually it's possible to plan before undertaking police surveillance and to make sure—' Her eyes widened, and she diverted her attention away from him. 'They're leaving.'

He turned and saw Murphy and his bodyguard marching away from the pub towards the junction with the main road.

'We'll follow but keeping our distance in case we're spotted.' He strode off.

'Hey. Stop going so fast. I can't keep up,' Birdie said, running up beside him. 'Let's go at a normal pace. We've got them in sight. Unless they jump into a car or taxi.'

Considering that Murphy was on the wrong side of the road to stop a taxi, Seb doubted they would be doing so straight away, but it certainly was a possibility once they reached the junction.

'In which case, we'll have to bring our surveillance to a close.'

'You mean we can't take off in a taxi saying, *"Follow that car!"*?'

'You've been watching too many action movies.'

'It would still be fun, though. Don't you think?'

'Maybe.'

Murphy and his man continued to the main road and walked straight past the entrance to the Underground station.

'Okay, they're not going to take the Tube. So, where are they heading?' Birdie bit down on her bottom lip. 'Murphy doesn't look the type to walk miles just for his health, not if his rather large stomach is anything to go by.'

'Agreed.'

They continued in pursuit until the two men stopped outside a small café. Murphy glanced over his shoulder, but not in their direction, and then pushed open the door and went inside.

Birdie and Seb hurried over and looked in through the window. The café was fairly busy, and Murphy and his man headed to the counter. Murphy spoke to the woman working there, and she nodded. The pair of them went around the back, past the counter, and through a door, closing it behind them.

'Now what?' Birdie turned to face Seb. 'I don't suppose we can go in there and order something to eat, and wait for Murphy to come back out.' She arched an eyebrow.

Was she serious? He couldn't tell.

'That would be out of the question because he'll recognise us, and he doesn't strike me as a man who would believe in coincidences.'

'I was joking,' Birdie said, rolling her eyes and letting out a sigh.

Could he feel any more foolish? He really had to get it together.

'I think our time is better spent returning to the flat and undertaking some research into Murphy and his connection with the café. From what he said, I don't believe he's anything to do with what happened to Pemberton but—'

'But he certainly has an idea of who might have done it. He clearly knew who paid off the debt, and if we can find that out, we'll have a head start.'

'My sentiments, exactly.'

They headed back to the Underground and, within thirty minutes, were back at Seb's flat, armed with an Indian takeaway, which they'd collected on their way.

'So, are you going to tell me what's wrong?' Birdie asked when they were seated opposite each other at the kitchen table.

He placed the fork he was holding on the plate. 'It's nothing.'

'Pull the other one, it's got bells on – of course it's not nothing. You've been acting totally out of character for most of the day. Now, either you tell me or I'll sit here guessing until I get it right. And believe me, I *will* get it right.'

'I don't doubt that for a moment,' he said, giving a wry smile. 'Okay—'

'Obviously, unless it's personal and you don't want to share.' Birdie took a mouthful of her meal, and sauce dripped down her chin. She wiped it away with a paper napkin.

'Of course it's personal. But I will tell you, and trust that you will keep it to yourself. I don't want to worry anyone.'

'Oh my God. You're not sick, are you? Tell me you're not.' Her eyes were glassy with tears.

'I haven't even told you, and you're welling up. This is exactly what I wanted to avoid.' He gave a frustrated sigh.

'No, I'm not. It's the curry that's making my eyes water. Come on. Spill.'

'I'm in perfect health, so there's no need to worry. But there is another issue that might be something or nothing. Recently, I've had the feeling that someone is trying to get me riled.'

'Riled? In what way?'

'Put me on edge. Worried. I'm not being overtly threatened, but there's an underlying tension. I've received several phone calls from withheld numbers which were ended when I answered. And twice it appeared a car was tailing me. Although, I might have been mistaken.'

'You're not. I'd put money on it. The question is, what are we going to do about it? Actually, there's more than one question. We also need to know who's doing it and why? Assuming that the calls came from burners, let's concentrate on the car following you. Did you get the registration number?'

'They were different cars. One a black Toyota Corolla, and one was a silver Mazda3. I wasn't able to see the plates. Both cars had one male driver, again too far away for me to identify.'

'Was it the same driver both times?'

'I don't believe so.' Seb drummed his fingers on the table. 'There's not much to work on, is there?'

'Can you think of anyone who wants to wind you up? Or threaten you? Someone from your past, do you think?'

'It's entirely possible. For now I just have to be mindful of it and hope it doesn't escalate.'

'Yeah, I agree. But now you've got me to keep an eye out, too. I've finished my curry, so hurry up, and we can start researching.'

'I'll save the rest for later.' He closed the container lid and got up from the table.

When they sat in Seb's study, Elsa lay down beside Birdie and snuggled up to her.

'I'm invisible to her when you're here.'

'She knows I'll give her a treat.' Birdie pulled out a doggie snack from her pocket and held it out for Elsa. 'I always keep some on me when she's around.'

'Ah. You're bribing her.'

'Absolutely not.' She laughed. 'Right, are we both looking into the café?'

'To start with, because that way it will take less time.'

They worked in silence, and all that could be heard was the clicking of laptop keys.

After fifteen minutes, Birdie closed the lid of her computer. 'I've got nothing. What about you?'

'The café is registered in the name of Rhys Richards, but so far, there's no connection between him and Murphy.'

'Shall I look on Richards' social media page and see if Murphy shows up there?'

'We don't want to waste too much time on a search that might not yield anything.'

Birdie nodded. 'Perhaps we should focus on the art gallery where Pemberton worked. Let's see if we can find out which painting was actually forged because that might help us.'

'I agree. We should visit them tomorrow.'

'I've got a better idea. Why don't I go on my own and see what I can find out without alerting them to who we are? For a start, we don't know what's going on with the insurance claim or what happened behind the scenes. I can pretend to be an art student and just have a chat with them. What do you reckon? Will it work?'

Would it? As far as he knew, Birdie wasn't particularly au fait with art, so would she be able to convince them that she was a student? Then again, knowing Birdie, it wouldn't be an issue.

'That's an excellent idea. You can go in tomorrow morning.'

Chapter 14

Birdie stood outside Nelson Art Gallery in Mayfair's Mount Street and sucked in a breath. She'd been to art galleries before, but nothing like this one. She wanted to create the impression that it was somewhere she was well used to visiting. Although she'd taken care over her clothes and make-up, she didn't have anything really fancy like Annabelle, but Seb had assured her that it wouldn't matter. She wasn't so convinced, judging by the people who were strolling down the street.

She'd practised trying to put on a posh voice in the mirror, but Seb had heard her and laughed. He told her to act natural and be herself because you didn't have to come from a certain type of family to be interested in art or to be shopping in Mayfair.

Birdie lifted her hand to push open the door and spotted the sign on the door. Opening hours were ten-thirty until four. Crap. It was only nine forty-five, which meant that she'd have to wait. She didn't want to hang around outside, so she took herself off down the street, looking for somewhere she could have a drink. She found a lovely café and ordered a coffee and what looked like a chocolate brownie from the counter.

She sat at a table by the window and watched the people walk past, except her mind kept going back to Seb and who was targeting him. If, in fact, there was someone. But she doubted he'd get it wrong. If anything, he might have played it down to stop her from worrying, even though they were partners and should share everything. It was probably because he'd been used to working alone and needed time to adjust. The same as she did. Joining Seb had been a massive risk. She invested all her house-deposit money, which had taken her years to save. But so far, she had no regrets. Even if it had only been a few days.

'Would you like a refill?'

Birdie glanced up at the sound of the waiter's voice and then down at her empty cup. She didn't even remember drinking it.

'No, thanks. I have to be going.'

She went to the counter to pay and nearly fell over backwards when they told her how much she owed. Twenty pounds for a coffee and cake. What the hell? She paid with her card, trying to act like it was no big deal. But seriously, that was ridiculous. And would definitely be put through expenses.

She made her way to the gallery, stopping to look in the windows of the shops she was passing. There was a jewellery shop where nothing in the window had a price on it. She could only imagine how much things cost. Actually, she couldn't.

When she reached the gallery, it was a couple of minutes past opening time, and she pushed open the door and stepped inside. Paintings lined the walls, and there were several white podiums dotted around with sculptures on them. She clutched her bag, which was hanging from her shoulder, to make sure she didn't knock into anything as she walked past.

Once she'd reached the centre of the gallery, a woman, who looked about the same age as Birdie and who'd been standing next to another slightly older woman, came towards her. She was dressed in typical Annabelle style, with a navy trouser suit, a pink open-necked blouse, and a single strand of pearls around her neck.

'Good morning, may I help you?' The woman smiled, and Birdie could see it was sincere. So far, so good.

'I'd like to have a look round if you don't mind. I'm studying for an art history degree at university here in London, and I've only just arrived from Market Harborough where I live. I thought I'd spend the day checking out galleries.'

Did that sound genuine? The woman didn't appear suspicious.

'Certainly. You're more than welcome to have a look around. We're currently exhibiting two Canadian painters, Lana Franklin and Vaughan Gregson, and you'll find their work on the first floor. Down here, we have some more traditional pieces of art and sculpture. My name's Natasha. If you'd like any information about any of our exhibits, please ask. I'll be over there with Daphne, my colleague.'

'Thank you.'

Birdie began scrutinising the pieces of art, all the time keeping her eye on the two members of staff. Judging by the waving of arms and the aghast expressions on their faces, whatever they were discussing was important. Birdie moved closer and hid behind one of the sculptures to listen.

'That's why I was surprised when Oscar asked me to work. In all my years here, it's never been so quiet. You'd have thought our regulars would have shown us some loyalty.' Daphne's voice was low, but Birdie was still able to hear every word.

'I know. Then again, the media did blow it all out of proportion by calling it a masterpiece,' Natasha said. 'I'm not saying that it wasn't valuable. I mean, who wouldn't want something worth a million?'

'Have you been approached by the press about it?'

'Yes, but I didn't give them anything. That's what Oscar said to do. But if we do speak to them, then surely they'd leave us alone. We could tell them the same as we told the police, that we don't know how the forgery got there. It's true.'

'You've got to admit, though, that the whole thing was really weird. For a start, how could the switch have happened?'

'I have no idea. Lord Somerton booked the painting in to be cleaned two weeks ago, and it was collected by our own driver, brought here, and put straight in the safe after Oscar checked it.'

'He couldn't have checked it very well then.'

Birdie took a step to the right because the voices had got quieter. The strap to her bag caught on the edge of the plinth and scraped it along the floor, making a loud noise. She grabbed hold of the statue to make sure it didn't fall.

'Crap.' Her heart pounded in her chest.

'Is everything okay?' Natasha called out, rushing over to her.

'Yes. I'm so sorry. The strap to my bag got caught. Luckily no damage.' She gave a relieved sigh.

'Don't worry. It's not in a very good position. I keep meaning to mention to Mr Devonport, our manager, about moving it.'

'Is that Oscar?'

Natasha frowned. 'You know him?'

'No. I couldn't help overhearing your conversation. I remember now reading about a missing painting. I hadn't realised it was from here.'

'Yes, unfortunately.' Natasha shook her head.

'I am curious about something. How did you actually discover that it was a forgery?'

'Our expert restorer had started cleaning it when he suspected something wasn't right, so he had the painting analysed using mass spectrometry, which is where they examine the chemical structures in the painting and can tell how old it is.'

'How long does the process take?'

'An initial assessment can be done within a day.'

That made more sense. Birdie had imagined these things would take weeks, but if all they'd needed was a basic assessment, then that made sense.

'Lucky that the expert was on the ball and spotted it. Do the police think it was swapped by someone who worked here?' Birdie asked.

'I don't know. Mr Devonport believes it might be Jasper, but no way do I believe that.

'Jasper?'

'Pemberton. He's Mr Devonport's deputy. Jasper has a deep loathing for all forgers. We've talked about it in the past. But not counting that, we only had two weeks' notice that the painting was coming in. How could Jasper have managed to find someone to create a forgery in such a short space of time? It's not like you can go online and search for an art forger. It doesn't add up.'

'So why does Mr Devonport think it is him?'

'Jasper's gone missing. He should have been at work this week, but he hasn't turned up, and we can't reach him on his phone.'

'Do you think the lord who owned it might have had something to do with it? He might have wanted to claim on his insurance.'

'How do you know about Lord Somerton? Are you the press?' Natasha's eyes narrowed.

Birdie held up both hands. 'No. I promise I'm not. Like I said, I overheard you talking to your colleague. And, to be honest, it did sound interesting, so I kept listening. I shouldn't have, really.'

'Okay,' Natasha said, albeit more hesitantly. 'But I don't believe it's to do with insurance. There are much easier ways to claim. Lord Somerton could have had it damaged or had it stolen from his home. Why go to all this trouble? Like Daphne and I were saying, it's all weird and doesn't add up.'

Maybe not to them, but Birdie saw it differently. If she had to guess, she'd say that the original never made it to the gallery in the first place. And if it was a good forgery, Oscar Devonport might not have realised at the time it was being placed into the safe. But it still begs the question, why go to such an elaborate performance?

'It's certainly a conundrum, that's for sure.'

'Anyway, you didn't come here to talk about that. Let me show you some of our pieces.'

'Thank you.' Birdie walked alongside Natasha to the back of the gallery.

They stopped beside one of the modern paintings on the wall. Birdie tilted her head to one side, trying to work out what it was about. But it still looked the same.

'Natasha.'

Birdie turned as a man emerged from a back office.

'It's Oscar,' Natasha whispered.

The man walked up to them, all the time looking

Birdie up and down. Was he assessing her ability to buy something? 'What's going on here?'

'We were talking about the paintings here. I've come to London to study art history, and Natasha was kind enough to show me around the gallery. I wanted to see one of the top galleries in the area. I hope that's okay.'

'Of course, we're always happy to welcome visitors. But I'm afraid you'll have to continue looking around on your own.' He turned to Natasha. 'I'd like you and Daphne to dust the shelves in the storage area. When were they last done?'

'Last week, I think. It could have been the week before.'

'Well, they need doing again. We can't allow dust to settle on any of the art. Feel free to browse.' He nodded at Birdie and then walked away.

'Oscar's not normally so sharp. It's this forgery business. I'd better go straight away. Please don't say anything about the missing painting – I shouldn't have said anything, really.'

'No problem.' Birdie crossed her fingers behind her back because, of course, she'd be telling Seb as soon as she saw him. 'I'll take a look around on my own.'

Birdie spent the next ten minutes looking at the displays on both floors. More because she wanted to work out where the safe might be housed. Natasha had left the door leading to the back open, but Birdie couldn't see anything out there. Devonport must have an office. Perhaps the safe was kept there. But it was impossible for her to see. He'd disappeared, and she hadn't seen where he'd gone.

Chapter 15

Seb had arranged to meet Birdie in Hyde Park, by Speakers' Corner, which he knew she'd find fascinating and was about a ten-minute walk from the art gallery. The park was one of his favourite places in London, and he often frequented it when in town, especially when he wanted to escape the hustle and bustle of city life and give himself time to think.

He hadn't needed it since living in East Farndon because he was surrounded by beautiful countryside, but he enjoyed being there nonetheless, and he had taken a leisurely walk around the park while waiting for Birdie.

'Seb.' At the sound of his name, he glanced up from where he was standing next to the soapbox and saw Birdie jogging towards him, a beaming smile on her face.

'I take it that the visit to the gallery went well.'

'Oh yes. It did, indeed. This is a great place for us to meet. I've always wanted to visit Speakers' Corner but never had the chance.'

'I thought you'd like it. Anyone can turn up and speak on a subject, providing the police consider their speeches are lawful. It's been around since the nineteenth century, and the likes of Marx, Lenin, and George Orwell all spoke here.'

'So, I could stand on a box, start speaking on any subject that I feel passionate about and be in illustrious company.'

That he'd like to hear.

'You could. The best time to visit is on a Sunday, because there are always people espousing their views.'

'After the case, maybe I will. We could come together. You know, I always enjoyed debating at school, whatever the subject.'

'Why doesn't that surprise me?' Seb laughed, imagining anyone trying to outwit Birdie in a debate.

'Because of my big mouth, you mean?'

'Not at all. Because you have views on all aspects of life and don't hesitate to express them.'

'That's just a more polite way of saying the same thing, which is typical of you. Anyway, this isn't getting us anywhere. My visit to the gallery was better than I'd hoped, so let's sit over there, and I'll tell you all about it.' Birdie pointed to an empty bench, and they strolled over to it.

'I'd been expecting you to suggest a café.'

In fact, he'd been looking forward to it and had skipped breakfast.

'Well, that's where you're wrong. I was early, and to pass the time until the gallery opened, I went to a nearby place and had a coffee and cake. Why didn't you tell me that shops around here don't open until halfway through the morning?'

'I suspect it's just the gallery because it's not like a normal shop. I'm sure you enjoyed your visit to the café, though.'

'I did. But don't get me started on how much it cost. No wonder only rich people can afford to live here. It's bloody ridiculous. I could get a three-course meal in Market Harborough plus change for what I paid.'

'Welcome to London and London prices.'

'In that case, I won't be moving here any time soon. I hope you're not intending to move the company here once Sarah returns because I'd take a lot of persuading.'

He certainly wasn't going to mention that it had crossed his mind, or Birdie would continually bring it up.

'We don't know what's going to happen in the future. I'm more interested in your visit to the gallery.'

Birdie turned to face him. 'Natasha, the woman who works there, was most informative. At least she was after I'd overheard her conversation with a colleague. I didn't discover the name of the painting that was switched, but I do know it belonged to a Lord Somerton and—'

'I know him. He's acquainted with my parents.'

Seb had known the family for most of his life. If Somerton was involved, it had the potential to be a tad on the difficult side.

'Oh. Well, two weeks ago, he booked the painting in for a clean, and when it arrived last week, it was put in the safe by the manager of the gallery, who didn't suspect that it was a forgery. So, either he didn't look carefully enough, or the painting was switched while in their possession. The manager believed that Pemberton might have been involved, but Natasha disagreed.'

Knowing what they did about Pemberton's dire financial situation and how cavalier his behaviour had been towards Annabelle and Felicity Allen, Seb wouldn't dismiss the man's involvement so readily.

'Did she say why?'

'Because Pemberton hates forgers. Yeah, I know, that's

a weak reason. But that aside, only having two weeks' notice to forge a painting isn't long, is it? Do you know how long it takes to forge a masterpiece? Actually, it's not a masterpiece. The media exaggerated. No surprises there. But it's still worth a lot of money.'

'Forgeries can take many hours because specific techniques must be employed to ensure the work appears to be the same age as the original. The problem at the moment is we don't know the exact painting. Did she volunteer the information?'

'No, and I didn't want to put her on the spot by asking because it would have been suspicious.'

'The thief would have had to have found a forger to undertake the work at short notice.' Seb sifted through his memory banks for names of any, but he hadn't ever come across any in his work.

'It's not like they'll be advertising their services on Google. Which makes it even more unlikely that it all could have been arranged so quickly. Which leads me to one conclusion.' Birdie paused and stared down at her lap, twiddling with the edges of her jacket. 'I'm sorry that he's a friend of the family, Seb, but I reckon that Lord Somerton could have had something to do with it.'

Silence hung in the air. Seb had already reached that conclusion but hadn't wanted to admit it. His parents would be devastated if it turned out to be true.

'And his motive?'

'Not for insurance purposes, because there are much easier ways to lose or damage a piece of art. Then again, if he was paid out for the forgery and had hidden the original, he could sell it on the black market and double dip. He'd have then made twice what it was worth.' Birdie raised her finger to her lips and gently tapped. 'I've just had a thought. The forgery only needed to be good enough to fool the gallery manager, and presumably, he wouldn't have examined the painting too closely because he wouldn't have suspected it wasn't the original. And if it's not a perfect forgery, then presumably two weeks might have been enough time to paint it without having to employ all the techniques you mentioned.' She leant back on the bench, a knowing smile on her lips.

'That's an excellent point. If the forgery was completed before the painting was delivered to the gallery, could it have been switched on the way there?'

'The gallery used their own guy to collect the painting from Lord Somerton's house. I didn't get the name of this man, but he would be worth interviewing if we can find out who he is. I didn't get a chance to ask Natasha because my conversation with her got cut short when the manager, Mr Devonport, came over. If that's where the switch happened, then it might eliminate Lord S from being a part of it.'

If it did, that would be a weight off Seb's mind. 'Is that Oscar Devonport?' he asked.

'Yes. Don't tell me you know him too.'

'I went to school with his younger brother, Stephen. Oscar was two years above us. I knew he worked in the art field but didn't know the exact place. My connection to him may turn out to be useful, but for now, I think our first port of call should be my parents to get Harold's contact details so we can question him. I'll see if they're available for a visit.'

'Harold?' Birdie frowned.

'Lord Somerton. Harold's his first name.'

'Can't you ask your parents to give you the details over the phone rather than going to see them? It will only delay things.'

'It's easier face to face. I'll give them a call to see where they are. I'm not sure whether they're in London or Winchester.' Seb pulled out his phone and pressed the key for his mother's mobile.

'Hello.'

'It's me, Mother. Are you in London, by any chance? I'd like to call in. I have something to ask.'

'Hello, darling. Yes, we are. We arrived last night. Is it urgent because we're busy today?'

'Yes, it is rather.'

'Would you like to come for dinner this evening?'

'Yes, that would be most enjoyable. I'll bring my new business partner, so you can meet her. What I'd like to ask you is business related.'

'Sounds fascinating. Of course you must bring her. I'll let Cook know to prepare two extra meals. It's nothing fancy, but I'm sure you won't mind that.'

'Good. Birdie and I will see you later.'

'Birdie? That's a strange name for a woman.'

'Her name's Lucinda Bird, but she prefers to be called Birdie.' He glanced across at his partner, who was glaring at him.

'How extraordinary. Lucinda's such a pretty name.'

'What time would you like us with you?' Seb asked, deciding it was best to move the conversation on.

'Seven-thirty, for dinner at eight. Got to dash. Your father's waiting for me, and I'm not ready. We have an appointment with the bank manager. Estate matters. See you later.'

'I'm looking forward to it.' He ended the call and returned his gaze to Birdie, who now had her arms folded across her chest and was staring ahead.

'Before you say anything, my answer is no. So you can forget it.' She turned towards him, her face set hard.

'I don't understand.'

'Yes you do. Stop pretending you don't. No way am I going to have dinner with your parents. That would be like… Well, I've never mixed with aristocracy before – not counting you, and you're different. I'll make a fool of myself by using the wrong cutlery or doing something totally stupid.'

'Don't be silly. It will be fine.'

'Stop patronising me and try to understand it from my point of view.'

'Sorry, I didn't intend for you to feel like that. But I'd like you to meet them. Then you can see that they're normal people.'

'They wouldn't even go to the funeral of Sarah's husband because of what he did. That was mean, when considering how Sarah desperately needed their support.'

Birdie was right. Seb hadn't been pleased with the way the family had left Sarah to deal with the death of Donald on her own. His mother had regretted it and had tried to make amends, but the damage had already been done.

'My mother's been in contact with Sarah since. There were extenuating circumstances, as you're fully aware.'

'I suppose so. What did your mum say when you told her about my name? And don't say "nothing" because it was obvious from the conversation.'

'Umm,' he hesitated, wondering what to tell Birdie.

'Don't tell me, let me guess. "But Sebastian, why would she want to do that? Lucinda is such a lovely name."'

Seb laughed, more at Birdie's imitation of his mother than anything else, which considering they hadn't even met, was quite accurate. 'Okay. You've got the gist.'

'Yeah, well, it's not the first time that's been said to me. It's easy for people to say when they're not the one who has to live with the name. But I still don't get why you want your family to meet your business partner. It's not like they've invested money into the firm.' She stared in his direction. 'Tell me they haven't.'

'No. It's all my own money. I haven't kept anything from you. Remember, I've already met some of your family.'

'Only my aunt because she was connected to the case we worked on. I hope you're not thinking that you want to meet my mum and dad now.'

'Only if you'd like me to.'

'I'm not sure they're up to hanging out with aristocracy. We don't have a butler, nor do we have a matching dinner service.'

'Birdie, you know that I'm not—'

'Got you. Every bloody time. It's so easy.' She smirked, leant in towards him, and gave a playful punch on his arm.

Seb shook his head. He was rather looking forward to seeing what his parents made of Birdie. He had no doubt that she'd make quite an impression, of that there was no question.

Chapter 16

'It's no good. I can't do it.' Birdie came to an abrupt halt on the corner of Ovington Square, Knightsbridge, where Seb's parents lived, determined not to go any further. She scanned the area; the imposing white, four-storey houses lining the square sent her heartbeat into overdrive.

'Can't do what?' Seb asked.

'You know full well what I mean. I can't come with you to your parents' house. It's going to be a total disaster and you really don't need me with you. It's not just knowing how to behave at dinner – although that's important – but I've never been in the company of a viscount before. What do I call him? Your honour? Your worship? My Lord? And then there's your mum. What do I call her, and do I curtsy? It's all very well for you, but you're used to this stuff. You're the closest I've been to an aristocrat, and you're different.'

She'd known all along that this was a mistake and was annoyed she'd allowed Seb to persuade her this far. She glanced down at the dress she'd bought earlier, at her insistence, even though Seb had said she needn't bother, and yes, okay, it was nice and she liked it, but it wasn't going to fit in with people who were friends with the royal family.

'You address a viscount and viscountess as *Lord* and *Lady* in conversation, but I can assure you, my parents will not expect you to call them that. Their names are Philip and Charlotte.'

'Well, I can hardly call them that when we've never even met before. Next, you'll be telling me to call them Phil and Charlie.' She ran her fingers through her hair.

'Now, that I'd like to see.' Seb laughed, and it sort of relaxed her a bit. 'Follow their lead. I'm sure they will tell you how to address them, although, if you're worried, just don't use their names in conversation. You're blowing this completely out of proportion, Birdie. Which is totally unlike you.' He paused. 'Well, it is like you. But you've never shied away from facing things head-on. Come on. They're people, that's all. People like you and me. You'll be fine.'

He cupped her elbow in his hand and pulled her slightly, forcing her feet to move forwards.

Was he right? Had she made more of it than she should have?

She sucked in a loud breath. 'Okay, but I'm warning you, if I do anything to stuff it up, then it's all your fault.'

'I will take the blame. But you won't do anything wrong, I promise. Here we are.' He stopped outside the third house from the end.

She stared up at the double-fronted white building with large windows and decorative wrought-iron balconies and clutched her chest. 'Here goes nothing,' she muttered.

She followed him up the four white stone steps to the door, and he rang the bell.

'Don't you have a key?' Birdie asked, confused. Who doesn't have a key to their parents' home?

'No. There are always staff here anytime I wish to visit. Whether or not my parents are in residence.'

'Wow. Now that could be handy on a drunken night out, and you can't find your keys.'

'It hasn't occurred yet.'

Before she had time to make another quip, the door opened and a man wearing black trousers, a white shirt, and striped waistcoat, who looked like he should have retired years ago, faced them.

'Good evening, sir,' the old man said, giving a slight bow of his head.

Holy moly. This was going to be worse than she'd imagined if even the butler bowed.

'Good evening, Bates. This is Birdie – we're here for dinner with my parents.'

'Hi.' She gave a half-smile, but the man didn't respond.

'You're expected in the drawing room, sir.'

'Thank you. No need to announce us. We'll find our own way.' Seb stepped inside.

Announce them? 'This is a mistake,' she mumbled under her breath as she followed Seb down a long corridor with high ceilings and ornate corner coving.

The door to the drawing room was open, and when they stepped inside, Birdie had to forcibly clamp her jaws shut. It was totally different from how she thought it would be. The two floral sofas were ancient and faded. There were three unmatching rugs on the floor and several small tables dotted around the room, each of them piled high with books. There was a dark wooden sideboard along one wall, which was full of photos in silver frames. It was like her granny's house used to be: old and comfortable.

Was this how the aristocracy lived? She'd never have guessed. Then again, all she had to go on was *Downton Abbey*, and that was set a hundred years ago.

'Sebastian, how lovely to see you.' A woman, who Birdie assumed was Seb's mum, placed the book that was in her hand on the cushion of the sofa where she'd been sitting and walked over to them. She had the same smile as Seb and was also tall – at least five foot ten.

'Hello, Mother. How are you?' Seb gave her a kiss on both cheeks.

'And you must be *Birdie*,' Seb's mother said, accentuating her name.

'Yes. Pleased to meet you, Your Ladyship.' The words had just come out, despite Seb's instructions. At least she managed to stop herself from giving a curtsy.

'My dear, we don't need to be so formal. Please call me Charlotte.'

Birdie glanced at Seb, who had a *told-you-so* look on his face. 'Okay.'

'Let's sit.' Charlotte gestured to the sofas, and Birdie followed Seb and sat beside him.

'Where's Father?'

'He got called away on some urgent business. Something to do with one of his charities. He won't be back for dinner, so it will only be the three of us. Will that cause a problem? I know you have a matter you wish to discuss with us.' Charlotte looked from Seb to Birdie, a concerned expression on her face.

'It's fine. We require contact details for Harold. Lord Somerton. Do you happen to have them? It's regarding a case we're working on.'

Charlotte frowned. 'We haven't seen Harold for a long time. Not since he divorced Veronica and married that young model. He no longer mixes in our social circle. And quite frankly, I was pleased. I couldn't warm to the young woman on the rare occasions that we met. It's a most peculiar alliance, and if you'd like my opinion, she was only after his title.'

'And money?' Birdie suggested. Surely that would have been a bigger draw for the model.

'Hardly, my dear.' Charlotte's laugh was dry. 'He's like most aristocracy – asset rich and cash poor. Mind you, she might not have known that at the time.'

'You have a very stereotypical view, Mother. Not every person who marries someone much older does it for ulterior motives.'

'If you say so, dear.' Charlotte made eye contact with Birdie and arched an eyebrow.

Birdie was warming to the woman already. It was the last thing she'd expected to happen. Although, she did agree with Seb about Charlotte's stereotypical assumption.

'But you still have his address and phone number?' Seb asked.

'Unless he's changed them. His estate is in Devon near Torquay, as you know, and he has a London house in Chelsea. I'll get his details for you after dinner. What case are you working on that involves him?'

Was Seb going to tell his mum about it, or should it remain confidential?

'Annabelle has asked us to look into the disappearance of Jasper Pemberton, and Harold's name has come up in our investigation.'

'Jasper's disappeared?' Charlotte's eyes widened.

'Along with a million-pound painting owned by Lord Somerton that was left at the gallery in which Pemberton worked, and that was replaced with a forgery,' Birdie said conspiratorially.

'Good gracious. And you believe they're connected?' Charlotte leant forwards, resting her elbows on her knees.

'It's what we are investigating at the moment.' Birdie nodded.

'Annabelle's received a threatening note asking for the painting to be returned. But she knows nothing about it.' Seb sighed.

'Why have you been tasked with looking into this and not the police? Surely this should be a matter for them,' Charlotte said.

'Annabelle's concerned that if it becomes common knowledge, it might damage a business deal her father's engaged in,' Seb replied.

'Oh my goodness, how typical.' Charlotte glanced at Birdie and shook her head. 'I like Annabelle very much, but sometimes her priorities are terribly misguided.'

'I did find it a little strange,' Birdie said, 'but I thought, you know, because she's so different from me, that it was okay to be like that.'

Charlotte laughed. 'My dear, you're most amusing. I'm assuming you mean because she comes from an aristocratic family that makes her different. Well, I can assure you that's nothing to do with it. We're perfectly normal, are we not, Sebastian?'

Birdie bit back a smile. Normal was hardly the way she'd describe them.

'Yes, Mother. Perhaps you could find the details for Harold now in case it gets too late after dinner.'

'If you insist.' Charlotte picked up the small bell that was on a small side table and rang it. Shortly afterwards, a woman came into the room. 'Angie, please will you fetch my address book? It should be on the desk in my study.'

'Yes, Your Ladyship.'

After a couple of minutes, Angie returned with the book and gave it to Charlotte, who handed it straight to Seb. 'You can find it. You'll be quicker than me.'

Seb opened the book, flicked through the pages, and gave it back to her. 'Thank you, Mother.'

'Aren't you going to write it down? Of course you're not. Silly me. You used your *super memory*. When—'

The door opened, interrupting her, and Bates came in.

'Dinner is served,' he announced.

Birdie followed Seb and his mum into a large dining room, which had the longest mahogany table Birdie had ever seen. There were three places set for dinner, and Charlotte indicated for Birdie to sit opposite Seb and she sat at the head of the table.

'How's Hubert?' Seb asked.

Seb's older brother was in line to inherit the viscountcy, but suffered from mental health issues, and at one time was unable to undertake all the duties expected of him. Seb had stood in for him on several occasions but he hadn't enjoyed doing so.

'He appears much better. Are you not in contact with him?' Charlotte frowned.

'Yes, when I can. But I wanted your opinion. He told me that he's still seeing the counsellor, which helps.'

'He doesn't like to discuss it with your father and me. You'll see him at the anniversary party and can judge for yourself then.'

'Yes, I'm looking forward to it.'

Birdie stifled a laugh. That hadn't been the impression Seb had given her.

'But he's certainly back to full strength on the work front. Although there was an incident last week at the estate, which caused some disconcertion.'

'Oh, what happened?' Seb asked.

'Several members of staff were approached by two men who wanted to know about the family. They weren't the normal type of visitor we have.'

'Did you contact the police?'

'Yes, Hubert did, but there was nothing that could be done because nothing happened. They didn't threaten the staff. They only asked questions. The police believe that they were probably passing through. They were only seen on the one afternoon.'

'Tell Hubert to make sure the ground staff are vigilant and let me know if it happens again.'

Birdie exchanged a glance with Seb. Was this related to what had been happening to him?

'I'm so sorry, Birdie. We must've been boring you by talking about family matters. Tell me a little about yourself,' Charlotte said.

'There's not much to say. I was born and live in Market Harborough, and I used to be a police officer. After meeting Seb— Sebastian, we worked several cases together and then he asked me to join him as a private investigator.'

'And why did you say yes rather than stay in the police force?'

'It wasn't an easy decision, but I was always getting in trouble for wanting to do things my way. I was more concerned with catching the criminals than obeying so many of the petty rules that were in place.' Did that make her sound like a rebel? 'Not that I don't think we shouldn't have them, just that they can get in the way.'

'She was an excellent officer, Mother. I'm very lucky to have Birdie working with me.'

'Well, I still don't understand the attraction of the work you do, and I know your father would have preferred for you to be working on the family estate, but we can see that it makes you happy. And I'm glad to see you working with someone like Birdie, who can certainly add some *enjoyment*.'

Warmth flooded Birdie's cheeks. Crap. Why did she have to blush?

'Well, it certainly makes life interesting. But what we need are some cases to get the business off the ground.'

'Preferably not following cheating spouses,' Birdie added. 'Because that can be extremely boring.'

'I'll be sure to let my friends know that you have opened the business, and if any of them have any work, they can contact you.' Charlotte paused for a moment. 'Providing it's not anything to do with divorce. Is that correct, Sebastian?'

'To be honest, at the moment, we'd probably take anything, but we would rather have something a little more interesting.'

'Like Annabelle's case.'

'Yes, exactly like that.'

'And if you're taking cases closer to London, we might get to see you more often.'

'Indeed.'

After dinner, they returned to the drawing room and sat down with a drink. Birdie didn't want to appear rude, but it was getting late, and Elsa was on her own. She was debating whether to mention it to Seb when the door opened, and an older man marched in. He was Seb's height, only much broader and imposing.

Seb jumped up. 'Father, I thought we might miss you.'

'Sorry to have missed dinner,' his voice boomed. He looked down at Birdie, who had also stood. 'You must be Sebastian's business partner, Bunty.'

'It's Birdie, dear,' Charlotte said. 'Her name is Lucinda Bird, but she doesn't go by that name.'

'Birdie it is then. I'm Philip, Sebastian's father. I hope you had an enjoyable evening.'

'Yes, thank you.'

'Sorry not to have spent some time with you, Father, but we have to leave. I'll see you at the party.'

Birdie breathed a sigh of relief. Seb's dad was scary.

'Don't worry, old boy.'

After saying their goodbyes, they left.

'Well, that wasn't as bad as I thought it was going to be. I like your mum. She's totally different from any of my family, but she was all right.'

'I'm glad you approve.'

'And you really need to see your parents more often. It was obvious from what your mum said that she doesn't see you enough. I don't understand why you don't visit them more.'

'I go as often as I can, but what you've got to remember is that every time, they try to persuade me to work for the estate.'

'I don't think your mum will anymore. What did you make of the strange visitors she mentioned? Connected to what's been happening to you?'

'I'm unsure. But I certainly won't dismiss it.'

'It could be totally unrelated, but at least you've been made aware of it. Let's hope that if anything else happens, they think to inform you.'

'I'll flick Hubert a text later and tell him.'

'Good. Anyway, the main thing is we now have Harold's details. So, plans for tomorrow?'

'Nelson Art Gallery and then Lord Somerton.'

Chapter 17

'Good morning. I'd like to see Mr Devonport, if he's available,' Seb said to the woman who'd approached him when he walked into the Nelson Gallery the following morning.

'I'll see if he's free. Please may I know your name and what it's regarding?'

'I'm Sebastian Clifford. It's a personal matter.' That was sufficient information for Devonport to remember him and not enough to alert him that Seb was visiting for anything other than social reasons.

The woman disappeared behind the counter and out through the back, leaving Seb time to take a look at some of the art on display. He was particularly drawn to one of the sculptures situated in the centre on a plinth. It was of a dog that looked remarkably like Elsa.

'Clifford.'

Seb turned. Oscar Devonport was striding towards him, a broad smile on his face. He'd hardly changed since school, apart from being a little thicker around the middle, and his closely cut dark hair was now streaked with grey and receding.

'Good to see you, Devonport.' Seb held out his hand, and the man shook it warmly. 'How are the family?'

'Stephen's a colonel now, as you most likely know, which means he's working all over the world, and we hardly see him. He married last year but no children yet. I've got four of the little blighters, aged between eight and two. Thank heavens for nannies. Without them, I'd be a walking zombie. Eleanor, too.'

Seb had only met Devonport's wife once, at a school reunion where partners were also invited. He'd taken Annabelle, and she'd spent most of the time chatting with Eleanor, who she knew from being on the social scene together.

'Good to hear everything's going well.'

'How about you? Are you still in the police force? I vaguely recall hearing through tittle-tattle from my parents that you'd had some problems.'

'I left the police after some nasty business in my team. I now have my own company, Clifford Investigation Services. Actually, that's why I'm here today. I'd like to ask you a few questions regarding a case we're working on. Is there somewhere private we can talk?'

'Of course, old chap. Come on through to my office – I'll ask Natasha to bring us some coffee, and we can have a catch-up. You can ask me anything you like.'

Seb wasn't surprised at how agreeable Devonport was being. Although his parents weren't part of the aristocracy, they did tend to mix in the same social circles as Seb's parents and were invited to the same events. So they had a connection. Not to mention that it was in his interest to be pleasant, in case Seb, or his family and friends, wanted to purchase items from the gallery.

He followed Devonport through to the back of the shop and waited while the man stopped to ask Natasha to bring them some coffee. Devonport's office was at the end of the corridor. It was modern, and on its white walls hung many paintings. There was a chrome-and-glass table and some easy chairs by the window. Devonport's desk, a table with no drawers, had an open laptop perched on it, and was towards the back. Behind it, there was another door. Was that where the safe was housed?

'Take a seat,' Devonport said, gesturing to one of the easy chairs. 'I'll just close the document I've been working on, and then I'm all yours.'

'Thank you.'

While he waited, Seb did a further scan of the office. There was a bookcase on one side, filled mainly with books on art, but apart from Devonport's laptop, there were no signs indicating towards the administrative side of the business. No filing cabinets, drawers, or documents lying around. It was almost like it was an office for show.

There was a light knock on the office door, and Natasha came in holding a tray with two white china mugs. She placed it on the coffee table.

'Thank you, Natasha.' Devonport walked over to the seating and perched opposite Seb. He waited until the woman had left the room before speaking. 'Now, how may I help you?'

'I'd like some information regarding your employee, Jasper Pemberton.'

'I'd probably say *ex*-employee. He's missed several shifts, and I've been unable to get hold of him by phone or at his flat. I can't have staff who are unreliable. It's meant I've had to be here all the time, which has played havoc with my schedule, and I've had to cancel a few appointments. I was planning to advertise his position this week.'

'It's believed that he's disappeared, and I've been asked to investigate.' Seb picked up his mug and took a sip of coffee.

'I see. So, what you're saying is it's not simply a case of him not coming to work because he was sick or couldn't be bothered?'

'We don't know yet.'

'But you've left the police, so why are they asking you to look into it?'

'I've been engaged by a third party.'

'I'm not sure that there is much I can tell you. I had no idea that he'd actually disappeared, only that he didn't turn up for work.'

'Did you think this behaviour, his not turning up to work, was unusual? Has he acted like that in the past?'

'No. In the main, he's a reliable chap. He did phone in sick a couple of times when I suspected he might've gone to a race meeting, but I had no proof. Other than that, I would say that he was reliable.'

'I understand that he disappeared at the same time it was discovered that the painting belonging to Lord Somerton was a forgery.'

Seb scrutinised Devonport's face, looking for any telltale signs about his knowledge of what had happened. But there were none. He seemed genuinely surprised that Seb knew anything about it.

'And you believe the two circumstances are related?'

'Hadn't you thought of that?' Surely the man wasn't so naïve that he hadn't made the connection.

'Yes, at first I did. But on reflection, I decided it wasn't the case because he was here when the painting's disappearance was discovered. It wasn't until two days later that Pemberton didn't turn up for his shift. I didn't connect the two.'

Was he being genuine? It would be foolhardy to have dismissed the connection so readily.

'Have you informed the police about Pemberton's absence?'

'No. They were called in when we discovered the painting was a forgery, and they questioned everyone who works here. That's me, Pemberton, Natasha, and Daphne who works two days a week. Now you've pointed it out, maybe I should have let them know.'

'What's the name of the stolen piece?'

Oscar hesitated. 'We haven't announced it publicly… But… it's going to come out sooner or later. It's *Sunset in Venice* by Allard.'

'I know of him. He's an impressionist. Not one of my favourites of that era.'

'But popular, nonetheless.'

'Returning to Pemberton, was he a good worker?'

'He was excellent and made a lot of commission. We're missing his input already. He had a way with our clients, in particular the women, that had them returning time after time.'

'We do know that Felicity Allen was a very good client of his.'

'Yes, he has a very close relationship with her. In fact, I often wondered if he… But no. Why would he when he has a lovely fiancé who…?' He paused for a moment, staring directly at Seb. 'Of course, you used to be involved with her yourself.'

Seb had no desire to go down that path because it would most certainly detract from his interview, and it wasn't relevant. 'That was a long time ago.' He waved his hand dismissively.

Devonport bit down on his bottom lip. 'And is she the person who has asked you to look into his disappearance?'

'My client's details are confidential. But I would like to know more about Pemberton. Can you think of any red flags that would give a clue as to why he might disappear? Was he more anxious than usual? More agitated? Did he seem distracted? Anything that you can think of.'

'Nothing that comes to mind... Although, I do remember overhearing him on a personal phone call, and by the sound of it, he wasn't speaking to a friend. It was difficult to work out what the conversation was about, but, at the time, I did wonder if it was to do with money because he'd asked me for an advance on his pay the previous week, and I had refused. I remember he used the words "I need more time", but then he saw me and moved away so I couldn't hear the rest.' He hung his head. 'I know what you're thinking. That I should have mentioned all this to the police. Shall I go to them now?'

'No. Leave it with me.'

Seb didn't want to mention Annabelle's note, but he would if Devonport pushed the matter. Going to the police now could put lives in danger.

'Okay. The whole matter has been bad for business as it is. If something else was added into the mix, then goodness knows how we'd recover. I already have a meeting with the big boss who's coming over from France to discuss the matter.'

'Is your position here in jeopardy?'

'I doubt it. I'm a shareholder in the company, and if they try to get rid of me, it could cause problems. But that doesn't mean they won't try to make my life difficult by moving me to another gallery or something. Up until now, we've been the most profitable gallery in the group. And I'd like it to remain that way, with me at the helm. School fees for four children aren't for the faint-hearted.'

'So I gather. Before I leave, I'd like to ask a little more

about the painting. Did Pemberton have access to the safe in which it was kept?'

Devonport glanced over towards the door behind the desk. Seb had been right in assuming that was where the safe was situated.

'I'm the only person with a key, but I suppose he could have got into the safe by taking mine. I often leave it on the desk because my staff are so trustworthy. At least, I thought they were.' He slumped in his chair.

'Do you believe the painting was swapped while it was in the safe, or do you suspect that the forgery was delivered to you and it escaped your notice?'

'That's something I've been deliberating over. When the painting arrived, it was protected by bubble wrap. I opened it and took a look before it went into the safe. It appeared like the genuine article to me. But I didn't look at it in great detail. I have since learnt that it was viewed as a very good forgery for what it was. By that, I mean that the painting hadn't been aged, but at first glance, it would have been hard to have discerned it was fake. We were lucky that our art restorer was suspicious and suggested that we investigate further. Which we did.' Devonport sighed.

His reactions appeared genuine, and Seb doubted that he was involved in the disappearance of the original.

'If it was a good forgery, there wouldn't be many people who could have executed it. Are you familiar with art forgers, and do you have any ideas who it could be?'

'I suspect it might have been done overseas. There's an excellent chap in France called Renaud, who I've never met but his work is known to be good. I've no idea how to locate him, other than I've got a feeling he might live in Paris or somewhere close. With your police connections, you might be able to find him.'

'I'm surprised you actually know his name.'

'Art forgery is big business. People commission work in the likeness of a famous painter and sell it overseas in those countries where there are people with lots of money and don't have any qualms about buying on the black market. Also, people who do have an original might have it copied so they can enjoy the painting while keeping the genuine one safe.'

Interesting.

'Thank you for your help. If you do remember anything, please give me a call.' Seb handed Devonport his card.

'I sincerely hope this matter is resolved swiftly. It's been very bad for business.'

'I can't promise, but once we find Pemberton, we may know more about what exactly happened. In the meantime, in the interests of keeping this quiet, I'd rather you didn't mention my visit to anyone.'

Chapter 18

'You lied to him,' Birdie said to Seb. On his return from his meeting with Devonport at the gallery, she'd heard him speaking to Lord Somerton and inviting himself around to his place on the pretext of wanting to discuss a charity that they were both interested in.

It had surprised her because it wasn't a tactic he usually employed.

'I didn't want to alert him about our real reason for the visit, in case he's involved, which he may be.'

'Will his wife be there?'

'I've no idea.'

'I've been looking into her career as a model before she married him three years ago. Her name's Edith Groom, and she comes from Kettering. She didn't have a fancy upbringing, and she left school at sixteen with very few qualifications after being spotted by a scout for a top London agency. She was very successful and lived in Paris for several years, making it her base while she travelled the world.'

'Paris is where a forger Devonport mentioned lives.'

'A bit of a coincidence, don't you think?'

'It's certainly worth looking into.'

'I've got an idea. If she's there, why don't you ask to speak to Somerton in private and leave me with her to see what I can find out? Because once you do start talking about the painting and Pemberton, Somerton might clam up. This way, we're doubling our chances of success.'

'Excellent idea. Let's go. I'll call us an Uber to take us to his home in Chelsea.'

Within twenty minutes, they had pulled up outside a row of terraced houses in Chelsea.

'Another fancy abode, I expect,' she said as they went up to the door, and Seb pressed the buzzer for Somerton's flat.

'Good morning, Sebastian. Come on up,' a voice said through the speaker, which she assumed was Lord Somerton.

The door clicked, and they walked inside.

'I'm surprised he actually answered the buzzer. Doesn't he have staff?'

'I've no idea what his situation is.'

'But clearly he's not as rich as your mum and dad because they have the whole house, and he only has a flat. Then again, viscounts are more important than lords, aren't they?'

'Harold is a baron, so in this instance, he is a lower rank than my father. But I don't know why you're so obsessed by it all.'

'I'm not obsessed. Just bloody nosy. And I suppose a little on the envious side. Sort of. Fascinated, really. It's all so different.'

They walked up the stairs, and when they reached the third floor, an old man, who she assumed was Lord Somerton, was standing by the open door of one of the flats.

'Sebastian, awfully good to see you.'

'You too, Harold. This is Birdie, my partner.'

'Oh.' Somerton stared at Birdie quizzically.

'He means business partner, not the other sort of partner,' Birdie said with a forced smile. Did she look too
common for Seb? Or was she overreacting? It could be her
age. It could be anything. And he wasn't the first to appear
shocked at the thought of them being a couple.

'I see. Good to meet you. What business are you in
exactly?' He held open the door, and they both stepped
inside the flat into a small hallway.

'Investigation,' Seb said.

'Very interesting, I'm sure. Come and meet Edith —
she's in the kitchen.'

Birdie gave Seb a nudge with her elbow, and he
nodded.

They followed him into the kitchen, which was on the
right. Leaning against the central island was a stunning
woman in her early thirties, with long dark hair that came
to just above her waist. Birdie couldn't help but stare; Edith
was mesmerising.

'Darling, this is Sebastian Clifford, the son of my
friends, who I've told you about, and his work partner.
Birdie. This is my wife, Edith.'

'Hello,' Edith said. 'Would you like a coffee? The
machine's on.'

'Yes, please,' Birdie said.

'Yes, that would be lovely, thank you. Harold, is there
somewhere we can speak in private first?' Seb said.

'Yes, of course. We'll go through to my study.'

Birdie waited until Seb and Somerton were out of the
room, and then she turned to Edith.

'You used to be a model, didn't you?'

'Yes, but when I married H, he asked me to give it up because he said it wasn't fitting for a lady.'

'Did you mind? It must've been a really exciting life, jet-setting all over the world.'

'It wasn't as glamorous as you think. It was hard work. Eighteen-hour days were common, just to get the right look on a magazine shoot. You'd have to go all day without eating because there was never any time. And, of course, being on a constant diet was expected. I'm glad to be out of it.'

Birdie stared at the ex-model. There wasn't an ounce of fat on her, even now.

'And now you're married to Lord Somerton. It's different, but still exciting, I expect, with the estate in Devon and the London home here.'

Edith gave a hollow laugh. 'It would be if we had enough money to enjoy it. I was shocked to discover how little he had. Fortunately, I'd got a nest egg put aside from during my modelling days, but that's not going to last forever. And it wasn't intended to be shared and used for living expenses.'

She wasn't backward in coming forward. Interesting.

'Yes, I've heard that certain members of the aristocracy have their estates but no money. He could sell this flat, no?'

It wasn't like they needed it. Not if they had some fancy stately home in the country.

'Yeah. He could. But if he did, I'd be gone. And he knows it. At least when I'm in London, I can meet up with my friends and have fun. I hate the estate in Devon. Have you ever been there? It must be the most boring place in the world. No one talks to me. Not even the staff, if they can help it. They're too loyal to H's ex-wife.'

Why was the woman divulging all this to a total stranger? Unless she was always like that. Had she got

Somerton wrapped around her finger? Was she the master-mind behind having the painting forged? And if she was, did Somerton know?

'I read about the painting belonging to Lord Somerton being stolen and the forgery found in its place. That must've been such a shock for him.'

'It was insured. And it's not like he'll even miss it. He has a very large collection of art in Devon. Apart from the paintings that the ex-wife was awarded during the divorce settlement.'

'Did she have many?' Birdie leant against the island in the centre of the room, giving Edith her full attention to encourage the woman to divulge more.

'It depends on who you ask. H thinks so, but some of the pieces she'd bought herself. I believe there were fifteen in total.' Edith went to one of the kitchen cupboards and pulled out four mugs, which she placed in front of the coffee machine. 'How do you like your coffee?'

'Milk and no sugar for both of us, please. Did you think it strange that the missing painting was forged in such a short space of time while it was at the gallery?'

Edith stopped what she was doing and turned to face Birdie. 'You seem very well informed about the whole incident. Is that why you're here? To question us?'

'Not at all. Seb told me he needed to speak to Lord Somerton about a matter to do with his parents.'

She was convinced that Edith knew more than she was saying, but she didn't want to risk pushing her.

'How are your parents? I haven't seen them for ages. Not since I married Edith,' Harold said to Seb once they were seated in his study.

'They're very well, thank you, and send their best regards.'

'So, what can I do for you, Sebastian? You mentioned wanting to discuss some charity work that we could engage in together. I must say, it was somewhat surprising to receive your call considering my social standing since my marriage to Edith.'

'I was a little economical with the truth when we spoke, Harold, because I wasn't sure that you'd agree to meet with me if you knew the real reason. I'm here to enquire about the missing painting and the forgery that was put in its place.'

The man stiffened. 'Why are you interested? I've spoken to the police and to my insurance company, and it's currently under investigation. What have you got to do with this? Do you work for either one of them?'

'No. I'm working for another party. I believe there may be a link between your missing painting and the disappearance of Jasper Pemberton, who worked at the art gallery.'

'I know Pemberton and his parents. I didn't know that he had disappeared, though. Do you believe he might have been involved?'

'It's a line of enquiry.'

'So, when you said you were in investigation, did you mean that you're a private investigator?'

'That is correct. When was the last time you saw Pemberton?'

'I don't remember exactly. I occasionally go into the gallery to see what paintings they're exhibiting and will talk to him if he's there. But I don't see him regularly. Maybe at a charity event occasionally, but nothing more than that.'

'So, you didn't deal with him when you arranged for your painting to be cleaned?'

'No. I spoke directly to Oscar Devonport.'

'Why did you choose this particular time to have the painting cleaned? Have you done the same for the rest of your art collection?'

The man hesitated. 'I was debating selling it to raise some capital and I wanted it to be in pristine condition. But that's strictly between you and me because I'm in the process of negotiating with the National Trust to take on the estate because of its historical importance, and for me to remain living there. Before they did an inventory, I wanted to see what the painting was worth and take it out of the equation.'

Somerton's admission gave him a motive for orchestrating the whole affair. Except... why then admit it?

'It could be suggested that the events went in your favour.'

Somerton's face clouded over. 'That, young man, is very presumptuous of you. You're now accusing me of criminal activity, and I don't appreciate it.' The man clenched and unclenched his fists several times, and Seb's interest was piqued; gestures made with both hands at the same time were often a sign that a person was lying.

'I was talking hypothetically.' Seb kept his voice light and nonconfrontational, wanting to elicit more information from the man, which he'd be unable to do if he wasn't trusted. Although he suspected that he'd already gone too far and Somerton would clam up.

'Well, you should be careful making that sort of accusation, my boy. Some wouldn't be so understanding. Is that all you wanted to ask me? Because if it is, then I suggest we call this meeting to a halt.' Somerton jumped up from the chair he was sitting on, and Seb did the same.

'I apologise for causing you any distress. I'm sure you appreciate that an investigation such as this means checking all avenues.'

'No, I don't, Sebastian. I've known you before you could even walk, and don't expect this sort of treatment. I won't have it.'

Somerton didn't give Seb a chance to reply. Instead, he marched out of the study and back to the kitchen. Seb followed.

'We're leaving now,' he said to Birdie once they were in the room.

'What about your coffee?' Edith asked, frowning.

'I'm sorry, we will have to give that a miss.'

They left the apartment, and once they were outside on the pavement, Birdie turned to Seb. 'What was all that about?'

'Somerton became very agitated when I suggested that it would be beneficial to him if the painting was stolen. He's currently going through the process of handing over his estate to the National Trust, and once a property is owned by them, he then just becomes a custodian. What did you learn from Edith?'

'Somerton's definitely strapped for cash. She's been using her own money, but that's running out, and she resents having to spend it. When I suggested they sold the London flat, she was adamant that wasn't going to happen. She'd leave him if she had to spend all of her time in Devon. Edith likes to go out with her friends when she's in London. I think it might be worth following her.'

'That's one option, but I think finding out who forged the painting and whether or not Somerton was involved is a better place to start.'

Chapter 19

'Do you know how many people have the surname *Renaud* in France? There are literally tens of thousands,' Birdie said, a frustrated edge to her voice because she'd been on the internet for over an hour, scrolling social media sites and newspaper articles trying to find their forger with no luck. The task seemed more and more insurmountable.

Seb glanced up from his computer screen. 'You should be confining your search to Paris and the surrounding areas.'

'I realise that, but it's still not easy. So far, I have no Renaud connected to an art gallery or being an artist. I'm now researching all the art galleries to see if any of them mention his name either on the staff or in their press releases and blogs. No wonder Paris is known as the cultural capital of the world – it's like there are galleries on every street corner … and before you say anything, yes, I realise that's an exaggeration.'

'New York has more art galleries than Paris, although it depends on your definition of gallery. There some bijou shops who would call themselves a gallery but which are not recognised as such. I'm assuming you're referring to some of them.'

'Yes. And if our man is a professional forger, it's likely he'll be in one of those rather than in somewhere high profile. What do you think?' Birdie rested her elbows on the table and stared over at him.

'I agree.'

'Do you know anyone in the Met's Art and Antiques Unit who might be able to assist us by any chance?' The thought had only just popped into her head.

'I used to before it was disbanded a few years ago. Now it's up and running again, I don't, but I'll contact Rob to see if he might be able to help. Why don't you research into some of the famous forgeries that have taken place over the past twenty years? That could provide a link, or at least give us something else to consider.'

Birdie opened another search and, for the next hour, was both immersed and fascinated by all the different stories reported regarding art thefts and forgeries of art from all over the world, although she focused specifically on those in France. There had even been art exhibitions devoted to famous forgeries, and the topic was studied at many universities.

'Art forgery is a massive business and worth billions. If only I was good at art, I could make myself an absolute packet. Shall I investigate people named Renaud who live in beautiful houses with lots of money? Then again, they wouldn't be able to do what they do because they'd be too high profile. Maybe this forger flies under the radar, and to do that, he'd have to lead a very ordinary life without drawing any attention to himself.'

'I've just heard back from Rob. There's a Bernard Renaud who has a small gallery in Paris. He helped the police during one of their enquiries about five years ago.

He was questioned regarding a number of paintings that were stolen from a holiday home situated on the outskirts of Paris owned by a British couple. He was only interviewed because they had patronised his shop while they were visiting.'

'If the French police ran the operation, how come the Met has details in their system?'

'It was a joint op, and they shared intel. It's quite common with special teams.'

'That does surprise me, knowing how fraught Anglo–French relationships can be sometimes.'

'Which is usually exaggerated and very often related to sporting events.'

'Okay, fine. Did they solve the case that Renaud helped on?'

'Yes, the pieces were found, and a syndicate of several people were prosecuted, but he wasn't one of them.'

'Well, at least now we have something to go on. I'll check social media first and see if he posts at all, although there's bound to be more than one Bernard Renaud. What other details did Rob send you? I might start there first.'

'His gallery is called Galerie Renaud, and it's situated in a small street off Rue de Lyon.'

'I'll see if he has a website.' Birdie keyed the name in, but nothing came up. 'That's strange. I thought every business had a website. All I can think is that it must be a very small gallery. I'll try Google Maps.' She found Rue de Lyon and then looked down some of the many side streets. She finally found the gallery, which was a door situated between two shops, with the words *Galerie Renaud* written on the front. 'It's not really a proper gallery. The front door is situated between a bakery and a pharmacy. Do you have a phone number for him?'

'Yes. I'll give it a call.' Seb pulled out his phone and

keyed in the number, and put it on speaker. It rang for several minutes and in the end, cut off without going to voicemail.

'Crap,' Birdie moaned. 'Too much to think we could be lucky enough to get hold of him straight away. Do you have an email address?'

'Yes, but I don't know how effective emailing him will be – he clearly doesn't want to be found if he has no website and no voicemail.'

'Although I haven't yet looked, I'm guessing that social media won't produce much either,' Birdie said.

'I think you're right. It might be best if we go over there and see him in person.'

Birdie's mouth opened. Was he suggesting they went overseas to one of her most favourite places in the world?

'You and me going on a trip to France? Oh my God, that's so exciting. I love it over there. But I haven't been since I was at school, and we went over for a few days to help with our French A-Level. Do you speak French?'

'Enough to get by but probably not as well as you if you studied the language to A-level standard.'

'I also took it as a subsidiary subject when I was at university.'

'Excellent. Then we'll be very well prepared.'

'When do you want to leave?' What should she pack? It depended on how long they were there, she supposed.

'We'll leave now. We'll just take overnight bags because we won't be staying there long.'

That answered that question.

'We're not going to get flights so quickly, surely.'

'We're not flying. We can either take the train from St Pancras to Paris, which will take around three hours, maybe a bit less. Or we can drive down to Folkestone and get the Eurotunnel across to Calais and drive to Paris, which will take six or seven hours. The plus side is that we won't have to worry about hiring a car.'

'Either works for me. But we might not have a choice so late in the day.'

'I'll take a look at what's available.'

He went back to working on his computer, and Birdie logged onto social media to see if there was anything on Renaud.

'I've booked us onto Le Shuttle. We can get the four o'clock crossing. I've also booked us into a hotel for two nights in case we don't finish our business in one day, and texted Jill to ask her to take care of Elsa for me. We need to leave in half an hour to be sure of making it to Dover in time.'

'Whoever said that PI work could be boring clearly didn't know what they were talking about. I love Paris.'

'This isn't going to be a sightseeing trip, Birdie. All we're doing is finding out what we can about Renaud. There's every chance that he's not the man we're looking for, and we will have wasted two precious days.'

Birdie rolled her eyes and made a loud tutting noise. 'I know that, but it doesn't mean I can't enjoy an unexpected trip overseas. It will give me a chance to practise my French, which is probably rusty by now.'

Within half an hour, they were in Seb's car, heading towards Folkestone. Fortunately, they'd left before rush hour, and although the traffic was heavy, Seb was able to keep a steady speed.

'I've been pondering over your suggestion that we follow Edith. Or at least make more enquiries into her,' Seb said. 'If we do get to meet Renaud, we'll mention her name and see if we can establish a link between them. Did you get the impression from her that the marriage was stable? If she has the original and is trying to sell it, is she likely to leave Somerton once she has money?'

Birdie stared ahead in thought. 'I'm not sure. I suspect she likes having a title and all the status it brings her, but she misses being with people of her own age. If we do find out that Renaud knows Edith, then that's a definite red flag.'

For the remainder of the journey to Folkestone they were relatively quiet. Birdie was engrossed in her own thoughts regarding her birth mother. Fingers crossed, the school her mother went to kept records going back that far.

She'd initially been worried that her parents would be upset about her desire to discover her roots. But they'd been supportive. They understood that she loved them and that they would always be her parents but that she still wanted to know where she came from. Like most people did. That was why TV programmes looking into celebrities' pasts and where they came from are so popular.

She started when her arm was nudged. 'Wake up, Birdie.'

'What? I haven't been asleep.' She shifted in her seat and sat upright.

'Yes, you have, and we're almost here.'

'I was resting my eyes, that's all. And maybe just drifted off there for a couple of minutes. Cars do that to me,' she admitted.

'It's fine. I enjoyed the peace.' Seb flashed a grin in her direction.

'Ha. Ha. Very funny. Are we going to stay in the car during the crossing?'

'Yes. It only takes thirty-five minutes.'

'Typical. I'd been hoping there'd be a restaurant on board so we can get something to eat. We should have stopped on the way.'

'I thought about it, but you were sound asleep, and I didn't want to wake you. We'll find somewhere to eat in Calais. You won't starve, I promise.'

'Good. Where's the hotel you've booked?'

'In Paris, about a ten-minute walk from the gallery.'

'Wow, the centre of Paris. It must be expensive.'

'It's a pension hotel, so fairly basic. But fine for us.'

'For me, you mean. I'm more used to slumming it than you.' She smirked.

'Don't start.'

'Joking.' She held up both hands, and he rolled his eyes.

'It will be too late to go there tonight, but we can make sure to visit Renaud first thing in the morning.'

Chapter 20

'Mmm. I could do this every day.' Birdie groaned with delight after taking a bite of her pain au chocolat. It was still warm, and the flaky, buttery pastry melted in her mouth. It was to die for.

They'd found a lovely café for breakfast, which was close to the hotel they were staying in. The room Seb had booked was basic. But she didn't mind. It was French, and that more than made up for it. They'd also had a very enjoyable evening out the previous night and had eaten at a café frequented by locals, which was always a good sign. And the food had lived up to her expectations.

Birdie was enjoying trying out her French after so long and was amazed at how much she could remember. In fact, she'd understood more than she could speak, which was interesting because she could hear what people around them were talking about. Which she then relayed to Seb so she could impress him. His French was also good, but hers was better. Not that she was in competition with him, but it was nice to outdo him at something for a change.

'You'd soon get fed up with delicious pastries. I know what you're like, remember.' Seb smiled.

'You're wrong. I'm really enjoying the relaxed way of life. Sitting outside watching the world go by. We should definitely consider moving the business and operating from here. It would be like one long holiday.'

'And you'd be bored within a week, and missing your friends and your cricket.'

He had a good point. Did they even play cricket in France? She didn't think so.

'Okay, I suppose you're right. But taking on a few cases from people living abroad might be nice. At least we'd get better weather. Not that it's hard. I can't believe the amount of rain we're getting at home. And it's meant to be summer.'

'You're forgetting that working over here would mean that we'd have to navigate a judicial system that we know nothing about and which, I believe, is extremely complex.'

'You're such a spoilsport.' She gave a loud tut and laughed.

'Have you nearly finished? It's time we went to look for the gallery.'

'I'm ready whenever you are. But maybe we should buy some more of these to have later.' She held up what remained of her pastry. 'They are totally the best I've ever tasted. Then again, they might be a bit stale later. I've got an idea. We'll return for breakfast tomorrow if we end up staying a second night.'

Seb paid, and they strolled down the Rue de Lyon until arriving at the tiny side street where Bernard Renaud had his gallery. A few metres down the road, they came to the oak door situated between the bakery and pharmacy that she'd previously identified. On the door, written in gold letters, was the name *Galerie Renaud*.

'This doesn't look much like a gallery. It's really dingy. Do you think it's a cover for his forgery work?' She wrinkled her nose. It smelt musty even in the doorway.

'That's what we'll find out.' Seb tried the door, and it was locked. 'Damn.'

'I'll pop next door and find out when he opens.' Birdie left Seb and pushed open the door to the bakery. The smell of warm fresh bread invaded her nostrils.

'*Bonjour*,' the assistant greeted her, smiling.

'*Bonjour. A quelle heure ouvre la Galerie Renaud?*' Birdie pointed in the direction of the gallery.

'*Aujoud'hui il ouvre à deux.*'

Not until two? Surely that can't be good for business.

'*Pourquoi si tard?*' she asked, wanting to know why it was opening so late.

'*Il a rendez-vous ce matin.*'

'*D'accord. Merci.*' Birdie left the shop and met Seb outside. 'It's not opening until two this afternoon because Renaud has an appointment. That gives us a few hours to kill, so what would you like to do?'

'Some sightseeing?' Seb suggested, a broad smile on his face.

'Perfect.'

Four hours later, after visiting the Louvre Museum, and then having lunch at a restaurant overlooking the Seine, they had returned to the gallery. This time the door was open, and the bell gave a little tinkle as they stepped into the dark, narrow hallway. There was an arrow on the wall pointing up the stairs with the gallery name below it.

They climbed the rickety staircase, and when they

reached the top, it opened up into a large airy studio which was well lit from windows on both sides of the room. Birdie had convinced herself it would be dark and seedy, but it wasn't at all. The walls were full of paintings, and in the far corner was a man sitting at a desk. He glanced up at them.

'*Bonjour,*' Birdie said, striding over to him. '*Parlez-vous anglais?*'

'*Un peu,*' he replied, holding up his forefinger and thumb a couple of centimetres apart to demonstrate that he meant just a little.

Surely he would speak more English than that? Most people in French cities did because of all the tourists. She'd have to test him out.

'*Êtes-vous Bernard Renaud?*'

'*Oui.*'

That was good. At least they had the right man.

'*Je suis Birdie.*'

'*Et je suis Clifford,*' Seb added, taking out his phone, pulling up a photo of the missing painting and showing it to the man. '*Reconnaissez-vous cela?*'

Birdie nodded her approval once Seb had asked the man in French if he recognised the photo.

'*Non,*' Renaud said, waving his hand.

'Are you sure?' Birdie said. 'Because we've been told that you do copies of paintings for people. And we think that this might be one of them.'

The man blinked several times. A sure sign that he was about to lie. '*Je ne comprends pas.*'

'He said he doesn't understand,' Birdie said to Seb.

'Yes, I got that.'

'I don't believe him. Show him the photo again.' Did he know more English than he was letting on. If so, why? Unless he had something to hide.

Seb held out his phone again, and the man looked at it and shrugged.

They were getting nowhere fast.

'I'm going to take a look around.' She slowly walked alongside one of the walls, looking at the paintings being exhibited, many of them of famous Paris landmarks. She spotted some more pieces leaning against the wall in the far corner with a cloth over them, and she slowly made her way over there, hoping not to alert Renaud as to where she was heading. When she got there, she took hold of the cloth, intending to lift it off the paintings.

'Oi, leave that alone!' a Cockney accent boomed out. Birdie jumped and let go of the cloth. She turned around. Renaud was marching over to where she stood, with Seb following close behind.

'You're English?' Birdie said, stating the obvious.

Now they were getting somewhere.

'Yeah. What of it?' Renaud snarled.

'You kept that quiet. Why didn't you tell us when we were asking about the painting?' Birdie glared at him.

'Because over here, I'm French and that works for me. And before you ask again, no, I don't know anything about the painting, apart from I recognise it as being the work of Allard, one of the lesser-known impressionist painters. In my opinion, his work is a poor imitation of Degas.'

'Yet it's still worth over a million pounds.'

'That's peanuts in the art world.'

'Well, it isn't in mine. Is it correct that you forge art for people?' Birdie placed her hands on her hips and locked eyes with him. 'Are there forgeries under that cloth?' She pointed to the paintings against the wall.

'Who the hell are you? The old bill? Because I've done nothing. You can't just come in here and start accusing me. I know what you lot are—'

'Shut up.' Birdie held up her hand to silence him. 'We're private investigators looking into the disappearance of a Jasper Pemberton in England, and also that painting my partner showed you.'

'Yeah. I read about that online. I didn't forge it.'

He would say that.

'But it is something you do,' Birdie pushed.

'Some people want a copy of a painting they own so the original can be kept safe. And some people want art in the style of a certain painter. So what? I'm not breaking the law.'

Was he telling the truth? She looked across at Seb, who was staring at the man intently. 'How do we know it's not yours? You could just be saying that.'

'Because my signature isn't on it.'

'Yeah, right. Of course it isn't. The signature would be of the original artist.'

'Look, every forger leaves a tiny mark somewhere on the painting to signify who did it.'

'That sounds ridiculous. Leaving a signature, however small, will provide proof that a forged piece of art isn't genuine.' An exasperated sigh escaped her lips.

'There are very few forgers around. No one else would know.'

She was getting nowhere. She'd have to carry out some more research to find out if he was telling the truth or just winding them up.

'Can you tell who forged this painting if it wasn't you?' Birdie grabbed Seb's phone from him and showed it to Renaud.

'Not from the photograph. I'd need to look at the original using a magnifying glass. Not something I'm prepared to do. I don't want to get myself a bad reputation.'

'Without giving anything away, do you know anyone

who would have the ability to not only copy this painting but possibly turn it around in a few days?' Seb asked.

'Whatever I say is off the record, right?' Renaud said, looking from Seb to Birdie and back again.

'We've already explained that we're not the police. We want to trace Pemberton and believe the painting will assist us.'

'First of all, I'd be very surprised if it was copied in just a few days because of getting everything right. It's a lengthy process and, to put in layman's terms, doesn't just involve paint on canvas.'

'It only had to be good enough to fool the manager of the gallery where it was taken to be cleaned. He gave it a cursory glance before putting it in the safe. It wasn't until it was taken out to be cleaned that the expert discovered it to be a fake,' Seb said.

Renaud pursed his lips and stared at them for a few seconds. 'Look, what I tell you better not come back on me. Find a guy called Jim Dempster. He was here for six months learning from me. Then he went back to England. He's a good forger.'

'So why are you giving him up?' There had to be a reason.

'He did the dirty on me. And that's all I'm saying. I don't forgive. Or forget.'

Hmm. Interesting.

'And do you really think it could be him, or are you just saying it to get him in trouble?'

Renaud rolled his eyes. 'What do you think I am? A child? There are very few decent forgers around. And when I say decent, I mean someone who can fool the curator of a museum or an independent checker. The only way of discovering a decent forger's forgeries is through chemical analysis. That's expensive and time-consuming. Dempster's good.'

'Where can we find him?' Seb asked.

'He lives somewhere on the south coast of England. And that's all I know. Conversation over. You can see yourselves out.' He pointed towards the stairs.

'Before we go, do you know Edith Groom?' Birdie asked.

Renaud's jaw tightened. 'No.'

'Your body language indicates that's untrue,' Seb said.

'Look, I've told you enough. No more questions. Got it?'

Birdie and Seb left the gallery and walked in silence until reaching the main road.

'Well, that was very interesting,' Birdie said. 'He definitely knows Edith, but more important is we now have a possible forger to find.'

'More than *possible*. I believe that Jim Dempster is *likely* the person we're looking for because, according to Pemberton's diary, he had two appointments with a JD.' Seb smiled.

'Oh yes. I'd forgotten. This means Pemberton probably commissioned the forgery, right? We've finally found our link.'

'I'll book Le Shuttle, and we'll leave first thing tomorrow morning to find him.'

Chapter 21

'Hey, Seb. I've finally found him.'

He glanced at Birdie, who had a self-satisfied grin on her face. She'd been on her phone looking for Dempster ever since they'd left Paris for Calais at six in the morning, which was over two hours ago.

They'd tried the previous day but had no success.

'That's excellent work. Where does he live?'

Seb returned his gaze back to the road ahead, which was a busy dual carriageway, and driving on the right side of the road rather than the left, meant he had to pay extra attention to not revert to driving on autopilot as it was so easy to do during long journeys.

'Close to Chichester, and you'll never guess in a million years what he does for a living.'

'Surely not an accountant or some other right-brained endeavour?' He took another quick look at Birdie, who returned his glance, a smug smile on her face.

'No. Try again.'

'I'd have thought he would have been like Renaud and

had a small art gallery or gift shop. Somewhere unobtrusive to hide his more lucrative occupation.'

'Nope. Believe it or not, he's an art teacher at the local secondary school. Why would he want to put himself through that when he clearly can earn megabucks without having to worry about talentless kids being let loose with pots of paint? I couldn't think of anything worse.'

'They may be well-behaved students. But, you're right, I wouldn't have guessed that. And you're sure it's him?'

'Renaud told us that he lives on the south coast, and he's got the same name. It's not like he's called John Smith or any other common name, so I reckon it's got to be him. I have a photo of him taken at the school prize-giving, so we'll easily recognise him. Shall we go straight to the school?'

He'd been about to suggest that. It was the most logical thing to do.

'Yes. Chichester's a couple of hours from Folkestone, but we should be there in time. Do we have his home address?'

'No. Only the school. We can wait outside until the kids leave. Or shall we go into the school and see the head teacher and ask to speak to him?'

Seb shook his head. 'To do that would run the risk of alerting him. I think our best approach is to wait for him to leave and follow him back to where he lives. We'll speak to him there and, hopefully, put him on the back foot.'

They reached St Paul's Academy, where Dempster taught, by three o'clock. Fortunately, it wasn't a large school, and there appeared to be only one car park. That would make it easier for spotting their man.

Seb parked in one of the visitor spaces, which gave them a good view of the entrance, and after Birdie had shown him the photo of Dempster, they both sat back and stared ahead, not diverting their gaze. At three-thirty on the dot, the doors opened, and the pupils piled out. After a further fifteen minutes, adults, presumably teachers, exited.

'I hope he doesn't have to stay after school for a meeting,' Birdie said.

'If he does, it still won't be dark, so we shouldn't miss him when he leaves.'

'Actually, hold that thought – there he is.' Birdie pointed towards a man coming out the entrance wearing casual trousers and a short-sleeved shirt and holding a bag. He walked towards the latest model Audi Q8, unlocked it, placed his bag on the rear seat, and climbed into the front.

'Excellent – we'll follow him.' Seb started the engine.

'Interesting choice of car for a teacher, considering how bad their pay is. It could be proof that he's our forger.'

'I wouldn't say proof, but it certainly points to him supplementing his income.'

They followed Dempster out of town until they reached Bosham, a village four miles outside of Chichester. Dempster pulled into the driveway of a double-fronted red-brick cottage in Shore Road, which overlooked the water. On the gate, there was a sign and an arrow pointing to the back garden saying *Art Gallery*.

'I think that confirms we have our man.' Seb parked further up the road from the house. Because of the low-level brick walls, they were able to watch Dempster get out of his car and go inside through the front door.

'How shall we approach him?' Birdie said. 'How about we follow the sign to the gallery and pretend we're here to look around? That way he won't be alerted and attempt to do a runner because presumably he does get people calling in.'

That made perfect sense to Seb. 'Yes, that is a good idea.'

They left the car and walked to the cottage. After following the arrow to the rear of the property, they reached a large outbuilding. On the wooden door there was a *Closed* notice, but underneath it was a phone number.

'I'll call his mobile, and let's hope he'll come out to see us.' Birdie pulled out her phone and keyed in the number. She put it on speaker.

'Jim Dempster speaking.'

'Hi. We're standing outside your gallery, and we'd love to take a look around. You were recommended to us by one of the locals. We're on the lookout for some local art to buy. I know it says closed, but is there any chance we could go in because we're only in the area today?'

'Well, you're in luck because I've just arrived home from work. Give me a couple of minutes, and I'll be with you.'

Birdie gave Seb a thumbs-up sign, and he reciprocated.

'Thanks so much. We really appreciate it.' Birdie ended the call. 'Well, that was easy enough. Did you hear the excitement in his voice and his sharp intake of breath when I said we wanted to buy something? Surely he can't be short of money after earning so much for the forgery.'

'Yes, I did. But remember, we don't know his financial situation, so it's pointless making a supposition. He may have considerable debts.'

'True.'

Within a couple of minutes, Dempster headed down the path, relaxed and smiling at them.

'Hello. Welcome to my gallery. Who told you about me? I'd like to thank them.'

'We were in the pub and asked the person behind the

bar if there were any small galleries around because we prefer to buy from them, rather than the large galleries which charge an arm and a leg for mediocre work. The man standing next to us mentioned you. Sorry, he didn't tell us his name. I'd say he was in his forties, around five foot ten and had dark blond curly hair that hung below his ears, touching his collar,' Birdie said.

'I think I might know who you mean. It was very kind of him. Come on through, and you can see all the paintings that I have for sale displayed on the walls.' Dempster unlocked the door and ushered them in. 'Have you come far?'

'From London. We've just travelled back from a short trip overseas to France,' Birdie said.

Once they were inside the square room, Seb and Birdie split up and started looking around. Most of the paintings were done in watercolours and featured local scenes. Seb glanced at Dempster, who was standing in a relaxed position to one side watching them, and decided to make his move.

'These are all very good, indeed,' he said, walking over to the artist. 'We've recently been to visit Bernard Renaud in Paris. I believe you're acquainted with him.'

Dempster stiffened. 'What's this all about? I thought you were passing through and wanted to view my work.'

'We're actually investigating the forgery of a painting by Allard called *Sunset in Venice*, and it was suggested to us that you might be the person to speak to.'

Panic marched across Dempster's face. 'And you've tricked your way into here based on something that bastard Renaud said, haven't you? He never did like me. Well, I'll tell you now, I don't know anything about forging paintings. And if you're not here to buy anything, then please leave.'

'We're going nowhere until you've answered our questions. We're investigating the disappearance of Jasper Pemberton. We believe he's involved in the forging of the Allard painting. In his diary, he had a meeting with a JD. I believe that's you?' Seb took a step towards Dempster, and he shrunk back.

'You don't know that,' Dempster muttered.

'Stop messing us around. If you want us out of here, then answer the questions,' Birdie said, marching over to them.

Dempster's frame sagged. 'I was asked to copy the painting. It's not a forgery in the strictest sense of the word. I didn't age the canvas or the paint. It had to be done quickly, and they didn't want my full service. I mean—' He sucked in a breath.

'And that's why you can afford the car you drive,' Birdie said.

'There's no law against me copying the painting. What people do with it is their business. I don't sell my copies or pretend that they're the genuine article.'

'You'll be considered an accessory if we report you to the police,' Seb said.

'I thought you were the police. That's what you said.' He looked daggers at Seb.

'We're private investigators. But we do have links with the police, and I'm sure they'll be interested in questioning you.'

'If you tell them about me, I'll lose my job and any other work that comes my way. There must be something I can do.' He momentarily closed his eyes, his self-assurance vanished.

'For a start, you can tell us who commissioned this piece of work,' Seb demanded.

'I don't know his name. He looked to be in his late thirties, and he was tall with closely cut blond hair. He spoke like you.' He nodded at Seb.

'Was this him?' Seb held out his phone and showed him a photo of Pemberton.

'Yes. He paid me cash and said he needed it quickly. I didn't ask questions.'

'How much did you charge?' Birdie asked.

'Thirty thousand. It would have been more if I'd spent longer on it, but he said it only had to pass a cursory inspection.'

'So you lied. You did know why the painting was wanted.'

'Not exactly. Look, I… It's just… I've told you everything I know. I don't want to be involved.'

'It's a bit late for that,' Birdie said.

'B-but—'

'We're going now,' Seb said. 'Don't mention our visit to anyone because if we find out you have, then we'll be forced to go to the police to inform them of your connection to the case.'

Chapter 22

Birdie folded her arms, leant against the wall, and stared at the new whiteboard she'd persuaded Seb to buy on the way back to his London flat the previous night. She much preferred a visual representation of a problem because it helped her to process it.

She picked up a marker pen and wrote Pemberton's name on the left, the name of the painting in the middle, and Lord Somerton's name on the right. She drew connecting arrows from each of the men to the painting. And under Pemberton's name, she wrote *Annabelle*, and under *Lord Somerton*, she wrote *Edith*. Under the painting, she wrote *Dempster (Renaud)* and a connecting arrow to Edith.

'Right. We know that Pemberton commissioned a forgery of Lord Somerton's painting, *Sunset in Venice*. We know that Somerton has financial problems and is handing over his property to the National Trust. We also know that he was thinking about selling the painting before that happened, and that's why he was having it cleaned. Finally, we know that Somerton's wife, Edith, lived in France – which gives her a connection to Renaud – and isn't prepared to live a pauper's existence. I think that's about it. Apart from the note.' She wrote *Note* under Annabelle's name. 'Now, how does this all fit together? Where is Pemberton, and what part, if any, does Somerton play?' She glanced across at Seb. 'Over to you.'

'Another point of note is that Pemberton paid thirty thousand pounds for the forgery. Money which he didn't have. An important question to ask, therefore, is, where did the money come from? I believe this is one of those cases where it's prudent to follow the money.'

Birdie added Seb's points to the board.

'Could it have come from Somerton? To his sort, an additional thirty thousand wouldn't mean much, so he'd still consider himself poor, even if he had that to spare.'

'I disagree. Thirty thousand is a lot of money, irrespective of who you are,' Seb said, drumming his fingers on the desk.

Was it? Birdie doubted Seb's parents would think so, but that was one thought she was going to keep to herself.

'It could be money from winnings. We know that Pemberton was a gambler. Somerton might be too. Suppose that he had some winnings and decided to invest it in a forgery of the painting. A spur-of-the-moment decision.'

Were they clutching at straws? It seemed a plausible explanation.

'Maybe. But this doesn't come across as a decision taken on a whim.'

'Do we think that Pemberton and Somerton were in it together? They know each other, but are they close, and do they regularly go to the races together?'

'We need concrete evidence if we are to connect them.

I'll look into some recent race meetings, and you investigate Somerton,' Seb said, pulling his laptop towards him.

Birdie's fingers flew over the keys, and soon she was absorbed in her research. Somerton didn't shy away from publicity, and there were hundreds, if not thousands, of articles about him, some of them not very flattering, especially when he got together with Edith. She'd finished reading an article from *Hello!*, where they'd invited the magazine into their home in Devon for a feature, when an article in a farming magazine that was listed right at the bottom of the fifth internet search page caught her eye.

'Bloody hell. I've found something interesting.' Excitement coursed through her as it always did when she was on to something. 'Somerton was involved in a company that went bankrupt twelve months ago. The company produced organic eggs, but on investigation, it was found that they didn't qualify for organic status because they'd been using chicken feed that contained additives. The company folded, and Somerton lost all the money that he'd invested. And according to this article, it was over a million pounds. If that's not incentive enough for him to nick his own painting and replace it with a forgery, I don't know what is.'

'Well researched. I think we need—'

'Hang on a minute.' Birdie stared at the screen. 'I've now found some photos of him taking delivery of a boat a few days after the company went belly-up. This isn't making any sense. How could he afford a boat after claiming to have no money and his wife agreeing with him? Do you think he's selling off his other paintings? Is there any way of knowing?'

'Not really. If the National Trust had already done their inventory, we might have been able to check but, according to Somerton, they haven't yet.'

'That's a shame. Have you found anything?'

'Not yet… Wait, no. It can't be,' Seb muttered.

'What is it?' Birdie looked up from her computer screen, her interest piqued.

'If this turns out to be something, then it puts a totally different complexion on everything that we've learnt so far.' Seb let out a worrying sigh.

'What? Stop talking in riddles and tell me.'

'Come over here,' Seb said, beckoning to her.

She slid her chair until next to Seb and looked at his screen, which was filled with a photo of a group of men at a horse-race meeting. 'Ohhh. There's Pemberton with Somerton, and looking a lot closer than *acquaintances*, I might add. When and where was this taken?'

'A few months ago, at Newbury Racecourse.'

'And this is what concerned you so much?'

There had to be more to it than that.

'No, it's him.' Seb pointed to a man who was on the edge of the photo. Only half of his face had been captured.

'I don't know who he is. And how do you know that he's with Pemberton and Somerton? He could've just been standing next to them.'

'That man is Liam O'Rourke. He's a well-known London gangster, and I was part of the operation that put him inside for ten years. He was released from prison six months ago, having received time off for good behaviour. If O'Rourke's involved, then it could result in something very nasty, and I certainly fear for Pemberton's well-being if he's got him. Especially if O'Rourke's the one who sent Annabelle the note. I don't like this one bit, Birdie. Not one bit.'

She'd never seen Seb looking so worried before.

'But how do you know he's with them? I can't see it myself.'

'Look at the way his posture is open. Although we can only see half of him, you can see an open hand gesturing in their direction. He's part of the group, I'm sure of it.'

'Shall we speak to Annabelle and find out if she's ever seen Pemberton with him?'

'No, I don't want to worry her yet. I think we need to contact Rob at the Met. Let's find out if O'Rourke's being investigated over anything or if they've got him under surveillance, because we certainly don't want to interfere in their investigation. This has taken a nasty turn. And if we're to save Pemberton's life, we need to act very carefully and stealthily without tipping off O'Rourke that we suspect him.'

'We don't actually know that he is involved.' Birdie glanced at Seb's arched eyebrow. 'Well, okay, we have Pemberton, Somerton and now O'Rourke together in one place. A very unlikely combination of people, so perhaps you're right.'

'I'm going to ask Rob if he can meet us today.'

'I'm surprised Rob didn't ask to meet us in the pub, knowing how much you two like to go out drinking,' Birdie said.

'When I mentioned wanting to discuss O'Rourke, he suggested that we came to Scotland Yard and meet in the cafeteria close by. Coffee and muffin?' Seb asked as they joined the queue.

'Sure. I'll find us a table.'

Seb joined her within a few minutes, and shortly after,

Rob arrived. Seb and Birdie both stood, and Rob pulled Seb into a bear hug.

'How are you doing, mate?' Rob said. 'It's great to see you. You're looking well. I can see PI work suits you.'

'It has its moments. And you?' Seb replied.

'Doing well, thanks. Doing well. And how's my favourite ex-detective constable?' Rob held out his hand for Birdie to shake.

'Good, thanks.'

'I take it you're keeping this one in check?' Rob nodded at Seb and grinned.

'I'm doing my best. But it's not always easy.' She glanced at Seb, who was laughing.

'You're probably wondering why I asked you to meet here, close to work,' Rob said once they were seated. 'When you mentioned O'Rourke, I thought it was best to keep our conversation on the down-low. The gang is firmly in our sights and, between you and me' – he leant forward slightly and lowered his tone – 'it's likely they've got someone here on the inside. We don't know for certain, but they certainly seem to be prewarned whenever we go on the offensive.'

Birdie frowned. 'Then why are you telling us in here? Surely that's going to alert whoever's on the take.'

'Because it's noisy, and people come and go. Believe it or not, this is one of the best places to have a private conversation. And we could be discussing the work that you're doing for us. Tell me why you're interested in the gang.'

'It's not the gang in its entirety. It's O'Rourke. We're investigating the disappearance of a Jasper Pemberton and think it's linked to the disappearance and forgery of a painting by Allard at Nelson Gallery in Mayfair. We've established that Pemberton was the one to commission the forgery, but we also know that he's been seen at the races with O'Rourke and the painting's owner.'

'If it involves O'Rourke, you should leave this to us. If there's something going on, then we will discover it.'

'That's not possible. We're working for Annabelle on a tight time frame,' Seb said.

'As in your ex?'

'Yes. She's engaged to Pemberton and has asked us to find him. Our investigation has led to O'Rourke, but having said that, we don't know for certain that he's involved. It might be a coincidence that he was seen with Pemberton at a race meeting. Do you have anything that might help in our investigation?'

'We haven't got anything on O'Rourke relating to the art world, so you can look into that. But if you uncover anything else, then I want to know immediately.'

'Okay,' Seb said.

'But be careful if you're looking into O'Rourke. You're not exactly his number one person, so if he discovers that you're investigating him, it might not be pretty.'

'I'm fully aware of that and will take all the necessary precautions.'

'Good. Now how long are you going to be in London?'

'Until we finish the case.'

'We need a night out together to catch up. You too, Birdie,' Rob said, rubbing his hands together.

'I don't get it. You can't meet anywhere other than close to your work to discuss O'Rourke in case it looks suspicious or someone overhears us, but we can have a night out?' Birdie frowned.

'We'll be drinking, and it doesn't matter who listens to our conversation because it will have nothing to do with work. There's more to life than that,' Rob said.

'I've never seen Seb drunk, so it will be a first.'

'Who said anything about getting drunk? We'll have a few beers, that's all. Thanks for your time, Rob. If O'Rourke is involved, then we don't have time to waste. He's a monster and wouldn't think twice about harming Pemberton or Annabelle.'

'Well, be careful,' Rob said.

'That's the plan,' Seb said. 'But if O'Rourke does anything to harm Annabelle, he'll live to regret it.'

Chapter 23

'Rob just cracks me up – he's so funny. And what's even funnier is that you're such good friends because you're so different from one another,' Birdie said as they left the pub, and headed to the Underground station to catch a train back to Seb's flat.

'You don't find me amusing?' Seb quipped, arching an eyebrow.

'Don't take it personally, but not in the same way that Rob is. I'm not saying that you don't have a sense of humour, because of course you do, otherwise, we wouldn't be working together. But Rob is so cool, and I like that when I was on the force, he never used his rank to belittle me or make me feel inferior.'

'I'd like to see him try. I don't know anyone who was able to put you in your place.'

'What about Sarge?' she said, referring to her old boss.

'You had him wrapped around your little finger. Why else would he have given me a lecture about treating you right when you left?'

'I didn't know that. I thought it was Twiggy.'

'Sergeant Weston, Twiggy, and every member of your team came up to me separately and made it plain what would happen if things didn't work out.'

Warmth flooded through her as fond memories of the team filled her head. When they got back to Market Harborough, she'd make time to visit the station and catch up with them.

'And you've only just told me this?'

'You didn't need to know. Anyway, returning to Rob. He's a good guy, and I'd trust him with my life. We go back a long time, as you know.'

'A bit like opposites attract, I suppose.'

'Something like that.'

They stepped onto the downward escalator, and as it reached the platform concourse, the void was filled by the rumbling sound of a train approaching. The pair turned the corner onto the platform itself, and within seconds, the train came out of the tunnel and slowed to a halt.

'Good timing.' The doors opened, and she made her way to a vacant double seat. Seb sat opposite her. There was no one close, which meant they could talk. 'What are our plans? Are we to report back everything we find to Rob and the rest of his team?'

'Only if we think it's relevant. Now we know his team might be involved, we'll have to tread carefully. I think our next step should be to find out where Somerton is and put a tail on him to see if he can lead us anywhere.'

'I've got a better idea. You follow Somerton, and I'll follow Edith – assuming they're still in London and haven't hightailed it back to their estate in Devon because they know that we're investigating.'

'I'll phone the estate to check.'

'I do hope this gangster friend of yours isn't involved because it's going to make life very difficult for us. Not to mention Pemberton, whose life could be in danger if he's double-crossed them, which, thinking back to Annabelle's note, could be the case.'

'I can assure you O'Rourke is no friend of mine.'

At the next stop, the seat next to them was taken, and so for the remainder of the journey they sat in silence, only talking about picking up something to eat.

They arrived at Seb's flat, armed with a takeaway from the Thai restaurant around the corner. Elsa was waiting at the door for them, her tail wagging so hard it was banging against the wall.

'Hello, girl, have you missed us?' Birdie bent down and rubbed her back. 'I bet you can smell our dinner. Come on, let's go into the kitchen.'

She took out some plates and put the takeaway in the centre of the table, all the time Elsa not leaving her side. They had such a good relationship. She'd love her own dog, but, of course, it wouldn't be practical and living at home with her parents meant they might have something to say about it. It wasn't as if she would be moving out any time soon. Not now she'd invested all of her money into Seb's business.

'I've just called the estate, and Lord and Lady Somerton are still in London.' Seb came into the kitchen and sat at the small round oak table.

'That's excellent. There's no point in tailing them tonight. Shall we start tomorrow?'

'Yes, we'll go to their flat in the morning.'

'How are we going to get there? If we're on foot and they take a taxi, then it won't be easy.'

'We'll take the car and make a decision once we see them leaving the flat. I imagine Somerton has his driver here, so we will be able to follow them, or at least one of them, if they go out separately.'

∽

The next morning, Birdie was up early, and she'd popped to the supermarket down the road to get them supplies for their surveillance.

'What are you doing?' Seb said when he walked into the kitchen as she was busy with her preparations.

'I've made sufficient rolls to last us all day, with a couple to spare. I also have nuts, fruit, and sweets for our snacks. Everything we need. Well, everything that I could find in the small supermarket down the road. I was annoyed that they didn't have my favourite muesli bars, but I can manage without.'

'A veritable feast. It's a good job we're taking the car.'

'I'm taking my rucksack as well, because if I end up following Edith on foot, I'll need to carry my supplies. Knowing my luck, you'll be the one in the car, and I'll be the one getting all the exercise. Do you have a spare key to the flat in case we split up and I want to come back sooner than you?'

'Yes.' He pulled out a key from one of the kitchen drawers and handed it to her.

'Thanks. When are you going to tell Annabelle what we're doing and where the investigation has led us? I'm surprised she hasn't been in touch already wanting an update.'

'She did message me, and I was vague in my response. I informed her we'd be in touch when we had something concrete to tell her. Fortunately, she's busy helping to organise a charity event, which means she's not breathing down our necks the entire time. Or, knowing Annabelle, wanting to accompany us.'

'I don't get her. How can she divorce herself from

what's happening so easily, especially after receiving the note? Is she at all worried, do you think?'

'Yes, I'm sure she is. But she's a great one for compartmentalising and not letting it get in the way.'

'That does make it easier for us, although I wouldn't be surprised if she's just trying to hide her feelings from you, because she's scared to show any vulnerability. That's what —' She stopped before adding her usual "you lot" because she was trying hard not to show any bias. 'Have I told you I am warming to Annabelle a little?'

'I had worked that out for myself. Not that it matters because we are professional investigators and shouldn't let our feelings interfere. That being said, you may discover soon enough a more pleasant side to Annabelle that she doesn't always reveal.'

'I realise that, otherwise why would you have gone out with her for so long? Right, let's have some breakfast and then we can get ready to go.'

They drove to the Somertons' flat and, fortunately, were able to park in a space that gave them a view of the front door.

'I wonder what time they get up and if we are going to be here for a while, because this is only one-hour parking, and we might not find another spot.' She gave a sweeping gaze of the surrounding area and couldn't see any other spaces available.

'If we're sitting in the car, we can risk it and only move on if a parking enforcement warden stops us.'

'Except that nowadays tickets are also issued from CCTV camera footage. Still, we can charge any parking fines we get to Annabelle as part of our expenses,' Birdie said, checking Seb's expression to see his response.

'It's a moot point because they're leaving the property.'

She glanced across the road and saw the couple stepping outside. They spoke to each other for a few seconds before a car drew up, and Somerton got in. Edith gave him a wave and then turned left and began walking down the road.

'Okay, it looks like I've drawn the walking straw. Didn't I tell you? I'll meet you back at your place later. You'd better hurry if you're going to follow His Lordship.'

Birdie jumped out of the car and immediately crossed the road, making sure to keep her distance while pursuing Edith. She couldn't help being envious of the woman who, even walking down the street, turned heads. She was tall, held herself upright, practically glided as she walked, and was wearing a stunning cream trouser suit with some high trainers. Because she was so tall, her strides were much longer than Birdie's, which meant keeping up with her wasn't easy.

They came to the entrance of an Underground station, and Birdie followed Edith to the platform for the Circle line and waited for a train. She kept her head down in case the woman turned and recognised her, but there were plenty of people on the platform, so Birdie felt safe. She'd pulled on a baseball cap earlier to hide her wild red hair, which could be a dead giveaway during undercover work. The train arrived after a couple of minutes, and Birdie got into the same carriage as Edith, who was seemingly oblivious to anything around her, as she had her phone out and she was concentrating on that. They got out three stops later at Notting Hill Gate, and Birdie followed her for several minutes until she turned into a quiet street that was lined by an elegant, white terraced building. The main entrance was flanked by white pillars, and a sign written in tasteful lettering on the glass at the top of the door read *Cashmere Hotel*. If you didn't know the place was there, it would have been easy to miss it.

Edith walked into the hotel, and Birdie stood in the entrance watching until the woman was out of sight. Birdie then went inside and drew in a breath. It was beautiful. Understated elegance was the best way to describe it. There was a sign pointing towards the reception, and Birdie could see Edith there, taking a key from the receptionist.

Had she booked a room?

Birdie followed Edith to the hotel restaurant towards the rear of the ground floor, and once in there, she approached a table where there was a man sitting alone. Edith kissed him on the lips and sat opposite. Birdie took a photo of the couple and then hovered in the background for a few minutes. This clearly wasn't a business meeting. They were holding hands and acting like a couple. Was Edith having an affair?

Birdie returned to the reception and sat in the corner out of the way. She took out her phone and gave Seb a call.

'It's me. Edith's met up with a guy in a hotel restaurant and has taken a room key from reception, so it looks like they're going to be here for a while. I've got a photo of him. I was debating going back to the flat to try and find out who he is. What do you think?'

'Yes, that's a much better use of your time.'

'How's it going following Somerton?'

'We're stuck in traffic, heading towards the East End. I'll keep in touch.'

Chapter 24

Seb kept his distance while following Lord Somerton's car, barely scraping fifteen miles per hour for most of the journey. He'd forgotten how tiresome driving in London could be. In Market Harborough, the traffic was a breeze when compared to the city.

He kept two cars between him and Somerton while they headed through Victoria, then crossing the Thames twice, crawling past the Tower of London, which was crowded with people as usual, until eventually, they ended up in the East End's Bethnal Green. Not somewhere Seb usually spent any time.

What was Somerton doing there?

The driver pulled up outside what looked like a nightclub called The Mermaid Club, and Somerton hopped out of the car, not waiting for his driver to open the door for him. Seb pulled into the side of the road, hovering on the double yellow lines, and kept an eye on Somerton while he walked up to the entrance of the club. Seb couldn't leave the car here to follow Somerton, or risk being clamped, so he headed for a nearby car park, found a space, and then used his phone to search for the club online. Not a nightclub, but a strip club, opening hours from eleven in the morning until midnight.

Why was Somerton at a strip club so early? It was barely eleven. Was it to see a show or for something else? It wasn't sitting right with Seb. There had to be a reason, and he wasn't going to find out by lurking in his car. It was a risk, in case he was spotted, but the photos on the website showed very low lighting inside, which should go in his favour.

Seb was stopped at the front door by a bouncer who charged him a five-pound entrance fee, which he paid in cash.

Inside was large, with a rectangular stage along one side that had three poles in the middle. A bar ran the full length of the other side of the room. Seb headed over and sat on a bar stool at the end furthest from the door. He scanned the place, looking for Somerton but was unable to locate him. Where was he? It wasn't possible for Seb to see the entire room, so maybe the man was in one of the booths.

'What can I get you?' the woman behind the bar asked, smiling as she headed towards him.

'A half pint of Guinness, please.'

He scanned the room again while waiting for his drink to be poured and noticed a door marked *Private*. Standing next to it was Somerton with a large, stocky man. The man opened the door, and gestured for Somerton to walk through, which was then closed behind him, leaving the stocky man outside, his back to the door with his arms folded.

Who could be behind the door that meant they needed security? And what had Somerton to do with them?

'Are you usually busy at this time of day?' he asked, turning to the bartender as she placed his drink on the bar.

'Not really. It gets busier late afternoon and right through until we close. The first show starts in twenty minutes, so you're not going to miss anything.'

Seb took a sip of his beer and laughed. 'That's good to know. Have you worked here long?'

'Me? I'm part of the furniture. I used to dance, but now I manage the bar. I'm too old for that.' She gyrated her hips and grimaced.

'If you've been here for all that time, you must know your customers well.'

'Yep. I'd say that seventy-five per cent of our customers are regulars, which is good because we know them, they know us, and we don't have any hassle. The other twenty-five per cent... Well, that's what we have security for, but we seldom have any trouble. Would you want to mess with Arte working on the door?' She stared at Seb. 'Then again, at your size, you can probably handle yourself. They're always on the lookout for security staff here. Are you interested? Probably not, the way you talk,' she added.

'That's correct. And to answer your question, I certainly wouldn't want to tackle Arte.'

'Wise move. The last person who tried lost most of his teeth and now walks with a limp.'

'Noted. Do you have a private area for parties? Through there, maybe?' He nodded over to the door Somerton went through.

'Yes, we do accommodate stag parties or private groups but not over there. That goes through to the boss's office. Upstairs, we have rooms for something more private. Is that why you're here? You're looking for a place for your stag party?'

'Me? No. I'm single. But my friend's looking for a venue, and he asked me to check the place out.'

'That explains it then.' She nodded.

'Explains what?'

'What you're doing in here, because you don't look like you belong. Now I know, would you like me to show you the rooms we have upstairs?'

That was exactly what he didn't want, but he'd have to feign interest.

'Are you allowed to leave the bar unattended?'

'It's quiet, so it will be fine for a few minutes.'

'Maybe a bit later. I'll sit here with my drink for now. I don't want to miss the show.'

In other words, he didn't want to risk missing Somerton leave the boss's office. Seb might not know why Somerton was there, but the fact he was seeing the owner could be important to the investigation.

'Whenever you're ready, love, you let me know, and we'll go upstairs together.' She winked at him.

Was she coming on to him?

'Thanks. Is this club part of a larger group? Do you have other venues around the country?'

'This is a one-off and has a private owner.'

'Oh, I see. What's his name?'

'You're asking a lot of questions. Are you a cop?' She narrowed her eyes.

'No, I'm not.' Seb held up both hands. 'I'm just curious, that's all, and I want to collect as much information as I can for my friend so we can start planning the stag party.'

'All you need to know is that we'll look after you and you'll have a good time. One you won't forget.'

'I don't doubt that, and I'm sure my friend will be keen to come here after I feed my impressions back to him.'

Seb glanced back over to the door marked *Private* just

as it opened. Out walked Somerton, and behind him was … Liam O'Rourke. His suspicions were confirmed.

The tall, wiry gangster was dressed in an expensive suit, looking more like a corporate lawyer than someone who was always prepared to shoot the head off anyone who betrayed him.

Seb hunched over his beer, keeping his head down but all the time watching. The two men shook hands, and O'Rourke slapped Somerton on the back in a friendly gesture.

This was evidence enough to convince Seb that O'Rourke was somehow involved in the disappearance of Pemberton and the painting. He waited for Somerton to leave, finished his beer, and left.

He squinted when he emerged into the daylight and caught sight of Somerton sliding into the back seat of his car, which had drawn up outside. There was no need to continue tailing the man. He'd rather get back to the flat to discuss his findings with Birdie.

Birdie flung her jacket over the back of the chair in the kitchen, turned away and then immediately turned back. She picked it up, went out into the hall, and hung it on the hook by the front door. Seb liked to keep everything neat and tidy, and he'd only moan if he'd seen it. She was the total opposite and couldn't care less if there was a mess around her.

She made herself a cup of tea, played with Elsa for a few minutes and headed into the study, where she fired up her laptop, determined not to stop until she'd identified the man hanging out with Edith at the hotel. She'd start by looking at photos in the media of Edith. He might appear in some of them.

It was made easier because she'd already done research into Edith, and so she knew where to look. She started with more recent photos of the ex-model, and there were plenty, but they tended to be Edith with Lord Somerton. So she went back in time to when Edith was modelling and single. That was way more interesting. There were hundreds of shots of Edith outside various trendy nightclubs and other places, always accompanied by lots of other glamourous people. But so far, no mystery man.

One of the photos Birdie called up onto her screen was taken at a charity event for a children's hospital four years ago. Edith was at a large round table, sitting next to a guy from one of Birdie's favourite bands.

While Birdie was staring at each person on the table, her eyes wandered to the table next door.

'Bingo.' She thumped the air. 'Got ya.'

Except, there was a slight problem. The only names listed in the article were people on Edith's table. Birdie wrote them down, just in case she needed to refer to them, and then searched other articles written about the event for other photos until she found the table she was looking for. The names were listed underneath, but she wasn't sure which of the names related to the mystery man. So she searched on social media until she matched a name to the face. Zac Trent, an American actor who'd also done some modelling work and was married to a prominent British actress. Was he still married to her? Birdie could find no photos or any articles about the couple. So either the relationship was over, or they'd managed to successfully keep themselves out of the limelight.

Birdie sat back in the chair, pleased that she had something to report to Seb. She glanced at her watch. He could end up being out all day.

It would give her some time to continue searching for her birth mother. She'd start with their school. She went onto the St Augustine School website and discovered that they had regular school reunions, and the social media pages for the school had photos of the events. She stared at all of them, scrutinising each person's face until finally, she saw Kim, her mother, standing in a crowd of other kids.

Birdie's heart thumped loudly in her chest. She couldn't believe it. She was getting closer to her birth mum than ever before. She returned to the page devoted to the school reunions. At the bottom was the name and phone number of the woman who organised them.

Without stopping to think, Birdie keyed in the number.

'Hello, Tina here.'

'Hi. My name's Lucinda Bird, and I'm contacting you because you're the organiser of reunions for St Augustine School. I found your name on the school website.'

'Yes, that's correct. Did you go to the school?'

'No, but I know someone who did, and I'm trying to find them. Her name at school was Kim Bakirtzis, and I wondered if you have her contact details?'

'Kim? Yes, I know her very well. We were in the same class together and were good friends until she moved overseas.'

'Yes, she went to Canada, didn't she?' Birdie said, wanting to make sure the woman understood that she really did know Kim.

'That's right. When she returned to England, she came to one of the school reunions, and we've stayed in touch ever since. It helps that she's in Croydon, which is where I have family, and we catch up whenever we can.'

Birdie's hand flew up to her chest. Croydon? Her dad

had a cousin who lived there. It was less than three hours from Market Harborough.

She sucked in a calming breath. 'Please could you give me her email address, or phone number, so I can get in touch?' Birdie forced her voice to sound neutral and not excited or nervous. She didn't want to blow what was the best opportunity she'd had since speaking to Kim's ex-next-door neighbour, Marie.

'I'm sorry, the Data Protection Act prohibits me from giving out her details. Especially to someone I don't know.'

Crap. Birdie knew that but had hoped that Tina didn't.

'I totally understand. What if I give you *my* email address and phone number, and you could pass it onto her?'

'Yes, that would work. Will she recognise your name?'

'Probably not. We just share a friend in common.'

'Oh. I thought you said that you knew her well.'

'It's complicated, but if you could please ask her to email or phone me, I would be grateful.'

Birdie gave Tina her details and then ended the call. She couldn't believe how close she was. And at least now she knew that Kim was in Croydon. She could kick herself for not finding out Kim's new surname. That was a real rookie mistake.

Chapter 25

The front door opened, and Elsa left Birdie's feet where she'd been sleeping and ran out of the study and into the hall, her tail wagging furiously.

'I'm in here,' Birdie yelled out.

She closed her laptop so Seb couldn't see that she'd been doing stuff relating to her birth mother. Not because he'd mind, but she wasn't in the mood to go through everything with him, and he was bound to ask how she'd been getting on. She just wanted to enjoy the excitement of getting one step closer on her own, in case talking about it took away some of the enjoyment. There was still a long way to go before any of her questions were answered. And that was assuming that they could be.

She heard footsteps on the wooden floor from Seb walking down the hall, accompanied by the pattering of Elsa's paws. They came into the room together.

'I wasn't expecting you back so soon.' Birdie said as Seb dropped his things on his desk and sat down. 'I thought you'd be hot on the tail of His Lordship for most of the day. What happened? Don't tell me – he, too, went to a hotel for a hookup with someone.'

'Nothing like that. I obtained sufficient information to warrant me returning home and for us to move forward on the investigation.'

'That sounds mysterious. I was about to go into the kitchen to grab something to eat so you can tell me in there. Are you hungry, or have you been ploughing your way through the rolls I left for you?'

Seb gave a lopsided grin. 'I completely forgot about them. They're still in the car.'

'Typical. You go back to the car, grab the bag, and I'll stick the kettle on. I'm guessing that you didn't have time for a drink either.'

'I had a half pint of Guinness.'

'I didn't have you down for being a morning drinker. Well, I'm sure you'd like a coffee, anyway.'

By the time Seb had returned to the flat, the kettle had boiled, and mugs were on the table, along with plates and the remaining fruit and crisps that had been in Birdie's rucksack that she hadn't eaten. He unpacked the rolls from his bag and spread them out on the table.

'Did you have any luck discovering the name of the man that Edith met?' Seb asked while they were eating.

'I certainly did. He's an actor called Zac Trent. I didn't find any evidence of Edith and him together, but I suspect they go back several years. I found photos of them at a charity event sitting at adjacent tables. Do you think we should interview him?'

'Maybe, but not yet. We now have other, more important, things to deal with. I followed Somerton to a strip club in Bethnal Green that I believe is owned by Liam O'Rourke. Somerton went through to the back to meet with him, and I saw them saying goodbye in a friendly manner. It certainly wasn't an antagonistic relationship.'

'Did Somerton appear scared of him?'

'Not that I could tell. After we've eaten, we need to look closely into the club and ascertain O'Rourke's connection to it.'

'Maybe we should start tailing O'Rourke to see if he can lead us to Pemberton.'

'That would be almost impossible with only two of us. He has security with him at all times, and they would be on the lookout. We'd soon be spotted.'

'Are you going to contact Rob to let him know about the relationship between O'Rourke and Somerton?'

'I've given it some thought and decided against it. All we know is that the owner of the missing painting is associating with a gangster. Rob's interest in O'Rourke is in respect to an international drug ring. Art fraud hasn't featured at this point. I don't believe that what we've discovered will assist him at all.'

'And, more to the point, you don't want him to warn us off the case,' Birdie added, arching her eyebrow.

'I admit that has been factored into my decision.' Seb's phone rang, and he glanced at the screen. 'It's Annabelle. I better take this because she'll be expecting an update.'

'Put her on speaker. It will save you from having to repeat everything.' Birdie sat next to Seb, rather than at the opposite end of the table where she had been, so she could hear more clearly. She leant forward and rested her chin in her hand.

'Hello, Annabelle,' Seb said, answering the phone and pressing the speaker key.

'There's been another one, Sebastian, and it's worse. I don't know what to do. Where are you? Can you come around? I can't carry on like this. I'm looking over my shoulder all of the time, checking to see if anyone's following me. I don't feel safe.' The words came tumbling out of her mouth at twice the speed of her normal speech.

'Take a breath, Annabelle. Another what?' Seb asked.

Birdie glanced at him and frowned. Didn't he get that she meant another note? What else could it be? He clearly wasn't thinking straight. Then again, did he ever when it came to Annabelle?

The sound of Annabelle sucking in a breath came from the phone. 'Sorry. I'll pull myself together. My behaviour won't help the situation. There was another note waiting for me when I got home this afternoon. It had been put through the letterbox like the other. No postmark, so I'm assuming it was hand-delivered. Shall I read it to you?'

Birdie shook her head. 'No. It's Birdie here, Annabelle. Leave the note on the side with the envelope, and don't read it out to us. We'll be over at your place soon and will look at it then.'

'Umm… Okay. If that's what you suggest. How long will you be?'

'We should be with you within the hour,' Seb said, pushing up his sleeve and checking his watch.

'Can't you be here sooner?' Annabelle begged.

'It will depend on traffic. It's very heavy at the moment. Lock your door and sit tight. Don't speak to anyone. We'll be with you as soon as we can.'

Seb ended the call and turned to face Birdie. 'What was your reasoning behind not having her read out the note to us? It might have given us a head start.'

'I doubt it would have. She's upset enough as it is. If she reads it out, she might get even worse and we're not there to help her. We need her to stay calm and not do

anything rash. The fact that she's losing it is out of character, and even though she said she'd pull herself together,
how long will that last? That's why I wanted her to leave
the note alone and not be tempted to read it again.'

'You made a good assessment. Let's go.'

Chapter 26

'You took your time,' Annabelle snapped, the moment Seb and Birdie emerged from the lift.

She turned away from them and headed back into the apartment. Birdie gave him a nudge in the ribs and pulled a face.

'We came by car, and there was a lot of traffic, Annabelle. I did explain that to you when you called,' Seb said once they'd walked inside the apartment and closed the door behind them. 'Are you okay?'

She glared at him. 'Of course I'm not *okay*. My fiancé is missing, and I'm receiving threatening notes. Why don't you engage your brain for once, Sebastian?'

Seb stiffened, the hackles rising on his neck.

'We're here now, Annabelle, so why don't you take us to where you've left the note, and we'll decide what we're going to do next.' Birdie's voice was calm and mature and much belied her youth.

'Okay. I'm sorry. I shouldn't have snapped. This is getting to me and I'm not good when I can't control the situation as I'm sure Sebastian will tell you.' Annabelle gave a hollow laugh and glanced over at him.

He couldn't remain angry with her. Not when placed in such a difficult situation.

They followed Annabelle into the kitchen. She gestured with an open hand to the counter upon which were the note and envelope.

After pulling on some disposable gloves, Seb picked up the typewritten note. '"Find Pemberton. Don't involve the police and that includes Clifford."' He frowned. There was no indication of how she was to contact them once she'd done what they had requested. Which meant one thing. She was being watched. It could be from outside. Or microphones or cameras had been planted in her apartment. Either way, they couldn't talk there. 'It looks like you need to wait for further instructions. Let's go for a coffee while we discuss it.' He glanced at Birdie, who was frowning and gave her a small nod to indicate that she should agree with him.

'Yes, that's a great idea. I'm hungry, too,' Birdie said. 'Come on, Annabelle, grab your bag, and we'll go out. I'm sure you're fed up with being stuck here on your own.'

They left the building and headed down the street. All the way, he was checking that they weren't being followed. Finally, when convinced that they weren't, he led them into a café. They ordered at the counter and went to an empty booth at the back where no one could hear them.

'You're being watched. I'm not sure whether it's by people in the street or cameras or microphones have been planted in your flat.'

Annabelle shuddered. 'How do you know? What shall I do?'

'They knew about me, and they gave you no way of

contacting them. I want you to go to your parents' house in Surrey and stay until this is over.'

'I agree. You need to leave,' Birdie said in a low, urgent voice.

'And once you're there you must stay inside the house.'

'Can't I even go for a walk in the grounds?' Annabelle asked.

'No. Because they're too extensive for you to be on view at all times,' Seb said.

'But surely—'

'But surely you want to stay alive? Do as Seb says. It's for your own good,' Birdie interrupted.

'I have several meetings lined up in London, not to mention other appointments.'

'Either invite them to your parents' house or cancel them,' Birdie said. 'If they can't wait, then find someone else to go in your place. Some things take priority, and this is one of them. The people who sent the note know where you live, and they know that Seb and I are involved in the case. We don't want to play into their hands. Leave your phone and laptop here in case they're getting to you through them. Buy yourself a burner phone to use instead.'

'How will I be able to contact people?'

'Take a photo of all your regular contacts and send it to me. I will write down my number for you, and when you get your burner phone, I'll forward the photo. That way, you can keep in touch with whoever you want,' Birdie said.

'Make it very small because we don't know who's involved. It could be someone you would never have suspected,' Seb said.

Annabelle's mouth dropped open. 'Oh my God. So you're telling me that a friend could have betrayed me?'

'We have to consider every possibility.' Seb didn't want

to frighten Annabelle, but she had to realise the severity of the situation she was in.

'I think your list should only contain immediate family and very close friends who you've known for years,' Birdie said.

'Agreed. Although, let me see it first, in case there's anyone on there that we should be wary of,' Seb added.

'I'll do whatever you suggest. I can't carry on like this.' Her voice was strained, and fear glinted in her eyes.

'Try not to worry. You'll be much safer there,' Birdie said.

'Don't tell your parents the reason why you're there. We don't need to worry them. Not at their age and disposition,' Seb said.

'You're right. It's best they're not alarmed. Before we go, are you going to give me an update on where the investigation is?'

Sebastian and Birdie exchanged a glance. 'What aren't you telling me? And don't say "nothing" because it's written all over your faces.'

Birdie sighed. 'You were going to find out soon enough, so it might as well be now. Jasper was definitely involved in the forgery. He actually commissioned it.'

The colour drained from Annabelle's face. 'Are you sure? I can't believe he'd do that.'

'Yes, we are. And we believe that he has the original with him, wherever he is. Which confirms what was told to you in the note.'

'I knew that Jasper had his faults, but underneath I thought ours was a strong relationship. We'd planned for marriage and children. To have a comfortable existence. Both of our families approve of us building a future together, but that's not going to happen now. I could maybe forgive a single dalliance with the woman you told me about. But now, with this? I can't do it.'

'I don't blame you,' Birdie said softly, resting her hand on Annabelle's wrist.

'But that doesn't mean I want him dead. Do you think they'll kill him if he doesn't give back the painting? We have to do something, Sebastian. We can't leave him out there.' Her eyes filled with tears.

'We're doing everything we can, Annabelle. You have to trust us.' Seb gave her shoulder a comforting squeeze.

'There is one more thing we have to tell you,' Birdie said. 'Lord Somerton who owned the painting—'

'*Harold* Somerton?' Annabelle said, pulling away from Seb's hold and sitting upright.

'The very same. We've now discovered that he's involved with a local gangster. A nasty piece of work. We haven't put together all the pieces, but there's got to be a connection. It's too much of a coincidence for there not to be.'

'In what way involved? Has Harold asked this gangster to get his painting back? And that's why they're threatening me because they believe I'm in cahoots with Jasper?'

'We don't know. That's why we want you away from here. This gangster wouldn't think twice about harming you if it furthered his goal. You're best keeping out of it and leaving everything to us,' Seb said.

'I have no choice but to trust you. Especially as I can't go to the police. But if they're watching or listening, they'll know that I've involved you, even though they said not to.'

And they would have already known that before sending the second note, Seb thought. So, were they expecting Annabelle to refrain from involving Seb, or did they want him there? And if that was the case, then why?

'You'll be away from here shortly, and they won't be able to find you,' Seb reassured her.

'If I leave now, they might see me and follow. Shall I wait until it gets dark? Unless… Do you think they'll have a tracking device on my car? Because if they do, then I won't be safe wherever I go.'

'That's a very good question,' Seb said, nodding. 'Possibly, yes, but don't worry, I have a way around this. I'll hire a car on your behalf and get it delivered to a place away from here. Can you get down to the garage belonging to your apartment without first going outside?'

'Yes, there's a lift that goes directly to the basement.'

'Good. And is that where the rubbish bins are?'

'Yes.' Annabelle frowned.

'We'll all go back there now and stay until it gets dark. Birdie and I will leave in our car, and it will look like you're still in the apartment to anyone watching from outside. Make sure to leave a light on. If they have cameras inside, then all they will see is you taking the rubbish out of the bin and heading out of the flat with it. We'll drive away, making sure that we're not followed and then head back to the basement coming in from the rear. We'll meet you in the car park and then drive you to where the hire car is parked.'

'That's a good idea, except what happens if they see me in your car?'

'You can lie across the back seat. There's no reason why they should see you because we won't go past the front entrance, and we'll take side roads all the way to the hire car.'

Had he covered every eventuality? He believed so.

'And once I'm out of the way, what's your next move?'

'Tomorrow, we'll be visiting His Lordship and putting pressure on him to find out what's going on,' Birdie said.

'And if that doesn't work, we'll speak to his wife, Edith, because it wouldn't surprise me to find that she's fully aware of the situation. Try not to worry. The main thing is that you're kept safe, and we can concentrate on finding Jasper.'

Chapter 27

'How annoying that they've gone back to Devon already. All I can assume is that Edith had the hookup with the actor, went back home to pack and then they left,' Birdie said as they began their drive to Somerton's estate first thing the next morning.

After ensuring that Annabelle was on the way to her parents with no one in pursuit, Seb had driven them to Somerton's London flat, only to find there was no answer. He then phoned the Devon estate and was told that they were expecting the couple later that evening. He hadn't wanted to drive down so late, so decided it was best to leave first thing in the morning.

'Maybe his business with O'Rourke was over, and that's when he decided to go back home.'

'Edith won't be happy. She hates it there,' Birdie commented.

'I expect it's the reverse for Somerton, being so much older and having been brought up there. If that is the case, it should go in our favour because he'll be more relaxed if we are talking to him in his own environment, away from the city. We might catch him off-guard, and he may let slip some useful information.'

The journey to Somerton's estate took them a little over three hours, and they drove down a winding drive until the stately home came into view. It was a magnificent example of English Baroque architecture, set in beautiful, landscaped gardens reminiscent of those designed by Capability Brown.

'Wow. Is this like the house that you lived in?'

'It's a little smaller than ours.'

'You're kidding, right? How many bedrooms do you think this one has?'

'Thirty bedrooms, forty bathrooms, and a large number of reception rooms. Most of which are unused, apart from by the staff and the family.'

'How do you know all that? Actually, don't answer – I know how you know. It looks amazing. They could use it for filming.'

'If Somerton succeeds in persuading the National Trust to take it on, they may well allow it to be used by the entertainment industry. It would make money for them. They would also open up the home to the public.'

'Isn't it already?'

'They open a selection of rooms for two months during the summer, and the gardens are also on show then. In the right hands, so much more could be done to ensure its financial well-being.'

'Yes. But who in their right minds would want people traipsing through their homes and around their gardens?'

'The public don't go into the private wings where the family live. Also, not all the gardens will be available to view.'

'Is your parents' estate open?'

'Yes. Out of necessity. The upkeep is phenomenal. It

works well. My parents have staff who take care of that, and my brother is also there to manage the estate.'

Seb parked his car on the gravel outside the front of the main house, and they walked up to the door.

'Are you sure we shouldn't be going round the back? There must be a side entrance. This is so grand.'

'Absolutely not.' He pulled on the rope to ring the bell. After a couple of minutes, the elderly butler answered. Seb recognised him immediately. He'd been with the family for decades.

'I'm here to see Lord Somerton. Tell him it's Sebastian Clifford.'

'Certainly, sir. If you'd like to step into the Great Hall, I'll let him know you're here.'

'Oooh. The *Great Hall*,' Birdie said, once the butler was out of sight. 'Look at all of these paintings. Some of them are massive.' She pointed to the back wall, which had several very large masterpieces.

'The house does have an extensive collection. No thanks to Somerton himself. He inherited most of them from his rather astute ancestors.'

After several minutes, the butler returned. 'Lord Somerton is in the conservatory. I'll take you through.'

Seb knew exactly where it was, having been to the estate many times over the years while growing up. However, he followed the man into the room, and the moment they entered, Somerton walked over to greet them.

'Sebastian, what are you doing here?' He smiled, but it was clearly forced and didn't reach his eyes.

'We'd like a further chat with you, Harold, in respect of our investigation.'

Somerton's face grew ashen. 'I believe I told you everything I know, but by all means, sit down, old chap, and you, too, young lady.' Seb and Birdie sat on the faded floral sofa that faced the walled garden, and Somerton reclined on an easy chair opposite them. 'Wilson, please make sure we're not disturbed.'

'Yes, sir.' The butler exited the room, closing the door behind him.

'I told you the last time we met to keep away,' Somerton said, his eyes flashing and his tone much darker now the butler had left the room.

'What were you doing with Liam O'Rourke at the strip club in Bethnal Green yesterday?' Seb dispensed with responding to the statement, not wanting to give Somerton a chance to collect his thoughts.

'What?' Fear shone from Somerton's eyes. 'Have you been following me? Who else knows you're here? This is serious. If anyone knows you're here, we could all...'

The man was clearly frightened, which could work to their advantage.

'Nobody knows we're here.' Seb kept his voice low and calm. 'But you still haven't answered my question. What were you doing with O'Rourke, a known criminal?'

Somerton tensed, his fists tightly balled in his lap. 'We've known each other a long time. For many years, in fact. We have a mutual interest in horse racing. That's all there is to it.'

'So why are you scared of him finding out we're here?'

'I-I... It's...'

'Are you aware that he runs a notorious gang in London and that he's recently been in prison?' Seb asked.

'Yes. I also know that you were part of the team who put him there... I mean, it's not that we've talked about you... Um... I just assumed... Well, I know you were in the police and...' His voice fell away, and he looked into his lap.

Seb's mind began to whirr. Somerton knew about his connection to O'Rourke. Annabelle received notes, one of which named Seb. Could all this be to do with him? Were all the strange things that had happened to him and his family also a part of it?

'Seb?' Birdie said. 'What's going on? Why have you gone quiet?'

Seb leant forward and stared directly at Somerton. 'Harold, I want the truth. And remember, I can tell if you're lying. Has all this whole situation got something to do with me?'

'I don't know what you mean.' Somerton averted his gaze.

'Yes, you do. Pemberton's disappearance. The forgery of your painting and its disappearance. The accusations made to Annabelle. The involvement of a man who despises me. What the hell is going on?'

'If I tell you, I'll need protection from him.'

'If you *don't* tell me, you'll need protection from me.'

The protruding Adam's apple in Somerton's neck quivered as he swallowed hard.

'Yes. You're right. It's about you.'

Birdie clenched her jaws together. She couldn't believe what she'd just heard.

Seb's expression was unreadable. Was he scared? Worried, even? Knowing Seb, he wasn't, because he could take care of himself. But against someone like O'Rourke, someone who clearly had it in for Seb and had an entire gang at his disposal? That was another matter entirely.

And why was O'Rourke targeting him? Surely it couldn't just be because Seb was on the team that sent the gangster to jail. It had to be something deeper than that. But what?

'Right. I want to know everything, and don't even think about leaving out the smallest detail,' Seb said to Somerton, his voice icy cold.

Birdie shivered. She'd never heard Seb like that before.

'And this is on the record.' She pulled out her phone, placed it on the coffee table between them, and hit the record button.

'I'm not talking if you're going to record it. I-I can't. No.' Somerton's voice was weak and hesitant.

'It's not up for negotiation. Now spill.' Birdie glared at him. So he realised it wasn't just Seb he needed to be wary of.

'I needed money. I was running out fast, and Edith was spending like it was water. I couldn't stop her. Didn't want to stop her in case she left me. We talked about it and—'

'Who's we?' Seb interrupted.

'Edith and me.'

Ha. So she was in on it. That didn't surprise Birdie. Perhaps Seb's mum had been right that Edith only married Somerton for the money.

'Carry on,' Seb said.

'We were trying to come up with a plan to find some more money, and we hit upon the idea of having a painting stolen and claiming the insurance. We worked out that we could make twice the money if the painting was forged and then have the forgery stolen. We could get the insurance money and then sell the original on the black market. Edith knew of a man in France who forged paintings, and we contacted him.'

'You mean Renaud,' Birdie said.

Somerton's eyes widened. 'You know him?'

'Yes. And we know that he pointed you in the direction

of Jim Dempster.'

'Oh.'

'Continue,' Seb demanded.

'We weren't sure how to go about arranging for the original to be sold once we'd had the forgery done. It was just coincidence that I bumped into O'Rourke one day, and so I asked him for a meeting, thinking he could help get rid of the original. By that time, I'd also thought about getting Pemberton on board because I knew he was in debt and would do anything, within reason, to make some money.'

'And O'Rourke agreed to help?'

'Yes. But it turned out differently to how Edith and I had imagined it would. We thought he'd use his contacts immediately and sell it on the black market and take a cut. But that wasn't his plan. He said that the painting would be sold eventually, but not until he'd used it to lure you to him. He must have done his research because he knew that Pemberton was engaged to Annabelle.'

'Why does he want to *lure* Seb out? He could contact him directly without going to all this trouble,' Birdie said.

'I don't know.'

'When he told you he wanted Seb, why didn't you go straight to the police? They could have protected you. You've known Seb all his life, and you were happy to put him in danger. I just don't—'

'Birdie, this isn't helping.' Seb held up his hand to silence her. 'Where's Pemberton now?'

'O'Rourke has him and the painting. And before you ask, I don't know exactly where apart from it's not going to be too far from London because he said Pemberton was going to be easily accessible.'

'What does that mean? Has he been kidnapped?' Birdie asked.

'Not in the strictest sense of the word. He went willingly, but he's not allowed any communication with the outside world. O'Rourke's men are guarding him.' He leant forwards and ran his fingers through his hair. 'This is going to end badly. I just know it. Why the hell did I agree to become involved?'

'Focus, Somerton. What was O'Rourke's plan for luring Seb out?'

'Umm… To use Annabelle. He warned me to say nothing if you approached.'

'Surely if O'Rourke wanted Seb to find him or Pemberton, then he would have wanted you to tell us that he was involved? And if he didn't, then why are you telling us?' Birdie didn't trust the man one bit.

'Because I regret getting involved. You have to believe me. Sebastian, I've known you most of your life, and your parents are dear friends of mine. I've done something stupid. I want to make it right, but I have to protect myself and my wife.'

'You've picked a fine time to suddenly get all remorseful. It's thanks to you that this whole thing has happened. If you hadn't been so greedy and your wife—'

'Enough.' Seb rested his hand on Birdie's arm. 'This isn't getting us anywhere. You can tell O'Rourke that we've been to question you about the painting, and you claimed to know nothing about it. He might be luring me out, but it's going to be on my terms and at a time I can control. Now I suggest you and Edith stay here and make sure you have staff with you at all times. Don't go out.'

'Are you going to tell the police? If the National Trust find out, there's no way they'll ever consider taking over the estate.'

'That should be the least of your worries,' Seb said, shaking his head.

Chapter 28

'If O'Rourke has Pemberton, then we need to find out where he's holding him,' Birdie said first thing the following morning when they were sitting in Seb's office.

It had been late when they'd arrived back at the flat the evening before, and after they'd eaten, all they wanted to do was sleep.

'First, we need to discover what properties O'Rourke owns and then analyse each location to see which is the most likely.' Seb drummed his fingers on the table.

'Easier said than done. Because he's not likely to own anything in his own name.'

'All he had in the past was the house he lived in with his family. A mansion in Essex. We weren't able to identify any others.'

'Tell me everything you know about his personal life. There might be something that will help.' Birdie picked up a pen and hovered over the paper, waiting to write down everything Seb could tell her.

'His wife is called Lena. They've been married for

thirty-two years, and they have two children, both girls, now aged twenty-nine and thirty. Meryl and Caroline.'

'Are they married? Does he have any grandchildren?'

'You'll have to check that. They weren't and had no children when I was part of the investigation into him.'

'Your consultancy work with Rob allows you access to the PNC, right?'

If he allowed her to use his Police National Computer credentials, it could speed up the research.

Seb shook his head. 'I know what you're thinking, Birdie, and that's not advisable. There are public databases that can be used to discover the owners of properties. Every time we access the PNC it's recorded, and we don't wish to send alarm bells. Especially as it's to do with O'Rourke, who's currently under investigation. And we know there's a mole in the team. Not to mention that if Rob's notified, he'll want to be involved. It's best to see what we can discover without using it.'

That made sense, and there were other ways of accessing the information. She'd start with social media.

Within a few minutes, she'd already found O'Rourke's daughters. They both posted often and hadn't made their accounts private.

'Hey, Seb,' she said, wanting to attract his attention. 'It turns out that O'Rourke has a grandson from Meryl, but he's only a year old, so it's hardly likely that there will be properties in his name. I'm going to try a combination of his daughters' names to look for company names. My Aunty Catherine and Uncle Peter called their house *Petrine, so* it's worth a try.'

'It's worth a try, but considering he's a notorious gang-ster, I'd be surprised if you discover anything.'

'Sometimes the simplest solutions are the best. I'm

going to look through the land registry and the various bill payers' databases. It will take a little longer than using the PNC but still doable.' She pulled her laptop towards her, and her fingers flew over the keys.

Half an hour later, she found something. 'Bingo.'

Seb glanced up. 'What have you discovered?'

'A company called Carmer Limited owns several properties in and around London. It's registered as a subsidiary of a shell company. I can't find details of any shareholders or employees.'

'Interesting. Well spotted. Look into the various properties they own, particularly those that are within a thirty-mile radius of London. O'Rourke would want Pemberton to be accessible.'

After an hour in which Birdie focused solely on her search, checking Google Maps for viable options, she announced her progress. 'Right. I've got somewhere that might be a good option. I've come across four houses owned by Carmer Limited that are within the area you suggested, and there's one that stands out as being suitable. It's in a village just outside of Guildford, thirty miles away, and is detached and on a large plot. Much easier to keep Pemberton out of the way there than either of the two terraced properties in Croydon or the semi-detached in Newham. What have you been up to?'

Every time she'd glanced across at Seb while she had been researching, his head had been lowered, as if he was concentrating on something. She hadn't liked to disturb him until she had a result.

'I've been going through in my mind everything that I was involved in to do with O'Rourke over the years. All of the team meetings we had. The actual operation that brought him down. I wasn't the only member of the team, obviously, but I am the only one who is no longer a police officer. Whether O'Rourke decided to target me first because of that, I don't know. And then we have to consider the fact that he's got someone inside the police force, according to Rob, so maybe he doesn't want to rock the boat there. It's possible that O'Rourke will target the others at a later date. But all this is tenuous. There's got to be something else, but I can't nail it down.' Seb sighed. 'Bring the house up on your screen so I can see it.'

He slid his chair around the desk, stopping next to Birdie.

'This is it, and here's the map.' She split her screen so he could see the actual property on one and an overview of the area on another. 'It's not so parochial that everyone will know each other, but not too busy that there are always witnesses around. I think we should drive out to take a look?'

'Yes, I agree. Seeing it in person will give us a better idea. We might even spot Pemberton in there. We'll go now.'

Within an hour, they were close to the property, the traffic not being too heavy.

'It's really nice around here,' Birdie said, staring out of the car window at the detached properties, all of which were slightly different from one another. 'Expensive, no doubt.'

'It's right in the middle of the commuter belt, so yes.'

Seb parked the car on the opposite side of the road to the house, which gave them a view of the front of the large red-brick detached property. There were two cars in the drive.

'I'll take a photo of those number plates so we can get them checked. Do you think Rob would do that for us?

Except then he'd know what we've been doing.' A thought came into her head. 'Actually, I've got an idea. Why don't I give Twiggy a ring and ask a favour? I can find out how he's managing without me.'

'Good idea. If you think he'll assist.'

She pulled out her phone and pressed the key for Twiggy's number.

He answered on the second ring. 'DC Branch.'

'Hey, Twiggy, it's me. Surely you haven't forgotten my number already.'

'Uh… I didn't look at the screen. How are you doing, Birdie?'

'I'm okay, Twig, thanks. But what about you?' she asked, referring to his illness. Was the dementia getting worse? Was that why he hadn't recognised her number?

'You know. Up and down, but I'm trying not to complain.'

'You not complain? That I'd like to see!' She laughed.

'True. I'll rephrase that. I'm trying not to complain any more than usual.'

Twiggy was well known for his moaning. Usually, it was directed at Evie, his wife, who had him constantly on a diet with very little success. All the bakeries in Market Harborough knew him by name.

'That's more like it. Well, don't push it too hard and remember, if you need any help or someone to talk to, then I'm here for you.'

'Thanks, Birdie. That means a lot. How are you enjoying your new role? We really miss you here. It's so quiet. Even Sarge mentioned how different it is without you. I hope Clifford's treating you right. Because if he isn't, I'll—'

'I'm enjoying it,' she interrupted before he could go on

about Seb. He wasn't her partner's biggest fan. 'How are Evie and the kids?'

'Driving me mad, as usual.' He laughed.

'I wouldn't expect to hear anything else. Anyway, I'm phoning to ask you a big favour. If I give you a couple of number plates, could you check them for me, please?'

'Are you trying to get me sacked? Sarge would go mad if he found out.'

'Please, Twig. We're trying to trace a missing person, and we believe his life's in danger.'

'And you couldn't possibly pass this case onto the police?'

'It's complicated. I wouldn't ask unless it was important. Will you do it for me, please?'

Twiggy tutted. 'Okay, let me have them. But you owe me one.'

Birdie read the numbers out to him at the same time as giving Seb a thumbs up.

'Both cars are registered under a company name, which is Grayson Limited.'

'Thanks, Twig, you're a lifesaver. We're in London at the moment. As soon as we're back, I'll call in to see you all. We can go out for a drink.'

She ended the call and turned to Seb. 'They're company cars owned by Grayson Limited.'

'That's one of O'Rourke's legal companies.'

'How do you...?' Her voice fell away. One day she'd remember not to ask him that same question. 'So now we need to find out if Pemberton's there or not. Where are your binoculars?'

'On the back seat.'

Seb had a pair that were small but exceptionally powerful. Birdie leant over, picked them up, and held them to her eyes, bringing the house into focus. She was definitely going to get herself some of these.

'I can make out two men in the front room on the left-hand side. They're both standing and talking to each other. Neither of them are Pemberton. Oh. Hang on a minute. Someone else has come into the room. It's him. Pemberton.' She lowered the binoculars. 'Now we know for sure that he's there and unrestrained.' She looked through them again. 'One of the men has left the room. Where's he going?' The front door opened, and the man came out and got into one of the cars. 'That must have been a handover,' she said as the man drove off. 'If there's only one of O'Rourke's men there with Pemberton, they must trust him not to attempt a getaway. You know Pemberton vaguely. What do you think?'

'I wouldn't say that I know him. But I doubt he'd try to leave if he believes that it would put Annabelle's life in danger. Unfortunately, we have no idea how deeply involved he is in O'Rourke's plan.'

Birdie's hand flew up to her mouth. 'Crap. Drive away now. We've been spotted. The man that's staying is looking straight at us. He's now left the room. Is he coming outside? Yes. The door is opening...'

Seb started the car and drove away at speed.

'Can you see if he's getting in his car to follow us?' Seb asked.

Birdie turned and craned her neck. 'It doesn't look like it. Hopefully, he only saw me, and I was blocking you. Although at your height... He didn't have binoculars, so that will go in our favour.'

'I need to see Rob to get him up to speed with all this. What we don't want is for O'Rourke to move Pemberton before we've got him.' He picked up his phone and pressed the speed-dial key. 'It's Clifford. We need to meet as soon as possible... I'm on my way.'

'*I* and not *we*?' Birdie said, frowning.

'Yes. I'll take you back to the flat. I want you to do a deep dive into O'Rourke. Anything you can find, however small, might be the key to us bringing this case to a satis-factory conclusion.'

Chapter 29

Rob had again suggested they meet in the cafeteria close to the Met, and by the time Seb had arrived, his friend was already seated at one of the tables. With hindsight, he should have taken a taxi or Tube, but his mind had been on the case and not on the logistics of getting there.

Birdie had been disappointed at not being allowed to accompany him, but she was better placed researching O'Rourke. If anyone could find something, it would be her. She might not have the research skills of Detective Constable Ellie Naylor at Lenchester Police, who he'd worked with in the past, but Birdie was still tenacious and had a nose for something that on the surface might appear perfectly normal but beneath it was rather more questionable.

He headed over to the table where Rob was sitting, not bothering to stop to get himself something to drink, which, as it turned out, wasn't an issue because there were two cans of Coke on the table.

'I bought you a diet cola. Is that still your drink of

choice after Guinness?' Rob slid the can over to Seb, who sat opposite him.

'Not so much. I tend to drink water these days.'

'Next, you'll be telling me that you've turned vegan,' Rob said as he picked up his can and took a drink.

'There's nothing wrong with that. But no, I haven't. I think that might be one step too far for my parents to cope with, considering they farm on the estate and their meat has a worldwide reputation. Their lamb rivals the New Zealand meat.'

'Do they farm organically?'

'Yes, they have done for years. They were one of the pioneers.'

His family seemed in the dark ages when it came to many things, but with the farming, they were at the forefront. Much of that was down to the influence of Hubert.

'Cool. Anyway, let's cut with the chit-chat. What's happened that warranted such an urgent meeting?'

'We know for certain that our investigation isn't linked to yours in respect to drug trafficking. It's much closer to home than that.'

Rob's brow furrowed. 'Do you mean what I think you do?'

'I have no idea, but I'll explain. This whole scenario has been set up in order to draw me out. O'Rourke planned it after Somerton had been to him with an idea about forging his painting because he was desperate for money. O'Rourke agreed to help on the proviso that the whole thing was geared towards hooking me. Pemberton is being held at a house in Surrey, but we're not sure how involved he is in the whole thing. The recent note to Annabelle mentioned my name and told her not to involve me or the police. O'Rourke would have known that saying not to bring me in was guaranteed to elicit the opposite response.'

'Why target you, though?'

'That question's been plaguing me, and I don't have a satisfactory answer. It could be to do with the operation which resulted in his imprisonment.'

'Who was on the team with you?'

'Davis, Hearn, Warrington, and me. We were the four main team members, although we had assistance from other teams when needed.'

'I see.' Rob strummed his fingers on the table. 'What I'm about to tell you stays strictly between us.'

'Of course. You can trust me to keep whatever it is confidential.'

'Warrington is now working on our team, and he's the person I have my eye on. I believe that he might be the officer O'Rourke has on the inside. At present, I have no proof, but I'm feeding different pieces of information to individual officers to see what gets back to O'Rourke. It's early days, but I'll get to the bottom of it.'

'We might be able to use this to our advantage.'

'What do you have in mind?'

'If we want to extract Pemberton while at the same time protecting Annabelle, we need O'Rourke to believe that he's lured me out. That I've discovered his involvement, and I'm going after him. Maybe you could confide in Warrington that I'm after O'Rourke, and if he passes it on, then you'll know he's the plant, and I'd have captured O'Rourke's interest.'

'Yes, that could work, but then what are you going to do?' Rob sighed, a worried expression on his face. 'You can't wait for him to come and find you.'

'I'll contact him myself and negotiate a meeting.'

'Yes, that's fine, but I don't want you to put yourself in

danger. During your meeting with him, we'll be close by and you can wear a wire.'

'We'll discuss it nearer the time. I'm not going to commit to anything. O'Rourke's not stupid. If he believes I'm wired, it could ruin everything.'

Seb had no intention of involving Rob when he met with O'Rourke, but he wasn't telling his friend that.

'Okay, keep me informed. Is there anything else you'd like us to do?'

'Birdie and I can't return to the house where Pemberton's being held because we were spotted, but if you could send some guys to check and see if they can discover if he's there voluntarily, that will help.'

'Okay, text me the address. I expect someone's reported a gas leak in the area, and we might have to send men in to investigate,' Rob said, grinning.

'Thanks. Let me know when you've told Warrington and also what you find at the house.'

Chapter 30

Birdie sat at the computer, with Elsa at her feet, and began her "deep dive", as Seb called it, into Liam O'Rourke. She'd already researched into him, so she preferred to call it an "*even* deeper dive."

She did her usual and started on social media, which was the place where most people let their guard down. She found his account, but it was hardly ever used, just the occasional antagonistic political meme since he'd been released from prison and a few posts before he was locked up. Prisoners weren't allowed to access the internet social media sites, nor were they able to check their email accounts. If anyone wanted to email a prisoner, there was a dedicated email address and the prison officers would print it off and take it to them. So it didn't surprise her that his social media presence was relatively dormant.

O'Rourke's lack of activity wasn't an issue because his account was public, which meant that she could see all his friends. So many people of his age and older were hopeless with social media and didn't realise how vulnerable they made themselves by not setting their accounts to private.

O'Rourke only had fifty friends, which was very low compared with most people in Birdie's experience, but it still gave her plenty to go on. She started systematically going through all of them. Many were his family, including Meryl and Caroline, and some of them were way more prolific than he was.

Two years ago, on all of his friends' accounts, there was continual posting about a tragedy relating to a Rose Connor.

Birdie keyed the name into a search engine.

'Crap. That's awful,' she muttered as she read through the entire story. Rose was O'Rourke's sister, and she went missing from her home in Spain after going down to the beach for a swim. She'd left her young daughter and husband at their house in Alicante but had never returned. Her towel and clothes were left on the beach, and despite her body never being found, she was presumed dead from drowning. 'That poor kid, losing her mum like that.'

All this happened during the time O'Rourke was in prison.

She chewed on her bottom lip. 'I wonder...'

She did another media search for around the time of the incident, but this time included O'Rourke's name and also the prison where he was being held.

Ha. She let out a low whistle.

'So that's what it's all about.'

'That's what what's about?'

Birdie shot up in the air. 'What the hell,' she yelled. Seb was standing opposite, smiling. 'How long have you been there? And more to the point, why didn't Elsa make a noise to alert me to the fact that you'd come home.' She took several deep, calming breaths attempting to slow down her pounding heart.

'She met me at the door and was doing her usual

leaping about, her tail hitting the wall and making a noise. I called out to you, but you didn't reply. You were so engrossed in your work that you didn't hear a thing. I take it that whatever you've discovered is important to the investigation.'

'You bet your life it is. I think I've found out why O'Rourke has got it in for you, and it's not because you put him inside, like we originally thought. Well, it is in a round-about way, but it's more down to the consequences of him being there.'

Seb pulled up a chair and sat next to Birdie, Elsa sitting by his side. 'I'm all ears. We both are.' He nodded in Elsa's direction and grinned.

'It's to do with his sister, Rose Connor. She lived in Spain with her family, a daughter called Chelsea and her husband, Shaun. Two years ago, she went missing, and it's widely believed that she drowned while out swimming. Her body wasn't found, but the coroner pronounced her dead. Her poor family. And leaving a young daughter. It's so tragic.'

Birdie couldn't imagine how hard it must have been for everyone. She'd have never coped if something like that had happened to her.

'Yes. It's a dreadful tragedy for the family. But how is this connected to me?'

'O'Rourke wanted to go to the funeral, which was being held in Spain, but he wasn't allowed, and it caused a huge riot at the prison. It was eventually brought under control, but it took several hours to do so.'

'And that's why he has a vendetta against me. He believed the decision not to let him go was down to me. I do remember that my opinion was sought, but I advised against it. If it had been in this country, it would have been different, but in Spain, we couldn't guarantee he wouldn't have absconded. We also had to consider the safety of any officers who were allocated to attend with him. But the ultimate decision wasn't mine. My opinion was only one of many. I understand how angry O'Rourke must have felt during such a difficult time. How did he discover that I was one of those officers who was consulted? Unless it was down to Warrington...' Seb's eyes widened.

'Who's Warrington?'

'An officer in Rob's team. This is confidential, and I'm appalled that I have broken the confidence so easily. He's the officer Rob believes might be working for O'Rourke.'

'Well, first of all, you know you can trust me, and I won't disclose what you've just told me to anyone. And second of all, I've discovered that you're human and do make mistakes sometimes.'

'I make mistakes all of the time.'

'I've also come up with another one. Well, not really a mistake but an omission. When you were trawling your memory banks for all of the times you were involved with O'Rourke, how come you didn't remember about being asked for advice regarding his release? I'd have thought that would have come up straight away.'

'That's a very good question. I expect it's because my mind has been focusing on other things. Like the phone calls and being followed. Except they do seem to have stopped. Anyway, back to business. I met with Rob and updated him. He's going to send some of his men to the house in Guildford to check on Pemberton. I told him that I'll be contacting O'Rourke to let him know that he's piqued my interest. Rob was also going to inform Warrington to see if he then passes it on to O'Rourke. Rob might be able to use that as evidence against him. He wants me to be wired, but that's not a good idea. He also wants to be informed after I've arranged to see O'Rourke so his team can be part of the operation. Again, not advisable, in case it impinges on Pemberton and Annabelle's safety.'

'Rob will go mad if you go behind his back.'

'We've got to do what is best for the case. In my view, what I'm doing is the correct course of action.'

'Even if it means putting yourself in danger?'

When Seb dug his heels in, there was nothing anyone could do to persuade him otherwise. It was okay. Birdie would've done exactly the same in this instance if it had been up to her. But that didn't stop her from questioning him. She had to make sure he was fully aware of the risks he was taking.

'I'll be careful. And make sure that you're kept informed at all times. Somerton should have O'Rourke's number. I suspect it will be the only way we can access it because the man no doubt uses a burner.'

'Lord Somerton, please. It's Sebastian Clifford,' Seb said to the person who answered his call.

'One moment. I'll see if he's available.'

He most certainly would be. Seb wasn't going to take no for an answer.

'He can't come to the phone,' the woman said after returning several moments later.

'Tell His Lordship that it's an extremely urgent matter, and if he doesn't speak to me now, I will send a police officer around to bring him to me.' It was an empty threat, but Somerton wouldn't know that.

The woman gasped. 'Y-yes, sir. I'll fetch him.'

Surely the phone was cordless. Why couldn't she take it to him?

Within thirty seconds, Seb could hear footsteps.

'Sebastian, what do you want now?'

'Give me O'Rourke's mobile number. I assume that you have it.' There was silence. 'Harold?'

'Umm… I do have it. B-but I can't let you have it.' His voice wavered.

'You can. And you will.'

'You don't understand. If I give it to you… You know what he's like. I-I can't do it.'

'Tell him I forced you. I don't have time to waste. Get me the number now, or I'll send the police around, and they will retrieve it from your phone.'

All Seb could hear was Somerton's laboured breathing. 'Okay. I'll do it.'

'Hurry up.' Seb looked over at Birdie and gave an exasperated sigh. 'What is wrong with the man?'

'I think he's caught between a rock and a hard place. He doesn't know who he's scared of more. You or O'Rourke.'

'I can hear him running back.'

'I've got it,' Somerton said, all breathless.

He called out the number, and Seb committed it to memory. 'Thank you.'

'What's going to happen to me?' The fear and weariness in Somerton's voice was clear. He wasn't a young man, and what he'd done could see him ending up in prison for much of the remainder of his life. 'I wish I'd never got involved with O'Rourke. I'm sorry, Sebastian.'

'It's a bit late for that. The police will decide what they're going to do. It's not my decision.'

'But you could put in a good word for me,' Somerton begged.

'After what you've done? I don't think so.' Seb shook his head in disbelief and ended the call.

He immediately keyed in the number for O'Rourke, putting his phone on speaker and placing it on the desk so Birdie could listen. It rang for a while before it was cut off. Was it because Seb's number wasn't recognised?

He tried again, and the same thing happened.

On the third attempt, his call was answered.

'What?' A voice growled.

'O'Rourke?'

'Who's this?'

'Clifford. I understand you're looking for me. You could've called instead of engaging in this ridiculous game of cat and mouse.'

With someone like O'Rourke, any sign of weakness would be pounced on. Seb wasn't going to give the man the chance. He was going to take the lead.

'Who gave you this number?'

Was Somerton wrong, and O'Rourke hadn't automatically suspected him?

'Do you wish to meet or not?' He ignored the gangster's question.

'Yes.'

'First, you release Pemberton from your house in Guildford.' Seb was convinced that O'Rourke wouldn't agree, but he wanted the man to know that they were well aware of Pemberton's location.

'No.' O'Rourke's voice showed no sign of being disturbed by how much Seb already knew.

Seb wasn't going to argue the point. He'd no idea how deeply involved Pemberton was, and he didn't want to waste time on him. Annabelle was his prime concern.

'I'm fully aware that this whole charade was designed to attract my attention. You've succeeded. I will meet with you alone, and we can discuss whatever it is you have on your mind.'

Seb was not prepared to negotiate with the man. That would be a sign of weakness.

'Come to my club in Bethnal Green.'

'No. We'll meet somewhere neutral. Meet me this afternoon at four. Speakers' Corner.'

'Done.' O'Rourke ended the call.

Seb's brow furrowed. 'That was a little too easy.'

Birdie rolled her eyes. 'You think? But more to the point, why did you arrange to meet him alone? That's ridiculous. I'm going to be there—'

'You heard the arrangement. We're going to meet outside, in a public place. I'll be perfectly safe. O'Rourke might bring men with him, and I don't want to jeopardise the investigation by them spotting you. Not to mention that you would need to be so far away that you wouldn't be able to assist if there was a problem. We also have Annabelle and Pemberton to consider. I can look after myself.'

If O'Rourke's concern was Seb, then he didn't want Birdie involved. He understood that his partner was worried and being protective, but this wasn't the time for her to be involved. O'Rourke was dangerous and, whatever his agenda, Seb would not risk Birdie's life.

'You're mad. This is one of those TSTL situations.' Birdie jumped up from her chair and began pacing the floor.

'I have no idea what you mean.'

She spun around to face him. '*Too stupid to live*. You know, in a film when there's danger lurking behind a closed door, and so someone goes through it.'

'This is nothing like that.' Did he really believe that?

'It totally is. Will you reconsider wearing a wire at least?'

'No. But I'll have my phone on record in my pocket.'

Birdie narrowed her eyes and glared at him. 'You're mad. You know he's never going to fall for that one.'

'He won't know. If I take two phones with me, one doing the recording and one to show him if he asks, then he won't realise. He's hardly going to pat me down if we're meeting in the open. Trust me. It will be fine.'

Chapter 31

Birdie paced the floor in the lounge of Seb's flat. What on earth should she do? She wasn't happy that Seb had gone out to meet O'Rourke on his own, even if it was at Speakers' Corner, which he thought was safe, but of course it wasn't. Nowhere was safe with a man like O'Rourke around!

O'Rourke could have posted his men all over the park, watching their every move during the meeting and covering every exit to make sure that Seb couldn't escape from them. They could follow him back to his car and beat him up, or worse.

Why didn't Seb get it?

He needed to understand that he couldn't protect everyone on his own. It was stupid.

'What do you think I should do, Elsa? Shall I tell Rob what Seb's up to?'

The dog looked up in response to her name being called, but other than that, gave no indication that she understood or that she had an opinion. Okay, so dogs don't have opinions, but they do get it when things aren't right and can make their feelings known.

'You're not helping. Seb said he'll be fine but, to be honest, I'm not sure. You know he thinks that he's invincible, but you and I both know that he isn't. No one can be. Wag your tail if you think I should trust that Seb knows best and to wait here for him, and not do anything.'

Birdie stared down at Elsa. Her tail didn't move, despite still staring directly at Birdie.

'Okay. Let's try this. Wag your tail if you think I should contact Rob and let him know where Seb has gone?'

Else's tail started wagging furiously. She had her answer. 'You do get it. I knew you would. Thanks. You've helped me make my decision. And I agree. It's the right one.' She bent down and gave Elsa a rub. The dog rolled on her back, and Birdie stroked her tummy. 'You love this, don't you? Well, you deserve it. And after I've phoned Rob, I'll get you a treat. Do you fancy one of those chicken sticks?'

Her words were greeted by another wag of the tail. Anyone who believed that dogs weren't intelligent and didn't understand what was said to them needed their heads tested.

Birdie pulled her phone from her pocket and called Rob's mobile. Luckily, she'd got his number from Seb a while ago, just in case she ever needed to contact him. At the time, Seb hadn't thought it necessary, but he'd given it to her anyway. Thank goodness.

'Lawson.'

'Rob, it's Birdie. Are you free to talk?' She didn't want him to be talking about O'Rourke in front of members of his team. Although being a detective inspector, he probably had his own office. Especially at the Met. Supposedly, no expense was spared there, although when she's brought it up with Seb, he'd said that was a rumour and totally untrue.

'I'm alone. What's the problem, Birdie?'

'Seb's going to kill me for this, but I'm worried and have to tell you. He's just left the flat to meet O'Rourke. The meeting place is Speakers' Corner, and because it's out in the open, Seb thinks it's fine. I don't know about you, but I'm not convinced. There are so many things that could happen.'

Was she overreacting? Seb had always been able to take care of himself, apart from when he was beaten up during their first case together. But that was because he was taken by surprise, and his attackers carried baseball bats.

'Thanks for letting me know, Birdie. He was meant to discuss it with me so we could be there as backup. I see he's still as stubborn as ever. But he's not rash. Never has been. There has to be a reason why he's done what he has. Also, there are plenty of CCTV cameras around that area, so I agree with him. I'm sure he'll be fine. But it's still a puzzle as to why O'Rourke has decided to single Seb out.'

'Well, I think I know. During my research into O'Rourke, I discovered that his sister died while he was in prison, and he wasn't allowed to go to the funeral, which was held in Spain. We believe that O'Rourke thought Seb had something to do with the decision, and now it's payback time.'

'I see. So it *is* personal. That does make a difference. To be on the safe side, I'll send a couple of men over to where they're meeting. I'll make sure they keep their distance. Seb won't even know they're there.'

If he believed that, he'd believe anything.

She gave a hollow laugh. 'I doubt you'll fool him. He notices everything, as you well know.'

'True. I'll make sure they're extra vigilant. Before you rang, I was about to phone Seb, but I'll let you know instead. I sent in a couple of undercover officers dressed as workmen to the house where Pemberton is being held. They said they were checking for gas leaks, and they were let into the house. They caught sight of Pemberton and reported back that he's not being held captive in a room, like you thought. But despite his apparent freedom, they did think he seemed very anxious. I wanted to discuss with Seb the implications of removing him from the environment at this stage.'

'I'll text Seb to discuss it with him, and let you know our decision.'

'Thanks, Birdie, and don't worry. Seb can look after himself. I'll send my guys over now. It was Speakers' Corner, wasn't it?'

'Yes.'

She ended the call and gave a big sigh. Would Seb think that she'd betrayed him and never trust her again? Perhaps she should tell him what she'd done and get it over with. She picked up her phone.

Heard from Rob. Pemberton fine in the house, but anxious. Do you want Rob's men to remove him? I've told him where you are, and he's sending men to watch. Sorry. Couldn't leave you on your own.

She hit send and stared at the phone for a few moments, praying that she hadn't totally destroyed their partnership before it had even got off the ground properly.

Chapter 32

Seb glanced at his watch. He'd been waiting for half an hour, and still no O'Rourke.

Why?

If the whole point of this stupid charade with Pemberton and the painting was to lure him out, then where was the man?

He scanned the area yet again, and there was no sign of any of the gangster's men. He'd give O'Rourke ten more minutes, and if he hadn't turned up by then, he'd leave.

He was yet to respond to Birdie's text. She'd annoyed him by going against his wishes and contacting Rob. But, truth be told, he might've done the same if the situation was reversed. Birdie was only looking out for him. Seb hadn't yet decided what they should do about Pemberton. On the one hand, if the police extracted him and O'Rourke discovered what they'd done, then who was he going to take it out on? But, on the other, Seb couldn't risk Pemberton getting hurt, whether or not he was a part of the plot. O'Rourke wasn't to be trusted, and he would have no qualms in harming Pemberton, especially if his only aim was revenge on Seb. Pemberton's safety should take priority.

He pulled out his phone and called Birdie.

'Are you okay?' she asked, answering straight away.

'O'Rourke is nowhere to be seen. It's most confusing, considering he was so adamant about our meeting.'

'Are you coming back to the flat?'

'I'll wait ten minutes more and make a decision. The alternative would be to visit the strip club in Bethnal Green, where he'd initially suggested we meet.'

'Are you mad? That's totally playing into his hands. You're not safe going there alone. It was bad enough you going to Speakers' Corner. Talking of which, are you annoyed at me for telling Rob where you'd gone?'

'I'm not ecstatic about you going behind my back, but I understand. Contact Rob and ask him to remove Pemberton from the house in Guildford. He needs to be out of harm's way, so suggest to Rob that he's taken to a police station. Pemberton will need to be interviewed regarding his part in the fraud anyway. Somerton should be arrested too, but we'll leave that until this is sorted.'

'I'm sorry, but I couldn't think what else to do. Please don't think you can't trust me. It was just that I was so worried for your safety.'

'I know that I can trust you. I—' He glanced down at the screen as another call was coming in. He recognised the number. 'I've got to go. I have a call from O'Rourke.'

He ended the call with Birdie and answered. 'Where are you?'

'There's no need for rudeness, Clifford. I'm phoning to let you know that I have something belonging to you.'

Seb winced at the smug tone in the gangster's voice.

'Explain.'

'While we're talking, your ex-girlfriend is being taken to a secret location.'

They had Annabelle. That couldn't be. How did they manage that?

'Why? We'd already arranged to meet.'

'Yes. And I'm not there. If you want to see the little lady alive and well, you will do exactly as I say.'

How could he have been so foolish as to fall for O'Rourke's compliance to meet with him?

'Okay. Proceed.'

'You'll put the following postcode into your car's satnav and drive straight there. It will take you sixty to ninety minutes. And don't think about involving your friend, Lawson. Or that partner of yours. Not that she could do much – she's hardly threatening. You come alone and tell no one, or the pretty face belonging to your ex-girlfriend will be ruined.'

Seb seethed. Had he really got Annabelle, or was it a lie to persuade him to go to this unnamed location? 'How do I know you really do have Annabelle?'

'You don't. But I'm telling you, she was contacted by one of my men who instructed her to leave her parents' house and drive to a location where she was picked up. If you're not there in ninety minutes, then what happens to her is your fault.' He gave a callous laugh. 'A nice long cut down the side of her face that will leave a lasting scar is where we'll start. If you don't believe me, then don't go, and her being scarred for life is down to you.'

'I'll be there. Give me the postcode.'

Seb had no choice. He had to trust that O'Rourke would let Annabelle go once he arrived. Which meant that at least Annabelle and Pemberton would be safe. Unless O'Rourke discovered that Pemberton had been rescued and decided to pay Seb back for that by harming

Annabelle. Although he'd know Seb hadn't been involved in the rescue because, at the time, he was at Hyde Park. Seb's head whirled with consequences. This was not the time to think. He had to act.

Seb returned to his car and keyed into his satnav the postcode he'd been given. He also put it into his phone to research exactly where he was going and the surrounding areas. The location was a remote building close to Binfield. He'd still got the second phone with him, which he placed in his jacket's long inside pocket. If O'Rourke demanded his phone, there was still the other one.

Seb went through the various scenarios of what was going to happen when he got to O'Rourke's location. He could take care of himself, but it would really depend on how many of O'Rourke's men were there, and also what the man had in mind for him.

He needed to get a message to Birdie but didn't want to text on either phone, despite the chances of O'Rourke having the wherewithal to tap Seb's phones being remote. Unless Warrington was involved. The best course of action would be for him to wait until he knew for certain that Annabelle was safe. He didn't want to put anyone else at risk. He also needed to consider that Birdie might be under surveillance by either Warrington or O'Rourke's men. He was in a catch-22 situation.

Thirty minutes away from his location, while stationary at some traffic lights, Seb set his second phone to record. He then continued on his journey and arrived at a remote house on the outskirts of the village, which had a large metal outbuilding to the right of it. In front of the house were three parked cars. He stepped out onto the gravelled drive, and the outbuilding door opened. O'Rourke walked out, followed by two of his bodyguards.

'Have you come alone?' The man's tone was cold and menacing.

'That's what we agreed.'

'Good. Because I'd have known if you hadn't. My spies are everywhere. You were wise not to involve anyone else.'

'You mean Warrington?' Seb was determined to get the admission on record.

O'Rourke frowned. 'You have been doing your work if you know about him. Well, he's outlived his usefulness. I'll have to find someone else.' O'Rourke shrugged and gave a hollow laugh.

'So you're not denying it then?'

'You'd better not be wearing a wire and trying to get me to confess.' O'Rourke stepped towards him until he was only three feet away.

'Take a look. I wasn't wearing one when I came to meet you at Speakers' Corner, and I had insufficient time to get one, considering I came straight here, as you well know, and I suspect you orchestrated that to prevent me doing such a thing. I also imagine that you had your men keeping an eye on me the whole time, so I suggest you ask them what I did when I left Hyde Park.'

'I know that you drove straight here.'

'Where's Annabelle?'

'All in good time.'

'We had an agreement. Me for her. I want to see her now.' He folded his arms and locked eyes with O'Rourke. He wasn't going to be intimidated.

'No, you're right. We did. And I'm a man of my word. As you're about to find out.' O'Rourke's icy tone cut through the air. 'Give me your phone.'

Seb handed it over and then the gangster turned and marched back into the outbuilding.

Seb followed him inside. There were storage racks filled

with boxes along one side and a fork-lift truck in the middle. In the corner, closest to the entrance, there was a desk, behind which Annabelle was seated. Her face was pale. She was petrified.

He hurried over to her. 'Annabelle. Are you okay?'

If they'd touched her, there'd be hell to pay.

Her chin wobbled, tears filling her eyes. 'I didn't leave the house at all. Not even when my parents tried to persuade me. And then I got the phone call on my mobile telling me to drive to Norbury Park. They knew my parents' car and where they were heading. They threatened to harm my parents if I didn't do what they said. I had to do as they told me. They warned me not to call anyone, so I didn't. I was too scared.'

His insides clenched. 'It's okay, now.' He put his arm around her shoulders and gave a squeeze. 'Did they harm you?'

'No. The man in charge said I could go when you arrived, but I don't know whether he meant it.'

O'Rourke marched over to them. 'Right. You.' He pointed to Annabelle. 'Outside now. One of my men will take you back.'

Annabelle looked from O'Rourke to Seb, fear in her eyes.

'She can take my car.'

Annabelle looked at O'Rourke, who nodded his assent. 'Go. Now. Before I change my mind and keep you here.'

'Will you be okay, Sebastian?'

'Of course. I'd like you to give a message to Lucinda.'

Annabelle gave a puzzled look. 'But I thought—'

'Did I say you could do that?' O'Rourke snapped.

'I was about to instruct Annabelle to tell *Lucinda* not to come searching for me. I fail to understand why that would be problematic?'

O'Rourke grunted and turned to speak to one of his men who was standing a few feet away.

'If I take your car, then how will you get back or...' Annabelle's words fell away, and a look of horror crossed her face.

'Don't worry about me. I'll be fine. Just make sure to deliver my message.' He pulled Annabelle into a hug. 'Use the satnav to get back to my flat. Birdie will be there.'

'Are you going, or what?' O'Rourke barked, glaring at Annabelle.

'She's going.' Seb handed her the key and watched while she left, clutching her handbag tightly to her body.

Once she'd left, he scanned the building to ascertain the best route to escape should it prove necessary.

O'Rourke was still talking with one of his men. Seb approached and overheard the words 'shipment' and 'sort it', but the moment he got close, the conversation stopped, and O'Rourke gestured for his man to go away.

'Well. I'm here now, as you requested. I know you believe it was my fault that you weren't allowed to go to your sister's funeral, but that wasn't down to me. It was a decision made by higher ranking officers in a different department.'

O'Rourke's jaw tightened. Seb had clearly touched a nerve. But if that was the reason he was there, then it could hardly be ignored.

'Don't lie to me. I know that you were the lead investigator when I was put in prison. I also know that you influenced the decision regarding me not being able to attend the funeral.'

Who'd been feeding him that information?

'You've been misinformed. Yes, I was part of the team who investigated you. And so too was Warrington.' Seb paused. 'Ah ... he's the one telling you about my input, and you're taking his word for it. Is that what this is all about? Revenge?'

'You call it revenge. I call it payback. Rose didn't die in a swimming accident. The coroner got it wrong. My sister was murdered.' A mix of hurt and anger flickered in his eyes.

Murder? Surely that wouldn't have been kept a secret. Someone would have informed the police.

'Are you sure? I understand her body wasn't recovered—'

'Are you calling me a liar?' O'Rourke grabbed a metal bar from the desk behind him and stepped towards Seb. His arm raised.

Seb stiffened. O'Rourke's temper was well known.

'No, no. This is the first I've heard about it, and I wanted to make sure. Put the weapon down so we can talk. Do you wish me to investigate Rose's death? Was all this a charade to test my capabilities?'

Seb couldn't think of any other reason for the whole missing-painting scenario.

'A test?' O'Rourke's hollow laugh was mirthless. 'No. I've just told you, it's payback. You're paying me back for what you did. Even if Warrington did exaggerate, you were still involved. And in case you're thinking of turning me down, be warned. There's no part of your life that I can't infiltrate. As I've already proved.'

'What do you want from me?'

'I know what happened to Rose. She was killed by a gang in Spain. They wanted to take over my drug operation. They thought I'd lost control because I was inside. But they were wrong. My men kept the business going. They murdered my sister as a warning. But it didn't work. I'm still in charge. I'm going after those Spanish bastards, and you're going to help.'

Chapter 33

A loud pounding on the door echoed around the flat, and Birdie grabbed hold of the desk. Who would be knocking like that? Was one of O'Rourke's men coming for her?

She jumped up from her seat and took hold of Elsa's collar. 'Come on. We'll check this out together.' She tiptoed to the front door, with Elsa following behind, her paws making very little noise.

She peeked through the peephole and let out a sigh of relief.

It was Annabelle.

Before she'd opened the door even a few inches, Annabelle barged in and grabbed Birdie by the shoulders.

'They've got Sebastian. They let me go when he got there. I didn't want to leave him, but he made me. O'Rourke wanted one of his men to drive me, but Sebastian insisted I took his car. I agreed because I was so scared. I don't know what they're going to do. He—'

She pulled herself away from the woman's grasp. 'Annabelle, stop. And take a breath. Come into the lounge, and you can explain everything.' She led the woman by the arm and guided her to the sofa, where they sat down. 'Now, tell me what happened. Slowly.'

Birdie sucked in a breath. Birdie's heart pounded in her chest. Was he going to kill Seb? But she had to remain calm if she was going to help her partner.

'I had a phone call on my mobile telling me to leave my parents' house and to drive to Norbury Park. They threatened to harm my parents if I didn't go. I had no choice. I was then taken to a house in the country.'

'Was it O'Rourke?'

'He was at the house I was taken to. He wasn't the driver.'

'Did O'Rourke's men harm you at all?'

'No. They were okay. They didn't really talk to me. O'Rourke said they only wanted Sebastian, and once he arrived, I could go. I waited in the corner of this warehouse-type building until Sebastian arrived. If they hurt him, I'll never forgive myself. I was the one who got him involved.'

'Don't blame yourself. There's more to it than that. We'll get Seb out of there. I want you to think hard. Is there anything else you can tell me that might help?' Birdie tensed. She had to do something. No way would she leave Seb in O'Rourke's clutches.

'Yes. Sorry, I should have told you straight away. Sebastian asked me to give you a message. He said you're not to go looking for him.'

Huh? Was he saying that to protect her? Surely he would know that wouldn't work.

'That makes no sense, Annabelle. He knows what I'm like. Did he say anything else? Come on, think.' Her voice came out harsher than she'd intended. The poor woman was in shock. 'I'm sorry. I didn't mean to snap at you.'

'He told me to use the satnav to get back here, which I did.'

'Okay. That makes sense because I'm assuming you didn't know where you were. Now, is there anything else he said, no matter how inconsequential it seemed at the time?'

'I don't know. I… Oh. I've just remembered something. When Sebastian asked me to give you the message, he referred to you as Lucinda. He's never done that before.'

Birdie's eyes widened. 'That's it. Now I get it.'

'Get what?' Annabelle frowned.

'I'm assuming he gave you the message in front of O'Rourke?'

'Yes. He was there at the time.'

'Very clever on Seb's part. I hate being called Lucinda. If anyone calls me by that name more than once, they'll wished they hadn't. By Seb referring to me as Lucinda, it means to ignore the message he was sending and flip it. He wants me to come after him. He insisted you take his car because of the satnav. If we check the history, we can see the exact location. Clever. Very clever,' she repeated.

'But you can't go on your own. It's too dangerous!'

'I'm not going to. I'll contact Rob Lawson. He knows about our investigation because it overlapped with one of his. We have to be careful, though, because O'Rourke has a man on the inside, and we don't want to alert him. Give me the keys to Seb's car, and I'll check the satnav and then get in touch with Rob. I might go straight there and not come back. You must stay here until we return. Help yourself to anything out of the fridge. Elsa will take care of you, and don't answer the door to anyone.'

'Thank you, Birdie. And I'm sorry if I've been a bit—'

'Forget it. I'm definitely an acquired taste. Then again … so are you.' Birdie grinned at Annabelle, who hesitated and then smiled in return.

'Just be careful.'

Birdie went down to the car park and found Seb's car. She turned on the engine to check the satnav and took a photo on her phone of the postcode identifying the car's last known location prior to arriving at the flat. She called Rob.

'Lawson.'

'Rob, it's me. Can you talk?'

'Yes.'

'O'Rourke kidnapped Annabelle, and Seb gave himself in exchange. He drove to the place they were holding her. He didn't tell me any of this. Annabelle is now back at Seb's flat. He sent a secret message asking me to come after him. I've got the postcode of the location from Seb's satnav, which I'll send to you. But we need to be careful because of your man on the inside, Warrington, isn't it?'

Crap. She hadn't meant to say the name of the person on the take. He'd know that Seb had told her.

'I'll get some men together. They'll have to be from another team, which means calling in a favour. O'Rourke and his men are likely to be armed, so we need to be careful.'

'Did you get Pemberton?'

'No. He wasn't there. The house was empty.'

'Shit. O'Rourke must know that we've found him. But I don't care about that. Seb's our main concern. I want to go with you. If O'Rourke thinks he can harm him, then it will be over my dead body.'

'Don't even joke about it – you don't know what he's like. I'll let you come with us because I know if I don't, you'll go anyway. But you'll stay in the car and not interfere.'

She'd agree to anything as long as she was part of the

operation. Whether or not she stayed in the car would depend entirely on what was going down.

'Shall I drive to you?'

'Get a taxi. Parking's a nightmare around here, and they can drop you off right at the front of the Met building. You're only about fifteen minutes away.'

Birdie ended the call and put her phone back in her pocket. Crap. She hadn't got any money. She raced back to the flat.

'It's only me. Don't worry,' she shouted as she opened the door and raced into the kitchen. 'I need some money for a taxi. She grabbed her purse from her bag, which was on the side and slipped it into her pocket.

'Where are you going?' Annabelle was sitting at the table, her hands wrapped around a steaming mug of coffee.

'I'm meeting Rob, and we're going to rescue Seb. It will be a change from the last time we got ourselves in a fix, when it was Seb who rescued me, so now we're even.'

Chapter 34

Before Seb and O'Rourke could talk further, the gangster was called away by one of his men. Seb took a few steps forward in an attempt to hear what the problem was. From the way O'Rourke was gesticulating, it was serious.

The more the men conversed, the louder their voices became, and Seb was able to ascertain that the shipment he'd heard mentioned before was drugs, and it had been intercepted by a Spanish gang on the way to the UK from the Port of Valencia. O'Rourke's men had managed to retain the shipment, although not easily won, and it was going to be delivered there soon.

The name Lopez was mentioned. It was familiar to Seb. Before leaving the Met, his work had focused on international syndicates involved in match-fixing and betting. Members of the syndicates were from gangs and criminal families, of which the Lopez family was one. They were also connected with drug and human trafficking. It was a nightmare for law-enforcement agencies because as soon as one syndicate was disbanded, there was another waiting in the wings to take its place. It was relentless.

Seb glanced over at O'Rourke, who was now heading back towards him. Whatever the man wanted, he'd play along until such time as he could escape, or they let him go. He'd already checked out the building for exits and noticed one at the rear, although he had no idea whether it was unlocked. His hidden phone had been on record the whole time he'd been there, so there should be enough evidence for Rob to arrest O'Rourke. He now had a chance to collect even more. Especially if he was still there when the drugs arrived.

'Problem with a drug shipment?' He wanted to make sure he'd recorded O'Rourke admitting it.

'Nothing I can't handle. And nothing to do with you. Yet. You've had time to think about my request. Got any questions?'

And now he could get O'Rourke to further incriminate himself.

'What do you need from me exactly?'

'You have access to the police. I want you to feed me information about their operations. And to feed information from me back to them.'

'What sort of *information*?'

'Anything I want them to know. I also need someone who can ensure that my operation continues to run smoothly and—'

'Boss?' One of O'Rourke's men interrupted. He was holding Pemberton in a tight grip and heading towards them. 'What do you want me to do with him?'

Pemberton stared ahead like a rabbit caught in a car's headlights. His normally immaculate hair was sticking out at right angles, as if he'd been continually running his fingers through it.

What was he doing there?

'Put him in the corner.'

'W-why am I here?' Pemberton squeaked.

'Because I say so,' O'Rourke sneered. He turned to Seb. 'We ruined your plan to rescue him.'

Seb shrugged. 'He's of no interest to me.'

'If you say so. I wonder what his fiancée would say if she knew.'

'Why should I care?' Seb waved a dismissive hand. 'You do realise that I no longer work for the police, so why do you think I can be of use to you?'

'You work as a consultant, and you're friends with DI Lawson. You have plenty of access.'

'How does this relate to taking down the Spanish gang?'

'You tell me everything the police has on them and help set them up. You also tell me about other gangs. Names. Locations. Operations. We're going to put them all out of business. I'll be the largest operation in Europe, and you're going to help me.' O'Rourke puffed out his chest, his menacing pale blue eyes locking with Seb's.

'Why should I agree?' Seb folded his arms across his chest and leant in slightly. He, too, could play the intimidation game. Especially now he knew that O'Rourke needed him.

For a fleeting second, the man tensed but immediately resumed his previous posture.

'I know everything there is to know about you. I know your family. Where they live. Their mansion in London and the country estate. I know your partner and where her family lives. She's very different to you. Does she know how posh you are?'

'I fail to see how that's relevant.'

'Just wondered. I also know about your ex and her family. There's nothing I don't know about you.'

'And if I agree to assist…?'

'They will all be safe.'

'And if I say no?'

Seb wasn't going to. Not to the man's face. But he wanted to record the threat.

'You really want to know? Well, I'll tell you. You won't go the same way as my sister because that's too easy. This will hurt you far more. Everyone around you will suffer. *You* won't need to look over your shoulder the whole time. But your friends, family, and work colleagues will. One by one, nasty accidents will take place.' A slow smile unfolded on his face, and it was all Seb could do not to punch it off him.

Seb let out a long sigh, wanting O'Rourke to believe that he was resigned to the situation. 'You've given me no option then. But I better have your assurance that nothing will happen to anyone I know. Or I won't be responsible for what happens to you.'

O'Rourke laughed. 'Are you threatening me? Listen to this,' he shouted so his men could hear. 'The viscount thinks he can get one over on me!' His face hardened. 'Don't even think about it, *mate*.'

Seb bit back a response. He'd pushed the man far enough.

'May I leave now?'

'Be my guest. Just one problem. Are you planning to walk? Because you gave your car to your ex-girlfriend. You can wait for one of my men to drive you.'

'My phone?' Seb held out his hand.

O'Rourke pulled it from his pocket and waved it in front of him. 'Your driver will give it back to you when you get to London. I'll be in touch soon. And in case you're wondering, you'll be well remunerated.'

Seb was tempted to tell him what he could do with his money, but, of course, he couldn't. However, if Birdie had been in the situation instead of him, he doubted that she'd have been able to refrain from telling O'Rourke. The thought amused him. But he needed to focus. Already, a plan was forming in the back of his mind. He assumed that O'Rourke would want to stay at the property to take delivery of the drugs. All that was needed was for Rob to catch him red-handed.

Seb would have to get a message to him. And he knew exactly how.

Chapter 35

'Let's go.'

Seb glanced down at one of O'Rourke's men, who was at least ten inches shorter than him, and dressed in casual clothes more suited to going for a round of golf. His appearance wasn't at all threatening.

'Do you have my phone?' Seb asked while they walked outside to one of the cars.

'It's in my pocket, and I'll give it to you later. You can sit in the front next to me.'

Seb ignored him, and opened the back door and sat behind the driver's seat. 'No, thanks. I'd rather sit here and stretch out. This isn't a great car for someone of my height.'

'Up to you.'

Seb turned side on and made a big show of stretching out his legs. 'You can drop me off at my flat – I assume you know where it is.'

Once they'd been driving for a few minutes, Seb surreptitiously removed his second phone from the inside pocket of his jacket to text Birdie.

I'm being driven home by O'Rourke's man. Important you get to where O'Rourke is straight away. He's expecting a drug shipment.

His phone had already been on silent, and the only sign that Birdie had replied was the vibration which couldn't be heard over the car engine.

I'm with Rob and his team. We're ten minutes away from the location.

Seb responded immediately with the car number plate and letting her know that he'd disable the driver in five minutes' time. He'd go back to the outbuilding with them to help deal with O'Rourke and his men.

'I understand that you're going to be working with the boss.' The driver made eye contact with him using the rear-view mirror.

'So it appears.' Seb's voice was emotionless.

'Well, don't even think about double-crossing him. Not if you want to survive. I've witnessed men who have, and the consequences aren't pretty.'

Had O'Rourke instructed him to make those comments?

'I'm sure they weren't.'

'Just so you know.' The driver shrugged and returned his gaze to the road in front.

After a couple more minutes, when Seb had gauged that Birdie and Rob would soon be on the scene, he sat upright in the seat.

'Stop the car.'

'No. My orders are to keep going until you're home.'

'I'm about to be sick, so if you don't want the stench of vomit in the car the entire journey, then I suggest you do as I ask.'

The driver shrugged. 'Fine, but don't try scarpering, or you'll regret it.'

'To where? I have no transport. Just pull in now. Please.'

The driver brought the car to a halt on the side of the road. There was no traffic. Seb got out, and the driver followed. His jacket was open, and the gun stuffed into his trouser waistband was visible.

'Hurry up.'

Seb removed his jacket. 'Hold this for me.'

As the man took hold of it, Seb grabbed him around the back of the neck and pushed him to the ground, pulling out the gun and throwing it to the side of the road.

'Get off me, you bastard.' The driver struggled, but Seb was too strong.

'Stop moving, or you'll end up hurt.'

'You'll pay for this.'

They stayed in that position for a minute or two until a car stopped on the other side of the road. Rob and Birdie jumped out and ran over, dodging the occasional vehicle across the road. Two more police cars and one van drew up behind them.

'You okay?' Rob asked.

'Yes. This guy needs to be kept out of the way so he can't warn O'Rourke.' Seb hoisted the driver to his feet and set him down beside his colleague. 'His gun's over there.' Seb nodded to the overgrown grassed area.

'Name?' Rob said to the man.

'No comment.'

'Your choice.' Rob signalled for a couple of officers in the closest police car to come over, and they handcuffed him. 'Put him in the back of the van and make sure he can't escape. And confiscate that gun.'

'Before you go, I want my phone.' Seb felt inside the driver's pocket and pulled out two phones. 'I'll take yours, too, in case you were thinking of phoning O'Rourke.'

'Search him for weapons or another phone,' Rob said to his officer before the prisoner was escorted to the police van. 'Have the drugs arrived yet?'

'Not that I know of,' Seb said. 'No lorry has passed us, but if they were driving from the coast, they'd have come from the opposite direction. If they're not already there, then I believe it won't be long until they are.'

'Right. Let's go.'

Seb followed Rob and Birdie back to the car, and he sat in the back as Birdie got in next to Rob.

'I was worried about you,' Birdie said, turning to him.

'O'Rourke had no plans to hurt me. He threatened me with harming everyone I know, but that was to persuade me to work for him. His goal is to become the largest drug dealer in Europe.'

'Today Europe, tomorrow the world,' Rob said with a hollow laugh. 'Such a shame we have to put an end to his megalomaniac ambitions.'

'I can't believe he thought you'd agree. You'd be the last person to go on the take. What an idiot.' Birdie rolled her eyes.

'When family and friends' lives are at stake, it makes a big difference. But, you're right, I had no intention of being any part of the man's empire.'

'Good work on finding his place. We had no idea it even existed. It's not registered to anyone connected to O'Rourke.'

'I didn't find it. He directed me to go there. A big mistake as it transpires.'

'It certainly was. When we get there, you two stay in the car while the team go in to arrest them. If the drugs haven't already arrived, we'll wait. What can you tell me about the layout of the place?'

'From my observations, there are two entrances. One

at the front where two of his men are positioned close by, and one at the rear of the building. I have no idea whether the latter is locked or not. To my knowledge, there are nine of O'Rourke's men in there, plus Pemberton.'

'Is he part of the operation?' Rob asked.

'I don't believe so. He was brought there by one of O'Rourke's men.'

'Did you speak to him?'

'No. But I could tell that he was scared.'

They drove to the property, stopping a little up the road.

'It looks like the drug shipment has arrived.' Rob pointed at the top of a truck that was just visible from where they were situated.

'Yes. That vehicle wasn't there earlier.'

Rob jumped out of the car to discuss with his team how they were going to approach the building.

'I can't believe we have to stay in the car. Surely Rob needs as many of us on the ground as possible,' Birdie said.

'You know why not. O'Rourke's gang are most likely armed, and we're not. Rob's team will all be armed and wearing protection and, again, we're not. Also, it's not a good idea for O'Rourke to know that we are behind this. He might have some people out there with eyes on Annabelle, or your family.'

'What?' Birdie exclaimed, her eyes wide. 'He's been tailing my mum and dad and brothers! Why the hell didn't you tell me?'

'I'm not certain that he's actually been following them. He informed me that he knows where you live. I took him at his word, but it might just have been a tactic to persuade me to work for him.'

'Okay, I get it. But once he finds out that the driver has

been arrested, he'll know that you might've had something to do with it.'

'Possibly. Here's Rob.'

Rob opened the driver's door and leant into the car. 'Remember what I said. Stay here and don't move. I'm going in another car.'

'Yes, boss,' Birdie said.

Seb got out of the car and joined her in the front, sitting in the driver's seat. 'I've got a better view of proceedings from here.'

'Not to mention that Rob's left the keys, so if it all goes wrong and any of O'Rourke's men try to get away, we can go after them.'

Chapter 36

Seb and Birdie watched in silence while the police cars and van drove into the drive of O'Rourke's property.

Birdie fidgeted in her seat. 'It's so annoying being stuck here. I want to be part of the raid.'

Seb glanced at her. Was she regretting being a private investigator and having left the police?

'You can't do that now you're no longer a police officer.'

'I know, but that doesn't stop me from wishing. And before you ask, I have no regrets about joining you. What? It's written all over your face. Plus, of course, mind-reading is one of my specialities.' She smirked.

'A very useful talent, which I'm sure we can utilise and—'

'Hey, look over there. There's someone running away.' Birdie pointed across the fields.

'Damn. That's O'Rourke.'

'We have to go after him. If we don't, he'll disappear, and then all hell will let loose.'

Birdie jumped out of the car and ran into the field, with Seb close behind.

O'Rourke was a speck on the landscape and getting smaller and smaller by the second.

They chased after the man until reaching a small forest. Seb came to a halt and held up his hand to signal the same to Birdie once she'd caught up with him.

'Now what?' she whispered.

'We listen.'

They remained motionless, ears pricked. The only sounds were the birds singing, and then, to the west, there began a repeated crunching sound. It had to be O'Rourke's footsteps as he trampled the twigs. Seb held his finger up to his lips, and he pointed in the direction of the sound.

If O'Rourke believed that he'd escaped without being noticed, then they had the advantage. Which they needed to maintain if they were to catch him.

They ran in the direction of the sound, trying to keep their footsteps in time with O'Rourke's so he wouldn't realise he was being followed. The forest was dense, and there was no sign of the edge. Suddenly, the footsteps stopped. Seb and Birdie came to a halt in a small clearing and listened.

The roar of a motorbike engine permeated the air, and the growl of an open throttle was enough to let them know it was heading in their direction.

The noise increased in volume until out of the trees appeared O'Rourke, mounted on a motorbike, heading directly at them, a gun in his hand which was pointed directly at them.

He shot wildly in their direction and Seb grabbed Birdie and pulled her to the side, both narrowly missing being hit.

O'Rourke swung the bike around and came hurtling at them again. 'You bastard. You'll pay for this,' he roared!

'Get behind the tree,' Seb yelled at Birdie, pushing her to the side.

O'Rourke was after him, not her.

Seb ran in the opposite direction, towards the trees, wanting O'Rourke to pursue him.

Adrenaline coursed through him with each footstep.

The throaty sound of the engine increased in intensity as the gangster got closer. Seb darted behind a tree. The only way to stop the man was to pull him off the bike.

He'd only have one chance.

He had to get it right.

Seb drew in a breath and waited until the bike was almost adjacent to the tree he was hiding behind. One second later, he jumped out and grabbed O'Rourke by the arm as he raced past, yanking him off the bike and throwing him to the ground. His gun went flying off in the other direction.

The bike shot off in the other direction, crashing into a nearby tree.

'Get the fuck off me!' O'Rourke shouted, rolling to the side, and pulling himself upright. 'You'll regret this, Clifford. You and anyone who knows you.'

'I'm prepared to take the risk.'

Seb grabbed hold of O'Rourke, pulled him until he was standing on his two feet, and twisted his arm behind his back.

'This is your last chance,' O'Rourke said, twisting his head around and locking eyes with Seb.

Birdie came running over. 'Are you okay?'

'Yes. Pat him down for weapons and phone.'

'I'd be delighted.' She ran her hands down the gangster's body and found a small knife in his sock and a gun shoved into his trouser waistband. She pocketed both weapons.

'You'd better watch out, too,' O'Rourke snarled at Birdie.

'Bite me. You're going down. And we won't be coming to visit.' Birdie pulled out her phone and keyed in a number. 'We've caught O'Rourke. We're heading back to you… No, we're fine. He's no match for Seb.'

'Rob?' Seb asked, glancing at Birdie.

'Yep. He'll be waiting for us.'

Seb frog-marched O'Rourke across the fields. The man tried to wriggle out of Seb's grasp but was totally ineffective against his height and strength.

When they returned to the outbuilding, Rob was coordinating the removal of O'Rourke's men and Pemberton from the warehouse, all of whom were handcuffed and being escorted to the police van.

'Rob,' Birdie called out.

The officer turned and made his way over to them.

'Here you are. Mr Bigwig himself,' Birdie said with a grin.

'He's been searched for weapons and a phone, which we have,' Seb said.

'Nice work, you two. Even if you did disobey orders.' Rob pulled out a pair of handcuffs, and cuffed the man behind his back.

Chapter 37

Birdie could hear Elsa's tail flapping furiously against the wall while Seb unlocked the door to his flat.

'It's only us,' she called out, pushing past Seb to get inside first.

She hurriedly gave Elsa a pat and then dashed towards the lounge with Seb following close behind. She knew how worried Annabelle must have been and wanted to let her know that they were okay.

As soon as Birdie got into the room, Annabelle rushed over. She pulled Birdie into her arms and squeezed so tight that she could hardly breathe.

'I'm so glad you're safe. I've been out of my mind with worry,' Annabelle said in her ear.

She'd never have imagined Annabelle would do or say anything so affectionate. It was weird, to say the least.

'We're fine,' Birdie said, gasping for breath as she was released.

Annabelle turned to Seb, who was standing beside them and gave him a big hug, too.

Birdie glanced at the bemused expression on Seb's face

and grinned. It was like they'd stepped into an alternative universe.

'Are you okay?' Birdie asked Annabelle once the hugging was over, and they were stood awkwardly, staring at one another.

'Yes. I think so. I've been sitting here waiting to hear what had happened. Praying that you were both okay. It gave me a lot of time to think about my behaviour towards you, Birdie. I'm sorry if I didn't treat you with respect when we first met. It was inexcusable. Please forgive me.'

If someone had told her that Annabelle was going to ask for her forgiveness, Birdie would have laughed into the middle of the following week. No way would she have ever seen that coming.

'You don't even have to ask. It cuts both ways. Remember when you came to Seb's house, and I was winding you up and made out I was his girlfriend? Your face was a picture while you tried to process how someone like me, totally not posh, could be with him. It was mean of me, but it was so funny. So let's call it quits. Okay?' Birdie held up her hand. 'High five.'

Annabelle smiled and high-fived back. 'Is it all over? Where's Jasper?'

'Yes, it's over,' Seb said. 'Jasper's in custody, and he may be charged for his part in the fraud. O'Rourke and his gang have been arrested and most likely will be charged for many things, including drug trafficking, but Jasper had no part in that—'

'That we know of,' Birdie said.

'I don't believe he is involved, but I'm sure Rob will elicit the truth.'

'And Harold Somerton?' Annabel said.

'We haven't been informed about what's going to happen to him and his wife, who was also complicit, but I suspect they'll be charged with fraud and possibly with wasting police time. It will be up to the Crown Prosecution Service to decide.'

'I've informed my parents that the engagement is off and they're going to arrange for the return of all the presents, which are being stored at their house. They will also let Jasper's parents know. I don't ever want to see him again, and there's nothing he can say that will change my mind. I realise now that he was only with me for my money and position in society.'

'From what I've learnt, you're well rid of him. He's—'

'Birdie, it's not your place to say that,' Seb said, his brow furrowed.

'Why not? Annabelle's now a friend. She doesn't mind me saying what I think, do you?'

Birdie glanced at Annabelle, whose eyes were twinkling. The change in the woman was quite incredible.

'I don't mind. I'd be honoured to count you among my friends.'

'So now you've got two of us ganging up on you, Seb. Perhaps you could join us as a PI, Annabelle? We would be the poshest investigators around.'

'No. I draw the line at that. But I do think the pair of you make a great team. In the past, Sebastian, I was extremely judgemental about the work you do. But I was wrong. You saved me from that awful gangster and I'll be eternally grateful.'

'O'Rourke wouldn't have involved you if he hadn't been after me,' Seb said, hanging his head.

'You can't blame yourself for that. It wasn't your fault. Thank you, both.'

'It's our pleasure,' Birdie said. 'Well, not our pleasure that you were kidnapped and were sent threatening notes. But you know what I mean. We both enjoy the work, and

Seb is very good at it, despite his background.' Birdie grinned as she looked across at Seb, who just rolled his eyes.

'Ignore Birdie. Her idea of fun is to tease me.'

'But you're such an easy target,' Birdie said.

'You complement one another, and I'll be recommending you to all of my friends. A number of them are involved in, or contemplating, divorce proceedings, and I'm sure they could benefit from your help.'

'Thanks. We're going for a drink to celebrate, would you like to come with us, Annabelle?'

'No. But thank you. I'll call a taxi to take me home. I've had quite enough adventure for one day.'

'I needed this,' Birdie said, picking up her glass of cider and taking a second large swallow. 'It's been a full-on and exciting few days.'

Although she told Sebastian otherwise as they waited in the police car, taking part in the police operation, however small her contribution had been, had given her cause to wonder whether she'd made the right decision leaving the police. The excitement of the chase and arresting the culprit had always been addictive. But then again, she'd also enjoyed the fact that they'd been able to investigate the case and do what they wanted without having to be bothered by police regulations. Not that Seb would have allowed them to cross the line … at least, not much. She was bound to miss the force, but … she'd made her decision, and it was a good one.

'Steady on. We're not in a rush,' Seb said, nodding at her almost empty glass.

'We're not on duty. We have nothing else to do now the

case is over. Although, we should make the most of this because if Annabelle is going to send all her divorcing friends to us, we could be spending a lot of time following people. Exactly what we don't want to do. I didn't have the heart to tell her we hate those sorts of cases because she wanted to do us a favour. Which was cool.'

'I agree. She simply wanted to show her gratitude.'

'She can show her gratitude when she pays us. I assume you're going to be sending her an invoice as soon as we get back.'

'Umm…' Seb hesitated.

Birdie locked eyes with him. 'Don't tell me you're thinking of not charging her. You know she can afford to pay. Just because we're now best buddies doesn't mean that we have to be out of pocket. I know her life was in danger, but that wasn't down to us. Well, in a way, it was down to us, I suppose, because she was the bargaining chip in O'Rourke's plan to get you to work for him. I still don't get why he had to come up with such an elaborate plan. It's not like you were in hiding. I'll never understand these people. Okay, you're right. We shouldn't charge her.'

She supposed it was the right thing to do, and if Annabelle did recommend them and they got some cases from it, then that would help get the business off the ground.

Seb's phone pinged. 'It's a text from Rob.'

'What does he want? Read it out.'

'Okay. He says: "Thanks for the Warrington recording. He's been charged. O'Rourke and gang have also been charged, and bail will be opposed. Thanks for your help. Sorry I couldn't make it for a drink. Things are hectic here. Send best wishes to my mate Birdie. Will catch up soon."'

'Send mine back to him. Let's hope O'Rourke doesn't have a lawyer who can get him off.'

'That's out of our control, but the evidence was certainly damning. Especially with my recording. He admitted everything to me.'

'Providing the evidence is admissible.'

'There's no reason why it shouldn't be.'

'We hope. You know, I still can't believe that O'Rourke thought that you'd be prepared to help him. And he's meant to be a feared gangster.' She rolled her eyes.

'You must appreciate that O'Rourke is used to being obeyed. It wouldn't have crossed his mind that I'd have refused.'

'Well, it was a stupid assumption to make. Anyway, at least we have one gang out of action. That's got to be good.'

'Until the next one steps up. It's a never-ending, cut-throat business.'

'The Spanish gang, you mean. The one who killed O'Rourke's sister.'

'Yes. If they move swiftly, they might be successful.'

'If they're in Spain, then it's up to the Spanish police to deal with them, not Rob and his mob.'

'When it's international crime, police forces will cooperate with one another.'

'Does this mean that Rob doesn't need us to work with him anymore?'

'No. I wasn't on that enquiry. But I'm hoping that soon we won't need the income from the consultancy work with him.'

'Not now we have all those divorce cases to look forward to.' She gave a wry smile, picked up her glass and tapped it against Seb's. 'Here's to a job well done.'

'And tomorrow, we'll head back home.'

'So you're beginning to think of Market Harborough as home now, are you?'

'I hadn't thought about it before. But in a way, yes. I believe I do. I've enjoyed being back at my flat in London and experiencing the city vibe, but the constant noise is not conducive to relaxation. It no longer feels like home. I believe that I much prefer to live in the country.'

'Does that mean you're going to sell up here?'

'Not yet. If at all. A place in London will always come in handy. But I'm certainly looking forward to getting back to East Farndon to walk in the fields with Elsa and enjoy a more balanced and relaxed lifestyle.'

'Until we get another case.'

'And before you say anything … one where we get paid.'

'Good. Because I'm totally over the freebies.'

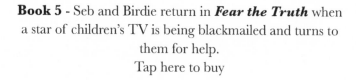

Book 5 - Seb and Birdie return in ***Fear the Truth*** when a star of children's TV is being blackmailed and turns to them for help.

Tap here to buy

Claim your free book

Read the Sebastian Clifford Series

WEB OF LIES: A Midlands Crime Thriller (Detective Sebastian Clifford - Book 1)

A trail of secrets. A dangerous discovery. A deadly turn.

Police officer Sebastian Clifford never planned on becoming a private investigator. But when a scandal leads to the disbandment of his London based special squad, he finds himself out of a job. That is, until his cousin calls on him to investigate her husband's high-profile death, and prove that it wasn't a suicide.

Clifford's reluctant to get involved, but the more he digs, the more evidence he finds. With his ability to remember everything he's ever seen, he's the perfect person to untangle the layers of deceit.

He meets Detective Constable Bird, an underutilised detective at Market Harborough's police force, who refuses to give him access to the records he's requested unless he allows her to help with the investigation. Clifford isn't thrilled. The last time he worked as part of a team it ended his career.

But with time running out, Clifford is out of options. Together they must wade through the web of lies in the hope that they'll find the truth before it kills them.

Web of Lies is the first in the new Detective Sebastian Clifford series. Perfect for readers of Joy Ellis, Robert Galbraith and Mark Dawson.

∾

SPEAK NO EVIL: A Midlands Crime Thriller (Detective Sebastian Clifford - Book 2)

What happens when someone's too scared to speak?

Ex-police officer Sebastian Clifford had decided to limit his work as a private investigator, until Detective Constable Bird, aka Birdie, asks for his help.

Twelve months ago a young girl was abandoned on the streets of Market Harborough in shocking circumstances. Since then the child has barely spoken and with the police unable to trace her identity, they've given up.

The social services team in charge of the case worry that the child has an intellectual disability but Birdie and her aunt, who's fostering the little girl, disagree and believe she's gifted and intelligent, but something bad happened and she's living in constant fear.

Clifford trusts Birdie's instinct and together they work to find out who the girl is, so she can be freed from the past. But as secrets are uncovered, the pair realise it's not just the child who's in danger.

Speak No Evil is the second in the Detective Sebastian Clifford series. Perfect for readers of Faith Martin, Matt Brolly and Joy Ellis.

∽

NEVER TOO LATE: A Midlands Crime Thriller (Detective Sebastian Clifford - Book 3)

A vicious attack. A dirty secret. And a chance for justice

Ex-police officer Sebastian Clifford is quickly finding that life as a private investigator is never quiet. His doors have only been open a few weeks when DCI Whitney Walker approaches him to investigate the brutal attack that left her older brother, Rob, with irreversible brain damage.

For nearly twenty-five years Rob had no memory of that night, but lately things are coming back to him, and Whitney's worried that her brother might, once again, be in danger.

Clifford knows only too well what it's like be haunted by the past, and so he agrees to help. But the deeper he digs, the more secrets he uncovers, and soon he discovers that Rob's not the only one in danger.

Never Too Late is the third in the Detective Sebastian Clifford series, perfect for readers who love gripping crime fiction.

HIDDEN FROM SIGHT: A Midlands Crime Thriller (Detective Sebastian Clifford - Book 4)

A million pound heist. A man on the run. And a gang hellbent on seeking revenge.

When private investigator Detective Sebastian Clifford is asked by his former society girlfriend to locate her fiancé, who's disappeared along with some valuable pieces of art, he's reluctant to help. He'd left the aristocratic world behind, for good reason. But when his ex starts receiving threatening letters Clifford is left with no choice.

With the help of his partner Lucinda Bird, aka Birdie, they start digging and find themselves drawn into London's underworld. But it's hard to see the truth between the shadows and lies. Until a clue leads them in the direction of Clifford's nemesis and he realises they're all in more danger than he thought. The race is on to find the missing man and the art before lives are lost.

A perfect mix of mystery, intrigue and danger that will delight fans of detective stories. '**Hidden from Sight**' is the fourth in the bestselling, fast-paced, Midland Crime Thriller series, featuring Clifford and Birdie, and the most gripping yet. Grab your copy, and see if you can solve the crime.

**FEAR THE TRUTH: A Midlands Crime Thriller
(Detective Sebastian Clifford - Book 5)**

**The truth will set you free...except when it
doesn't...**

Private investigator Sebastian Clifford and his partner
Birdie, step into the world of celebrity when a star of children's TV turns to them for help. She's being blackmailed
by someone who knows about her murky past and she's
desperate to keep it hidden. But silence comes at a price,
and it's one she can't afford to pay.

Clifford, who knows better than anyone what it's like to be
punished for one mistake, agrees to help. But, as they dig
deeper, they discover that everyone has secrets, and some
are dark enough to kill for. Can they find the blackmailer
before it's too late and save the reputation...and the life...of
a beloved star?

'Fear the Truth' is the fifth in the best-selling Sebastian
Clifford thriller series, and is a perfect blend of mystery,
mayhem and danger. Grab your copy now and see if *you*
can face the truth.

Also by Sally Rigby: The Cavendish & Walker Series

DEADLY GAMES - Cavendish & Walker Book 1

A killer is playing cat and mouse……. and winning.

DCI Whitney Walker wants to save her career. Forensic psychologist, Dr Georgina Cavendish, wants to avenge the death of her student.

Sparks fly when real world policing meets academic theory, and it's not a pretty sight.

When two more bodies are discovered, Walker and Cavendish form an uneasy alliance. But are they in time to save the next victim?

Deadly Games is the first book in the Cavendish and Walker crime fiction series. If you like serial killer thrillers and psychological intrigue, then you'll love Sally Rigby's page-turning book.

Pick up *Deadly Games* today to read Cavendish & Walker's first case.

FATAL JUSTICE - Cavendish & Walker Book 2

A vigilante's on the loose, dishing out their kind of justice…

A string of mutilated bodies sees Detective Chief Inspector Whitney Walker back in action. But when she discovers the victims have all been grooming young girls, she fears a vigilante is on the loose. And while she understands the motive, no one is above the law.

Once again, she turns to forensic psychologist, Dr Georgina Cavendish, to unravel the cryptic clues. But will they be able to save the next victim from a gruesome death?

Fatal Justice is the second book in the Cavendish & Walker crime fiction series. If you like your mysteries dark, and with a twist, pick up a copy of Sally Rigby's book today.

~

DEATH TRACK - Cavendish & Walker Book 3

Catch the train if you dare...

After a teenage boy is found dead on a Lenchester train, Detective Chief Inspector Whitney Walker believes they're being targeted by the notorious Carriage Killer, who chooses a local rail network, commits four murders, and moves on.

Against her wishes, Walker's boss brings in officers from another force to help the investigation and prevent more deaths, but she's forced to defend her team against this outside interference.

Forensic psychologist, Dr Georgina Cavendish, is by her side in an attempt to bring to an end this killing spree. But how can they get into the mind of a killer who has already killed twelve times in two years without leaving a single clue behind?

For fans of Rachel Abbott, L J Ross and Angela Marsons, *Death Track* is the third in the Cavendish & Walker series. A gripping serial killer thriller that will have you hooked.

~

LETHAL SECRET - Cavendish & Walker Book 4

Someone has a secret. A secret worth killing for....

When a series of suicides, linked to the Wellness Spirit Centre, turn out to be murder, it brings together DCI Whitney Walker and forensic psychologist Dr Georgina Cavendish for another investigation. But as they delve deeper, they come across a tangle of secrets and the very real risk that the killer will strike again.

As the clock ticks down, the only way forward is to infiltrate the centre. But the outcome is disastrous, in more ways than one.

For fans of Angela Marsons, Rachel Abbott and M A Comley, *Lethal Secret* is the fourth book in the Cavendish & Walker crime fiction series.

~

LAST BREATH - Cavendish & Walker Book 5

Has the Lenchester Strangler returned?

When a murderer leaves a familiar pink scarf as his calling card, Detective Chief Inspector Whitney Walker is forced to dig into a cold case, not sure if she's looking for a killer or a copycat.

With a growing pile of bodies, and no clues, she turns to forensic psychologist, Dr Georgina Cavendish, despite their relationship being at an all-time low.

Can they overcome the bad blood between them to solve the

unsolvable?

For fans of Rachel Abbott, Angela Marsons and M A Comley, *Last Breath* is the fifth book in the Cavendish & Walker crime fiction series.

∼

FINAL VERDICT - Cavendish & Walker Book 6

The judge has spoken......everyone must die.

When a killer starts murdering lawyers in a prestigious law firm, and every lead takes them to a dead end, DCI Whitney Walker finds herself grappling for a motive.

What links these deaths, and why use a lethal injection?

Alongside forensic psychologist, Dr Georgina Cavendish, they close in on the killer, while all the time trying to not let their personal lives get in the way of the investigation.

For fans of Rachel Abbott, Mark Dawson and M A Comley, Final Verdict is the sixth in the Cavendish & Walker series. A fast paced murder mystery which will keep you guessing.

∼

RITUAL DEMISE - Cavendish & Walker Book 7

Someone is watching.... No one is safe

The once tranquil woods in a picturesque part of Lenchester have become the bloody stage to a series of ritualistic murders. With no suspects, Detective Chief Inspector Whitney Walker is once again forced to call on the services of forensic psychologist Dr Georgina Cavendish.

But this murderer isn't like any they've faced before. The murders are highly elaborate, but different in their own way and, with the clock ticking, they need to get inside the killer's head before it's too late.

For fans of Angela Marsons, Rachel Abbott and L J Ross. Ritual Demise is the seventh book in the Cavendish & Walker crime fiction series.

∾

MORTAL REMAINS - Cavendish & Walker Book 8

Someone's playing with fire…. There's no escape.

A serial arsonist is on the loose and as the death toll continues to mount DCI Whitney Walker calls on forensic psychologist Dr Georgina Cavendish for help.

But Lenchester isn't the only thing burning. There are monumental changes taking place within the police force and there's a chance Whitney might lose the job she loves. She has to find the killer before that happens. Before any more lives are lost.

Mortal Remains is the eighth book in the acclaimed Cavendish & Walker series. Perfect for fans of Angela Marsons, Rachel Abbott and L J Ross.

∾

SILENT GRAVES - Cavendish & Walker Book 9

Nothing remains buried forever...

When the bodies of two teenage girls are discovered on a building site, DCI Whitney Walker knows she's on the hunt for a killer. The problem is the murders happened in 1980 and this is her first case with the new team. What makes it even tougher is that with budgetary restrictions in place, she only has two weeks to solve it.

Once again, she enlists the help of forensic psychologist Dr Georgina Cavendish, but as she digs deeper into the past, she uncovers hidden truths that reverberate through the decades and into the present.

Silent Graves is the ninth book in the acclaimed Cavendish & Walker series. Perfect for fans of L J Ross, J M Dalgliesh and Rachel Abbott.

$\sim$

KILL SHOT - Cavendish & Walker Book 10

The game is over.....there's nowhere to hide.

When Lenchester's most famous sportsman is shot dead, DCI Whitney Walker and her team are thrown into the world of snooker.

She calls on forensic psychologist Dr Georgina Cavendish to assist, but the investigation takes them in a direction which has far-reaching, international ramifications.

Much to Whitney's annoyance, an officer from one of the Met's special squads is sent to assist.

But as everyone knows…three's a crowd.

Kill Shot is the tenth book in the acclaimed Cavendish & Walker series. Perfect for fans of Simon McCleave, J M Dalgliesh, J R Ellis and Faith Martin.

∿

DARK SECRETS - Cavendish & Walker Book 11

An uninvited guest...a deadly secret....and a terrible crime.

When a well-loved family of five are found dead sitting around their dining table with an untouched meal in front of them, it sends shockwaves throughout the community.

Was it a murder suicide, or was someone else involved?

It's one of DCI Whitney Walker's most baffling cases, and even with the help of forensic psychologist Dr Georgina Cavendish, they struggle to find any clues or motives to help them catch the killer.

But with a community in mourning and growing pressure to get answers, Cavendish and Walker are forced to go deeper into a murderer's mind than they've ever gone before.

Dark Secrets is the eleventh book in the Cavendish & Walker series. Perfect for fans of Angela Marsons, Joy Ellis and Rachel McLean.

∿

BROKEN SCREAMS - Cavendish & Walker Book 12

Scream all you want, no one can hear you....

When an attempted murder is linked to a string of unsolved sexual attacks, Detective Chief Inspector Whitney Walker is incensed. All those women who still have sleepless nights because the man who terrorises their dreams is still on the loose.

Calling on forensic psychologist Dr Georgina Cavendish to help, they follow the clues and are alarmed to discover the victims all had one thing in common. Their birthdays were on the 29th February. The same date as a female officer on Whitney's team.

As the clock ticks down and they're no nearer to finding the truth, can they stop the villain before he makes sure his next victim will never scream again.

Broken Screams is the twelfth book in the acclaimed Cavendish & Walker series and is perfect for fans of Angela Marsons, Helen H Durrant and Rachel McClean.

Writing as Amanda Rigby

Sally also writes psychological thrillers as **Amanda Rigby**, in collaboration with another author.

REMEMBER ME?: A brand new addictive psychological thriller that you won't be able to put down in 2021

A perfect life...

Paul Henderson leads a normal life. A deputy headteacher at a good school, a loving relationship with girlfriend Jenna, and a baby on the way. Everything *seems* perfect.

A shocking message...

Until Paul receives a message from his ex-fiance Nicole. Beautiful, ambitious and fierce, Nicole is everything Jenna is not. And now it seems Nicole is back, and she has a score to settle with Paul...

A deadly secret.

But Paul can't understand how Nicole is back. Because he's pretty sure he killed her with his own bare hands....

Which means, someone else knows the truth about what happened that night. And they'll stop at nothing to make Paul pay...

A brand new psychological thriller that will keep you guessing till the end! Perfect for fans of Sue Watson, Nina Manning, Shalini Boland

~

I WILL FIND YOU: An addictive psychological crime thriller to keep you gripped in 2022

Three sisters...One terrible secret

Ashleigh: A creative, free spirit and loyal. But Ash is tormented by her demons and a past that refuses to be laid to rest.

Jessica: Perfect wife and loving mother. But although Jessica might seem to have it all, she lives a secret life built on lies.

Grace: An outsider, always looking in, Grace has never known the love of her sisters and her resentment can make her do bad things.

When Ashleigh goes missing, Jessica and Grace do all they can to find their eldest sister. But the longer Ashleigh is missing, the more secrets and lies these women are hiding threaten to tear this family apart.

Can they find Ashleigh before it's too late or is it sometimes safer to stay hidden?

Acknowledgments

This book would not exist without the help of many people. Thanks to Rebecca Millar for being such an incredibly insightful editor and for pushing me to make the book the best it can be. Thanks also to Kate Noble for being such an amazing proof reader.

To Stuart Bache, thanks for yet another fabulous cover.

I would especially like to thank my advanced reader teams. Your input is invaluable and I'd be totally lost without you.

Finally, thanks to all my family for your continued support.